ARAMINTA HALL was a journalist for nine years before becoming a full-time writer. She is married with three children.

From the reviews of *Everything and Nothing:*

'*Everything and Nothing* is a beautifully written, completely gripping novel that plays on the unsettling notion that sometimes the least safe place is your very own home'   EMILY MORTIMER

'An assured debut takes the Mary Poppins myth and turns it into a menacing tale of the enemy invited in ... Araminta Hall has turned the perfect nanny trope into something much more disturbing. Imagine a mash-up of Mary Poppins with Stephen King and you get the general idea ... What makes this smartly written first novel so disturbing is its moral ambiguity; Hall keeps us engaged with all the characters, even the duplicitous Agatha, right up until the end. I suspect that this will be the first of what promises to be a new genre: the nanny chiller'   DAISY GOODWIN, *Sunday Times*

'This gripping novel will chill the working parent to the bone ... Hall's debut novel is a confident and compelling read. Evoking that kind of subconscious empathy with characters is a real skill – and Hall displays it masterfully'   *News of the World*

'Chilling and suspenseful'   *Sun*, BEST OF 2011 BOOK PICKS

'A suspenseful and emotive examination of a family in meltdown ... Hall's tale is told assuredly and touches on the darkness, tensions and unhappiness behind the façade of daily family life. It's a skilfully executed debut novel that nestles perfectly alongside the dark, nuanced psychological thrills of Daphne du Maurier and Sophie Hannah'   *Waterstone's Books Quarterly*

'An unsettling, menacing read'

'This is a brilliant book – very well written and thought provoking. I read it very quickly as I just couldn't put it down and had to keep reading to see what happened next ... Highly recommended'

'This is a dramatic read featuring sinister events'

ARAMINTA HALL

Everything and Nothing

Harper
Press

Harper*Press*
An imprint of HarperCollins*Publishers*
77–85 Fulham Palace Road
Hammersmith, London W6 8JB

This Harper*Press* paperback edition published 2011

1

First published by Harper*Press* in 2011

A catalogue record for this book
is available from the British Library

This novel is entirely a work of fiction. The names, characters
and incidents portrayed in it are either the work of the
author's imagination or are used fictitiously.

ISBN 978-0-00-741395-9

Typeset in Dante MT by G&M Designs Limited,
Raunds, Northamptonshire.
Printed and bound in Great Britain by
Clays Ltd, St Ives plc

MIX
Paper from
responsible sources
FSC **FSC® C007454**
www.fsc.org

FSC is a non-profit international organisation established to promote the
responsible management of the world's forests. Products carrying the FSC
label are independently certified to assure consumers that they come
from forests that are managed to meet the social, economic and
ecological needs of present or future generations.

Find out more about HarperCollins and the environment at
www.harpercollins.co.uk/green

To my own perfectly imperfect family,
Jamie, Oscar, Violet & Edith

The grey-haired man began to laugh again. 'First you tell me that marriage is founded on love, and then when I express my doubts as to the existence of any love apart from the physical kind you try to prove its existence by the fact that marriages exist. But marriage nowadays is just a deception.'

The Kreutzer Sonata, LEO TOLSTOY

EVERYTHING AND NOTHING

The tube spat Agatha into one of those areas where people used to lie about their postcodes. Although why anyone would ever have been ashamed to live here was beyond Agatha's understanding. The streets were long and wide, with trees standing as sentry guards outside each Victorian house. The houses themselves towered out of the ground with splendour and grace, as if they had risen complete when God created the world in seven days, one of Agatha's favourite childhood stories. They were stern and majestic, with their paths of orange bricks like giant cough lozenges, their stained-glass window panels in the front doors reflecting light from the obligatory hallway chandeliers, the brass door fittings and the little iron gates which looked as correct as a bow tie at a neck. They even had those fantastic bay windows, which looked to Agatha like a row of proud pregnant bellies. You never saw anything like this where she had been brought up.

The address on the piece of paper in Agatha's hand led her to a door with an unusual bell. It was a hard, round, metallic ball which you pulled out of an ornate setting and was probably as old as the house. Agatha liked the bell; both for its audacity in daring to protrude and its undaunted ability to survive. She pulled the ball and a proper tinkling sound rang somewhere inside.

As she waited, Agatha tried to get into character. She practised her smile and told herself to remember to keep her hand movements small and contained. It wasn't that she couldn't be this person or even that this person was a lie, it was just that she had to remember who this person was.

The man who opened the door looked ruffled, like he'd had a hard day. A girl was crying in the background and he was holding a boy who looked too old to be sucking on the bottle clamped in his mouth. The house felt cloyingly warm and she could see the kitchen windows were all steamed up. Coats and shoes and even a bike lay across the hall.

'I'm sorry,' said Christian Donaldson, as she supposed him to be, 'we're in a bit of chaos. But nothing terminal yet.'

'Don't worry.' Agatha had learnt that people like the Donaldsons secretly, or maybe not even secretly, liked to appear chaotic.

He held out his spare hand. 'Anyway, Annie, I presume ...'

'Agatha actually.' His mistake unnerved her and she tried to save herself from instant rejection. 'Well, Aggie really.'

'Shit, sorry, my fault. I thought my wife said ... she's not home yet.' His flustered response reassured her. They were just one of those families. He stood back. 'Anyway, come in, sorry, I'm keeping you standing on the doorstep.'

The wailing girl was sitting at the kitchen table and the kitchen itself looked as though a small and mutinous army had attacked every cupboard, spilling all their contents onto every available surface.

'Daddy,' screamed the girl from the table, 'it's not fair. Why do I have to eat my broccoli when Hal doesn't have to eat anything at all?'

Agatha waited with the child for the answer, but none came. She hated the way adults found silence sufficient. She looked at the man whom she hoped would employ her and saw a thin film of sweat on his face which gave her the confidence to speak. 'What's your favourite colour?'

The girl stopped crying and looked at her. It was too interesting a question to ignore. 'Pink.'

Predictable, thought Agatha. Her daughters were going to like blue. 'Well, that's lucky because I've got a packet of Smarties in my bag and I don't like the pink ones, so if you eat that one tiny piece of broccoli I'll give you all my pink Smarties.'

The girl looked stunned. 'Really?'

Agatha turned to Christian Donaldson, who she was relieved to see smiling. 'Well, if that's okay with your dad.'

He laughed. 'What's a few Smarties amongst friends?'

Christian couldn't stand the girls who moved into his house to look after his children. He wondered what he looked like to this one. He wanted to explain that he was never usually home at this time, that it was only the result of a massive row he'd had with Ruth at the weekend. Something about his children and responsibility and the fact that she'd be sacked if she took another day, all of which simply boiled down to how bloody brilliantly self-sacrificing she was and what a selfish shit he was. Besides, after a full day of childcare he felt like his kids had flung him against a wall and he was too tired to think of anything to say. And where the fuck was Ruth anyway?

The girl didn't want tea but she did allow Betty to lead her into the part of the sitting room overrun by plastic toys. Christian pretended to busy himself in the kitchen, shifting piles of mess which Ruth would properly home later.

Other people in his house always shrunk it for Christian. It became all it was in the eyes of guests. Two small rooms knocked together at the front and a kitchen unimaginatively extended into the side return. Overcrowded bedrooms and a space squeezed into the roof. It felt like a fat man who had eaten too much at lunch, gout ridden and uncomfortable.

When he had been fucking Sarah they had always met at her flat, for obvious reasons. But that had been worse. As he had lain on her creaking double bed, he would feel old and foolish surrounded by posters for bands he didn't even recognise, stuck onto walls whose colour he knew hadn't been chosen by anyone who lived there. He would find himself perversely longing for the subtle shades and carefully crafted beauty of his own house. And what a trick for his mind to play because he had so hated Ruth when she had cried over builders running late or been

4

more excited by the colour of a tile than the touch of his hand.

There had been a park bench which had also reminded him of his wife during that time. Predictably, because don't all affairs need a park bench, he would sometimes meet Sarah there and it had an inscription which read: *For Maude, who loved this park as much as I loved her*. He had imagined an old man whittling the letters to make the words, tears on his gnarled face, a lifetime of good memories in his head. All of which was of course crap as no one had good memories any more and the bench had no doubt been gouged by some council machine.

Not that it would have been enough to stop him anyway. Ruth had been so easy to fool it had almost cancelled out the excitement, and this annoyance had spurred him on. He had always worked unpredictable hours and his job in television had often led him far from home, so staying away over night was commonplace in their marriage. More than anything though he had felt vindicated. He told himself that Ruth had always smothered him, that she had repressed his true nature, that his real self was a fun-loving, carefree guy who had never wanted to be tied down. That ultimately someone like Sarah suited him far better.

She probably hadn't, though. Although he still felt muddled, still found it hard to get any clarity around a situation that had descended into such stomach-churning detritus, it was hard to place any decent feelings. Two women pregnant at the same time and yet only one child to show for it. One strange little boy who still, at the age of nearly three, never ate, hardly spoke and followed your movements like eyes staring out of a painting. Christian worried that Hal had absorbed his mother's misery in the womb in the same way that some babies are born addicted to heroin. A key turned in his front door and he realised that his hands had grown cold in the sink.

Ruth was always going to be late, but still she felt like a naughty child. Christian wouldn't understand. She hadn't even got the necessary words to explain why she had always known she wouldn't leave the office at six, but had arranged the interview for seven. Not that she had been able to predict the rain, of course, which jammed the tube so you felt you would suffocate even in the ticket hall. It unsettled her; the way the rain lashed at the city nowadays, the way the clouds darkened so quickly and furiously, without any warning. She couldn't remember it having been like that in her own childhood and she fretted over what she would tell her children about the world they were growing into.

She could tell the girl was already there, just as she could tell the house had sunk even lower. Ruth was used to leaving every morning closing her eyes to the tangled sheets falling off all the beds, the washing exploding out of the laundry basket, the food drying onto plates in the sink, the fridge compartments that needed cleaning, the dirty hand prints on all the windows, the fluff which multiplied like bunnies on the stair treads, the unre-turned DVDs scattered around the machine, the recycling which needed transporting from beside the bin to the boxes at the front of the house, the name-tags not sewn into Betty's uniform. The magnitude of these tasks pulled at her back like a bungee rope all the way to her office. But this evening she thought they might at last have tipped from mess to squalor. She wondered if Christian had done it on purpose to punish her for keeping him from his stupidly important job where he got to pretend that he was an indispensable person every day of the working week. Light household duties, she had written in her advert; she wondered what that might consist of and decided on the usual laundry so that at least they would look like they held it together to the outside world. And food shopping; they had to eat, after all.

From the hall Ruth could see the girl on the floor with Betty. She looked so young, they could almost have been playmates. On the tube coming home Ruth had been hit by panic. Going back to work after two weeks immersed in childcare had jolted her and filled her mind with doubts. The final showdown with their last nanny was also still lodged in her brain. The weeping girl standing in the doorway with her bags already packed and her mind resolutely made up, saying she couldn't take one more night listening to Betty screaming. I have to get some sleep, she'd said, forgetting surely that Ruth was the one who got up to the little girl hour after bloody hour, scaling each night like a mountain climber.

Then last week she'd found herself checking Christian's texts, something she hadn't done in over a year. Worse than the checking though was realising that she almost wanted to find something. That it would be more exciting than washing another load of socks or trying to make supper out of whatever was in the fridge. And she was too old to still be a deputy editor, wasn't she? It had been a terrible mistake to have refused the editorship Harvey had offered last year.

'I don't get it,' Christian had said when she'd wept to him over her final decision. 'What's the big fuss? If you want the job, do it; we'll get more help. No big deal.'

'No big deal?' she'd repeated, the tears straining again against her better judgement. 'Do you think your kids are no big deal?'

'What do you mean? Why are you bringing the kids into this?'

'Because obviously I'm not refusing the job for me.'

He'd sighed. 'Oh God, please not the martyr act again. Why is your refusing the job anything to do with the kids?'

Ruth felt consumed by an annoyance so intense she worried she might stab her husband. 'Because if I take this job I'll basically never see them.'

'What, like all the quality time you spend with them now?'

'How can you say that? Are you saying I'm a bad mother?' Ruth had felt as though she was losing her grip on the situation.

Christian poured himself more wine. 'I'm saying that we both made a choice, Ruth. We both decided to pursue our careers. I'm not saying we're right or wrong. I'm saying you can't have it all.'

'You seem to manage it.'

'No, I don't. I'd love to see more of them, but we bought a house we couldn't afford because you wanted it and we have a massive mortgage.'

'It wasn't only me, I never forced you into buying it.'

'I'd have been as happy somewhere smaller.'

But the truth was that Ruth was sure Christian did have more than her. He pursued his career with a single-minded focus and, as a result, had done very well. He didn't feel guilt at being out of the house all day and so he could relish the time he spent with their children. For some primeval reason it didn't appear to be his role to know about when their vaccinations were due or even whether or not they should have them. He didn't feel compelled to read endless parenting books or to worry that his working caused behavioural problems in his children. He never took a half day to attend Christmas concerts or sports days, but if he happened to be around and turned up everyone noticed and thought he was a great father.

It was all these little injustices which wore away at Ruth until she felt as though her marriage was nothing more than a rocky outcrop being relentlessly lashed by the sea. And it wasn't even as if she could articulate any of this to Christian, or he to her. And so they flailed along like blind bumper-car drivers, occasionally causing each other serious injury, but mainly just cuts and bruises.

'You got her name wrong,' said Christian as soon as Ruth walked into the sitting room. 'It's Aggie.'

Ruth sat down without even pausing to take off her coat because both Betty and Hal were trying to climb on her. 'Oh, I'm sorry, I must have misheard you on the phone.'

'I couldn't get away.' Ruth realised she was apologising as much to Christian as Aggie. 'You know, first day back and all that.' She smiled at Aggie and mouthed over Betty's head, 'It's been a nightmare.' Who was she trying to be here?

'Why don't you put a DVD on for them?' she said to Christian, and then felt the need to say to Aggie, 'We don't normally let them watch TV after five, but we'll never finish a sentence if we don't.'

The girl nodded, watching the children fight over which DVD they were going to see. In the end Christian lost his temper. 'Look, I'm putting on *Toy Story*. It's the only one you both like.'

Betty started to wail but they all kept their smiles fixed.

'It's either this or nothing,' Christian shouted as he jabbed at the machine.

'So.' Ruth turned to Aggie. 'Sorry about that. Right, well, let's see. I suppose Christian has filled you in on us a bit.'

The girl blushed and tried to answer but nothing came out.

'Sorry, Betty commandeered her,' said Christian.

Ruth felt defeated before she'd even begun. 'So you haven't said anything about Hal yet?'

'No, not yet, I was waiting for you.' And there it was, the perfect get-out.

Ruth composed herself. 'Sorry, Aggie, let me explain. Hal's nearly three and he's never eaten anything. Not ever. He lives off bottles of milk. I've taken him to the doctors but they say he's perfectly healthy. Maybe a bit behind developmentally; I mean, he hardly speaks, but apparently that's not overly worrying. We don't know what to do next. I've got an appointment with a great nutritionist in a few weeks, but I guess our most important question to you is how you feel about food?'

Agatha looked at the back of Hal's head. She liked the idea of looking after a freak. And she'd babysat and nannied for enough of these ridiculous women to know what to say. She imagined the Donaldsons' fridge, all green and verdant and organic at the top, but beating in the cold heart of the freezer would be the fat-laden, salt-addled reality.

'Well, I think what you feed kids is reflected in their behaviour. Obviously I try to get them to eat five fruit and veg a day and I only buy organic, but I'm not evangelical or anything. I think the odd sweet or biscuit is fine.'

Ruth nodded approvingly while Christian stared oblivious out of the window. 'That's pretty much how we feel, but we've had such problems with Hal. The doctor says we should go with it for now. She even told me to try giving him things like chocolate to get him used to the idea of eating. But that's absurd, don't you think?'

Agatha thought it sounded sensible. She had been brought up on a diet of frozen burgers, oven chips and chocolate. Pot Noodles, if she was lucky. And it hadn't done her any harm. But of course she shook her head disapprovingly.

'And what about discipline, where do you stand on that?'

'I do believe in rules.' Agatha could remember her last employer screaming at her children after telling Agatha in her interview that she thought a raised voice was a stupid voice. They were fucking priceless these women. 'But I think they should be rules we'd obey anyway, like be polite and kind and don't hit or snatch, those sort of things. And I don't like to threaten anything I'm not prepared to carry out.' Agatha wasn't confident she should say this as Ruth Donaldson was in all likelihood another of those crazy women who wouldn't be left in charge of their kids if they lived on the local estate but somehow got away with it because they lived in half-a-million-pound houses and knew a few long words. But then again these women were usually addicted to parenting programmes and so had a fair idea for how they should be behaving even if they couldn't manage it themselves.

'I put on the advert light household duties, are you okay with that? I meant a bit of laundry and keeping things a bit straight and maybe a bit of food shopping.'

'Oh, absolutely, that's fine. Of course I'd do that.' That was the part Agatha liked the best. Putting everything into its right place. Sorting the house and making her employers marvel at her efficiency. She had been a cleaner many times in her life and she always proved herself indispensable. A lot of these families lived in near slum conditions. Agatha had learnt that they were the sort of people who you'd look at from the outside and wish you could be part of them. You'd covet their clothes and their house and coffee maker and £300 hoover and fridges in bright colours. But they couldn't even flush their own toilets, most of them. They didn't understand that the world had to be neat and that keeping things in order was very simple.

'And as you know, Christian and I both work long hours. I try to be home for seven, but Christian never is. Are you okay with that? Maybe sometimes putting them to bed?'

'Of course, I'm used to that.' By the end of most jobs Agatha would have preferred it if the parents had disappeared; she liked to imagine them vaporised by their own neuroses. Handling children was always so much easier than adults.

'So, Aggie, tell us about yourself.'

Agatha was used to this question now, she knew these types of people liked to pretend they cared, but it still roused a dread inside her. The other answers hadn't really been lies. It wasn't like she was going to feed the kids crap whilst hitting them and shovelling the dirt under the sofa. She was going to be a good nanny, but she couldn't tell these people about herself. She had experimented with a couple of answers in the past few interviews, but she'd found that if you said your parents were dead they felt too sorry for you and if you said they'd emigrated they still expected them to call. This was the first time she'd tried out her new answer: 'I was brought up in Manchester and I'm an only child. My parents are very old-fashioned and when I got into university to study Philosophy my dad went mad. He's very religious, you see, and he said Philosophy was the root of all evil, the devil's work.' She'd seen this on a late-night soap opera and it had sounded plausible, or maybe fantastic enough to be something you wouldn't make up.

Ruth and Christian Donaldson reacted exactly as she'd expected, sitting up like two eager spaniels, liberal sensitivity spreading across their faces.

'He said if I went he'd disown me.'

'But you went anyway?'

Agatha looked down and felt the pain of this slight so hard that real tears pricked her eyes. 'No, I didn't. I could kick myself now, but I turned down the place.'

Ruth's hand went to her mouth in a gesture Agatha doubted to be spontaneous. 'Oh, how awful. How could he have denied you such an opportunity?' She was longing to say that she would never do anything so terrible to her own children.

'I stayed at home for a while after that, but it was terrible. So many rows.' Agatha could see a neat suburban terrace as she said this with a pinched man wagging a finger at her. The air smelt of vinegar, she realised; maybe her mother had been a bad cook or an obsessive cleaner, she wasn't sure which yet. She wondered along with this kind couple sitting in front of her how he could have been so mean. 'I left five years ago and I haven't spoken to them since.'

'But your mother, hasn't she contacted you?'

'She was very dominated by my dad. I think they've moved now.'

'Do you have any siblings?'

'No, it's just me. I'm an only child.'

'Poor you,' said Ruth, but Agatha could already see her working out that they were getting a nanny who was clever enough to get into university, and for no extra cost.

When Agatha got back to her grotty room in King's Cross she felt tired and drained. She was still trying to work out why she might have told the Donaldsons she was called Aggie when no one had ever called her anything but Agatha. She supposed it must have sounded friendlier and she'd have to go with it now. Her room-mate's mobile was ringing. She answered with a curt hello and then started waving madly at Agatha. Lisa was prone to wild mood swings, so Agatha didn't take any notice until she heard what she was saying.

'Oh, she was amazing, we were so sad to lose her … yes, she had sole care of both of them, I work full time … No, it was because we decided to move out of London, to get the children a bigger garden.' Lisa started to pretend she was sucking a massive penis as she said this which annoyed Agatha, she fucking had to remember the script. 'In fact, we nearly stayed just to keep her.' Fake laughing, Lisa miming sipping a glass of champagne. 'Oh, it's so hard, isn't it, all that juggling.' Lisa put her hand over the phone and mouthed fucking tosser at Agatha, who smiled obligingly. If Lisa fucked this up she might hit the stupid bitch. 'No, no, ring anytime, but really, I couldn't recommend her highly enough.' Lisa threw her phone onto the bed and made a sucking noise with her teeth. 'Man, those posh types are gullible. They almost deserve to be done over, innit?'

'Thanks,' said Agatha, fishing her last twenty-pound note out of her wallet and handing it over to Lisa. If you wish for something hard enough it will happen, someone had once told her, or maybe she'd seen it on a film. She didn't care, all she cared about was wishing herself out of this hellhole and into the Donaldsons' home as quickly as possible.

'Do you want Indian or Chinese?' asked Ruth as she rooted through the spare kitchen drawer overflowing with wrapping paper, old packets of seeds, a spilt box of pins, paint colour charts and numerous other bits of tat for which they would never again find a use.

'Don't care,' answered Christian, pouring them both wine. 'I'm knackered.'

The children had only been in bed for fifteen minutes and Ruth was sure Betty would be down any minute with some excuse like wanting a glass of water and then she'd lose her temper, which would mean the only real time she spent with her daughter would be about as far from quality as you could get. But how long could she be expected to go on surviving on so little sleep? It wasn't a euphemism to say that sleep deprivation was a form of torture; there were doubtless thousands of people right now in prisons around the world sleeping more than she was. Christian had developed the ability to sleep through

Betty's crying and she'd long since stopped trying to wake him. Survival of the fittest, she found herself thinking most nights, dominant evolution. It was no wonder Betty cried all day; Ruth would do the same if she could.

Christian noticed it was nearly nine and couldn't help feeling as if he'd wasted his day. He'd lied to Ruth earlier and told her he'd managed to get a bit of work done when all he'd accomplished was approving the advert for the new admin assistant for his department. He felt physically wrecked. Why did Betty cry so much? And why wouldn't Hal eat? He knew they should talk about it but also felt too tired to bring up these explosive topics with Ruth. Because his wife always had the energy for a fight, if nothing else.

'So what did you think of her?' she was asking.

'Fine, how about you?'

'I thought she was great and her referee couldn't give her enough praise.'

'Right.' Christian sat down at their long wooden kitchen table, which had been designed for a much larger and grander house and made their kitchen feel as foolish as an old woman in a mini skirt. Ruth had bought it from an antiques fair in Sussex where they'd walked round a massive field filled with Belgians selling old bits of furniture which would be burnt in their own country but went for hundreds of pounds over here. He could remember the Polish builders laughing at Ruth when they'd been renovating the house and a pair of wall lights had gone missing and she'd asked the foreman if maybe one of the men might have taken them. To us, he had said, throwing his hands in the air, they are pennies. Christian had felt hated by those men. Actually not hated, more contemptuous. He knew they laughed at him in their own language, wondered at what mad man would spend thousands on a fucking house.

'But do you think we should hire her?'

Christian tried to think of a reason to hire or not to hire. Their last nanny had seemed great until she'd left with no more warning than the time it had taken to say the words. He couldn't even picture the new girl properly, but he did remember that she'd made Betty stop crying. 'She seemed great. Do we have a lot of choice?'

Ruth looked grey. 'No, but is that a good reason to hire someone to look after your children?'

'Look, do it. If it doesn't work out we'll re-think.' He put his hand over hers and got a flash of passion from the touch of her skin. She did that to him sometimes.

She tucked her hair behind her ears. 'Okay, good plan, Batman.' It was what she said to Hal and it sucked his desire right out of him.

Agatha's room in the Donaldsons' house was so perfect it made her want to cry. It was right at the top, which made her feel cocooned, all those people between her and the world. And it was painted in a light blue that she had once read was called duck-egg blue, which was a colour she could imagine cosy American mothers using. Jutting out of the far wall was a large white wooden bed festooned in squishy, fluffy cushions which gave the impression you were floating in the clouds as you drifted off to sleep. And her own little bathroom behind a door she'd thought was a cupboard, where Ruth had kindly put some expensive-looking lotions and potions. Best of all though the only windows were on either side of the roof so you couldn't see the street and instead could stare at the sky in all its different guises and pretend you were in any number of countries and situations. It was the sort of room Agatha had dreamt of, but never imagined she'd inhabit.

Ruth and Christian seemed very concerned she had everything she needed and immensely grateful that she had agreed to take the job, when it should have been the other way around. She smiled and laughed all weekend, but was itching for them to leave on Monday morning so she could get stuck in. She had plans for the house and kids. First she would sort and tidy and then she would get Betty to stop crying all the time and finally she would get Hal eating. Life was simple when you set out your targets in basic terms.

The house was dirtier than she had given it credit for. The Donaldsons' cleaner had been taking them for a ride because anywhere you couldn't see had been left untouched for years. Under the sofas and beds were graveyards for missing items which Agatha couldn't believe had ever been of any use to anyone. The inside of the fridge was sticky and disgusting and the lint in the dryer must surely be a fire hazard. All the windows were filthy and the wood round them looked black and rotten, but really only needed wiping with a damp cloth. The bread bin was filled with crumbs and hard, rotten rolls and the freezer was so jam-packed with empty boxes and long-forgotten meals that it looked like it was never used. There were clothes at the bottom of the laundry basket which smelt mouldy and which Agatha felt sure Ruth would have forgotten she owned, simply because they needed hand washing. Cupboards were sticky from spilt jam and honey, and the oven smoked when you turned it on because of all the fat that had built up over the years. Agatha would never, ever let her future home end up like this. She would never leave it every day like Ruth did. She would never put her trust in strangers.

'How's the new nanny?' Sally, her editor, had asked as soon as Ruth had arrived at work that first Monday, to which she'd been able to reply truthfully, 'She seems great.' And at first she had, in fact still now, a week since Agatha had started, she seemed great. It was just that she made Ruth feel shit. Ruth suspected her feelings to be pathetic, but the girl was too good. Her house had never been so clean, the fridge never so well stocked, the food she cooked every night was delicious and the children seemed happy. It was a working-mother's dream scenario and to complain was surely akin to madness; but before Aggie she had always found something perversely comforting in bitching about the nanny, in secretly believing she could do a better job. Ruth knew enough however to know that she undoubtedly could not have done a better job.

Ruth had given up work after Betty was born but she had only lasted a year and the memory of that time still resonated deep inside her. Ruth was a coper, sometimes even a control freak. She prided herself on her ability to get on with life, to run at it full tilt without wavering, not to be afraid to try, to not even be afraid to fail. But life with Betty had been different.

She had started so positively, with such high hopes and expectations. She was going to always have fresh flowers on the table, bake bread and cakes, read to Betty every day, take her for long walks round the park, teach her the sounds that animals made and smother her in kisses. At first it had been like the best drug she'd ever taken, pure euphoria accompanied her everywhere. It reminded her of the feeling she used to get lying on a hot beach and feeling as if the sun had penetrated her body, warming every organ. Before, of course, the ozone layer was wrenched apart and the sun became carcinogenic.

The warmth however came from within her and what she had achieved. There is a moment after giving birth when you have come through the shit and the blood and the vomit and the sensation of being split in two and turned inside out and the pure unadulterated terror when you realise that, like death, no one else can do this for you. And that moment is heaven. It is pure bliss. It is spiritual and yet earthy. You know your place and accept it for maybe the first time in your life. You are like other women and spectacularly set apart from men. And this feeling lasts, often for months.

But like every drug, it had its come down, a come down which took Ruth by surprise. She could remember the moment exactly. She had been cutting carrots in the kitchen, thinking about how she could save a bit of supper for Betty's lunch the next day, when her brain shifted. She physically felt it, like a jolt in her skull. One minute she was in the moment and the next her hands were disconnected from her body. She watched them performing the mundane task of cutting and couldn't feel them. She tried a different job, filling the pan with water, but it was the same. She thought she might faint and went running in to Christian, who was watching football on the telly and couldn't understand what she was going on about. Why don't you go to bed, he'd said, you must be knackered, what with all that getting up all night. I'll do supper, bring it up to you on a tray.

But sleeping did nothing for her. She woke the next morning covered in sweat, her heart racing. When she sat up in bed her head spun and the room tilted when she went to the bathroom. She begged Christian to stay at home because she must be ill, but he looked at her as if she was mad and asked if she remembered that his new show was going out that night.

Ruth pulled herself together because babies hold all illnesses apart from their own in contempt, but the world remained distorted. From then on everything she had jumped and skipped to only twenty-four small hours before became as hard as leaving a new lover in a warm bed on a cold winter's day. She started to feed Betty from jars, Christian's supper was often absent, the cleaning went undone for weeks on end. She began to hate the park in the same way that she had once hated flying, something she couldn't ever imagine doing again. Even the women whom she was starting to make friends with now seemed foreign, the language they spoke disconcerting and meaningless. She was never going to be as competent as they were, days were never again going to wash over her, fear was beginning to limit her every moment.

Ruth had felt as though she was disappearing. Her bones felt slushy in her body so that sometimes she was sure she was going to faint in the park or fall down the stairs while holding Betty. She worried constantly about what would happen to her precious daughter, who she loved as ferociously as a mother lion. She calculated that if she died just after Christian left for work that would be twelve hours Betty would have to spend alone. Certainly she'd be scarred for life if not seriously injured or killed. And when he spent the night away on a programme she couldn't sleep for anxiety, feeling as if she was falling through the bed and into oblivion when in truth she was simply exhausted.

Things came to a head when going to the supermarket became terrifying. She recognised the irony. Here she was, a woman who had backpacked round Asia, spent a year at an American university, moved to London after meeting Christian only once and worked her way up a very greasy career ladder, now paralysed by the thought of a few aisles of food.

Ruth tried to grab onto the person she had been but couldn't find herself however hard she looked. She remembered a confident woman, but it was like watching a film, the idea that she would ever climb back into that skin impossible. After nine months at home she realised that it was only going to get worse. She looked at all the women in the park and marvelled at their selflessness. There was an army of women out there, she realised, who had made the ultimate sacrifice, themselves for others, and she had nothing but respect for them.

The Monday that Aggie started should have been insignificant for Christian. He prayed she'd work out because he couldn't bear the eruption of stress from Ruth if she didn't. They'd have to go through all those tedious conversations again about her staying at home when they both knew she never would. Full-time motherhood hadn't suited her, but still she would flirt with the idea. He couldn't understand why Ruth was so prepared to waste both of their precious time on arguments that had no answers or endings. She could worry about anything and nothing with equal importance, so that sometimes his head spun and he felt as though he was on a rollercoaster.

But Ruth seemed happy when he'd left and Aggie had already been in the kitchen fixing breakfast for Betty and ignoring the fact that Hal wouldn't eat, something which he'd always silently believed to be the best policy. But Ruth would insist on fussing round him so much at every

meal. He wondered how she had the energy and opti-
mism to start every day thinking Hal would eat, to go to
the trouble of putting food in front of him at every meal,
to dance around him with the spoon, begging and pleading. If Christian had a say he'd have stopped offering Hal
anything and then given him a few biscuits after a couple
of weeks. It was odd how Ruth never considered that the
GP might be right. But he never said anything because
decisions like this were always Ruth's remit. He was
scared to get involved in the important stuff, not just
because of the argument he could so easily cause, but
also because he'd be setting a precedent and more would
be expected of him in the future.

Carol, his production manager, reminded him they had
the interviews for the new admin assistant when he got
in, which sounded boring, but nothing too serious.

'I've narrowed it down to three,' she was saying. 'Do
you want to see their CVs before we go in?'

But he was already reading his emails. 'No, thanks.
Anything I should know? Any of them only got one leg?'

She laughed. 'No, nothing like that. They all seem
great.'

He had a meeting with the Chairman at ten who
wanted to know how the contract with Sky was going,
which took up two minutes, and then they spent half an
hour laughing about the new reality show from the weekend. By the time he got out Carol was annoyed with him
because their first interviewee had been sitting in reception for ten minutes and he'd obviously forgotten. Right,
right, Christian had said as he'd grabbed a cup of coffee
on his way in.

They sat at a Formica desk in a room which someone had designed to look jaunty by adding a couple of round windows framed in acid colours. Touches like this depressed him as he hated anyone pretending that work was fun. It wasn't like he had a bad time, but he wouldn't choose to be there. Which wasn't what Ruth thought. Ruth constantly told him that he'd rather be at work than at home, that he was better friends with his colleagues than his actual friends, that he probably worked on programmes he didn't have to only because he enjoyed it. Christian found the last accusation hard to fathom. Firstly, it wasn't true and he wouldn't do it, but secondly what would be so wrong about him enjoying something? Ruth seemed to live with a constant yoke of resentment around her neck and couldn't bear it if he had more fun than her. Sometimes he considered compiling a fun chart like the children's star charts and they could tick off the minutes they'd each enjoyed during the day and at the end of the week the loser would get an afternoon to themselves. The flaw in this plan was that they would both have to be honest and both have to have the same perception of fun. Ruth, for example, claimed that going out for lunch with Sally was all right, but because she was always on her guard it wasn't exactly fun. Jesus, he wanted to say, take what you can.

The door opened and Sarah walked in. They were both thrown so immediately and physically off guard that Christian couldn't pretend to Carol that he didn't know her. He also couldn't help but wonder if Sarah might have engineered the situation.

'Do you know each other?' asked Carol.

Christian stood up. 'Sorry, I didn't know you were coming in. Yes, we used to work together at Magpie.'

Carol, thankfully, was hard-skinned. 'Well, I did say you should read the CVs.'

Sarah had changed. She was a lot thinner and her face was paler. She'd also let her hair revert to its natural colour, which was much darker than Christian had realised, and her clothes were more demure. She was much, much more attractive and Christian felt himself start to sweat. He couldn't think what to say and let Carol do all the talking, which she enjoyed so didn't notice his silence. Sarah stumbled over her answers and rubbed her blotchy, rash-covered neck, which made Christian remember things he shouldn't.

As she left, Christian felt the air move and was relieved when Carol said, 'Sorry, I misjudged her. She was so confident last time. That was awful. What was she like at Magpie?'

'I can't remember. We didn't work directly together, I don't think she was there long.'

Carol tossed Sarah's CV into the bin. 'I think we can forget that one then.'

The next girl was much better than Sarah and even the third, who had hygiene problems, would have been preferable. After they were done he told Carol he had a meeting and left the office. Christian walked towards the park, a dull pain building behind his eyes and rang Ruth.

'You okay?' he asked.

'Not bad. Busy.'

'Are you?'

'No need to sound so surprised.'

'I wasn't, I just …' He searched for what he wanted to say, but there was nothing he could articulate. He wanted her to tell him he was being stupid.

'Look, did you want something?' she said now and he could see her perfectly, the phone wedged between her ear and her shoulder, her fingers tapping on the keyboard. 'It's just that I want to leave on time tonight, give the kids a bath.'

'No, nothing. It's fine.' But even as he was pressing the red button on his phone he was thinking about Sarah.

April was Agatha's favourite month of the year. It held all the promise without any of the disappointment. She had tried to get Betty to walk to school before, but the little girl had complained so ferociously about wet shoes and a cold nose and the wrong gloves that she'd given up. Now though she made it a fun adventure, through the park and along fairytale streets. Betty was not a hard child to figure out; she needed positive reinforcement, a term Agatha had learnt from one of the numerous child-care books she'd hidden under her bed. You had to pre-empt Betty. You had to watch her and that bottom lip and when you saw it begin to tremble you had to say something like, Don't you hate that little girl's boots, they are completely the wrong shade of pink? or, Did I ever tell you that Cinderella thought that eating two ice creams in one go was really greedy? or, Washing your hair makes it grow faster.

But nothing was going to be properly achieved until the girl was allowed to sleep. Agatha had lain awake most nights since her arrival at the Donaldsons', listening to the pointless drama occurring on the floor beneath her. Betty woke at midnight every night, almost to the second, and yet her cries obviously pulled Ruth from a deep sleep as Agatha heard her bumping and banging on her way to her daughter's bedroom. She'd start the night relatively tolerantly, but by the third or fourth wake-up she'd be shouting, saying ridiculous things to the child like she was going to die if she didn't sleep soon and then expecting Betty to fall into a peaceful state. Sometimes she'd take her to the loo, turning on all the lights and making Betty wash her hands. It was proper madness and Agatha itched to be allowed to intervene; she reckoned she could have Betty sleeping through in a week.

The morning was warm; the air felt like a kiss on your skin and when Agatha opened the kitchen window she could smell the sap.

'Would you like to plant a vegetable garden?' she asked Betty and Hal, out of nowhere. She hadn't planned on speaking those words, which scared her as Agatha believed she'd given up spontaneous speech a long time ago. She mustn't let herself get too comfortable.

'What's a vegetable garden?' asked Betty.

'Well, it's like an ordinary garden, but instead of growing flowers you grow vegetables.'

'Why?'

'To eat, silly.' Agatha was starting to sweat, she'd only been there a month and re-planning the Donaldsons' garden was too much.

But Betty was already brimming over with excitement. 'Can we grow tomatoes? And carrots? And chips?'

Agatha laughed. 'We'd have to grow potatoes and make them into chips. I tell you what, I'll call your mum and ask if it's okay and if it is we'll do it.'

'Can I call? Can I call?' shouted Betty, already reaching for the phone.

The message Ruth listened to when she left the caverns of the tube was garbled and she couldn't make out what Betty was saying. Something about growing carrots on the patio. Shit, not another school project she'd forgotten. She remembered how last year she had pinned the list of what Betty needed for the school nativity play to the fridge and then forgotten all about it. Gail had called on the morning of the play to say that Betty was hysterical because she needed a brown T-shirt and brown trousers by twelve o'clock that day. So instead of being able to make the editorial meeting she'd spent a frantic hour in H&M, crying when the shop assistant couldn't find Betty's size.

She dialled home now and Betty picked up, immediately pleading with her. 'Can we do it, Mum? Please say yes.'

'Say yes to what? I couldn't hear you properly.'

'Aggie is going to make our garden grow vegetables. That we can eat. But only if you say yes.'

Ruth had an image of Aggie digging up their whole garden, turning it into some sort of allotment. 'Where in the garden, darling?'

Betty started to whine. 'I don't know. Please don't say no, Mummy. You're no fun.'

Ruth felt a strong surge of annoyance with Aggie. 'Can you put Aggie on, sweetheart. I just want to find out where she wants to do it.'

'I'm sorry, Ruth,' Aggie said as soon as she got on. 'I know I should have spoken to you first. It's just that I opened the window this morning and everything smelt so fresh and I've been reading about how if you get children to grow their own food they're more likely to eat it and so obviously that made me think of Hal and I've been meaning to mention it to you.'

Aggie's enthusiasm rubbed off on Ruth and she immediately lost her annoyance. Besides, the appointment with the nutritionist that she'd had to re-schedule because of the advertisers' lunch she'd forgotten about was only a few days away and wouldn't that be a good thing to say. 'It sounds like a great idea,' Ruth said as she approached her office. 'Get what you need and I'll pay you back.'

Ruth thought she probably should call Christian and check that he liked the idea as well, but the day rushed at her as soon as she was by her desk. She tried to tell herself to remember to call him later.

Agatha felt pleased with herself. Her improvisation about getting children to grow their own food to make them eat wasn't something she'd read, but it was something which should have been written down and, as such, it had been a good thing to say. Finding a garden centre in West London was hard, but not impossible. Agatha got the children to think about what they wanted to grow and then she wrote a list: tomatoes, carrots, potatoes, beetroot and celery. It seemed like a good, clean start. She got a cookery book down from a large white wooden shelf unit that looked like it should have gone on top of a dresser, but Ruth had fixed to the wall. The paint was flaking off it and Agatha had already mentally re-painted it. She showed Hal the pictures of the vegetables and explained to him that he would have to try whatever he grew because it was a miracle that you put a seed in the ground and it turned into a plant you could eat. He was interested enough to take the bottle out of his mouth.

Betty was impossibly good on the bus and in the garden centre. She behaved like a proper little lady all the way around and was so good that Agatha allowed her to choose an organic chocolate bar at the till.

'It's so fun, hanging out with you,' she said, making the little girl beam with pride.

All the way home they talked about the best way to plant. Agatha had bought a cheap manual in the book section of the garden centre and she read to the children from it on the bus. It sounded like a fairytale anyway. You had to dig a patch of ground and mix in some compost. Then make rows and plant your seeds just under the surface and not too close together. You had to protect them from marauding insects and take good care of them with lots of water and even a bit of food. And then they would reward you with lots of juicy goodness that would run down your chin when you bit into them and make you glad to be alive. 'All the best things are worth waiting for,' Agatha repeated from somewhere when Betty asked her how long it would all take.

The spot they chose was in the bottom right-hand corner, because you could see it from the kitchen window and it wasn't going to interfere with any precious plants. Agatha started by marking out the area and then digging a trench. It was much harder work than she'd anticipated, but now she'd started she was definitely going to finish. The children were so excited that they didn't once ask if they could go in and watch TV. Hal brought his trucks into the garden and ran them through the disturbed soil so that Agatha could see how they were traversing mountains and building new futures. Betty took her little shovel from the shed and begun turning over the soil in the middle of their patch. It took two long hours, but by lunchtime there was a patch of virgin soil waiting to be cultivated.

Agatha made herself and Betty tuna sandwiches for lunch. She had decided to stop offering Hal anything for a while, even though this was exactly against Ruth's instructions. She didn't even question his requests for bottles. She had read in one of her books that making a child feel like eating was an issue was not advisable. The same went for children who wouldn't go to bed. Apparently it was negative attention and because kids crave any sort of attention, however much they get, if you made a fuss about them not doing something they would continue not to do it just to get the attention. It made sense to Agatha and she planned to pay no attention to Hal's not eating, but lots to anything he might put into his mouth that wasn't a bottle. And if ever she was left alone with the children overnight she would let Betty into her bed and cuddle the girl all through the night.

They sat in a patch of sunlight on the patio, Agatha and Betty munching on their sandwiches and Hal slurping a bottle, surveying their new territory. Agatha imagined they were in America, pioneers carving out their own place in the world. Hal sidled over to her, placing his head on her lap, his signal that he was tired. Agatha stroked his head as he sucked and in minutes his eyes were closed and the bottle had fallen to the ground.

'That's handy,' she said to Betty. 'Now he's asleep we can get on with the job.'

Betty beamed because there was nothing she liked more than being made to feel superior to Hal. Agatha picked him up, a dead weight of trust in her arms, and carried him into the house. She buried her face into his neck and smelt his peculiar scent of yoghurt and cotton. She laid him on the sofa and kissed his damp, red cheek. Something twisted in her chest.

Agatha never stopped until she had completed what she set out to do. Unfinished tasks weighed heavily on her mind like her father's pheasants hanging in his game store. Working for all the women who had left their children in her care over the years had proved to Agatha that when she had her own house and family she would not be able to work herself. Which presented a problem in that she would have to marry a man who earned enough to keep them all. She wasn't sure where she would meet this man, as she didn't have any friends and never went anywhere that wasn't connected to the children. And even if she did, she didn't much like men anyway.

By teatime the three of them were banging a miniature fence around their new vegetable patch, pretending to be giants standing over a country they had excavated for food. Agatha planned to cover it with a fine mesh she had bought earlier to guard against snails and birds. Betty and Hal were ecstatic that finally they were going to be allowed to plant the seeds they had bought so long ago. Agatha made the neat furrows they needed, not letting the children help, and then stood over them as they dropped their tiny offerings into the earth. Hal couldn't be persuaded to keep to his row or to drop one seed at a time, but still Agatha felt proud with what they had accomplished. She let them watch TV while she finished off the labelling and the netting.

Christian tried to call Ruth on his way home because he'd found a message from Carol stuck to his computer when he got out of his monthly management meeting saying she'd forgotten about the MTS awards that night and wouldn't be home till late. All he got was her voicemail. Very occasionally he wondered if she would ever pay him back by having her own affair. The thought of another man touching her made him nauseous, but he supposed he would have to be graceful about the whole thing if she did. He doubted that she would, though; even in revenge she was likely to be fair.

When he opened his front door he felt an air of calm which had settled like a fine layer of dust. There didn't seem to be anyone in. He dropped his bag in the hall and went into the kitchen where he could see the remnants of Betty's dinner. There didn't seem to be a place laid for Hal, but Ruth could be trying a new technique so he hardly even registered it. He heard noises in the garden and made his way outside. Agatha, Betty and Hal were bent over a patch at the bottom of the garden and both the children were talking at once. Betty turned when she heard him and ran across the grass like a battering ram. She was filthy and he couldn't stop himself from worrying about his suit as she hurled herself at him. Children, he had noticed, had no respect for personal boundaries. They often acted as though they would climb inside you if they could, pressing their face up against yours, fiddling with your clothes and speaking over your words. But he checked himself and tried to match her glee.

'Come on, Daddy,' she was screeching. 'Come and see what we made.'

He followed the urgent pull of his daughter's hand to a dirty patch of his lawn which he could have sworn had been grass when he'd left that morning but now was a mangy patch of earth surrounded by a cheap and ugly fence. He didn't know what he was looking at.

'We're going to be eating them soon,' Betty was saying.

All Christian wanted was a beer. 'Eating what?'

'The vegetables, silly.'

'Toms …' He strained to hear what his son was saying, but it got lost on the air.

Christian looked imploringly at Agatha and she laughed. 'We made a vegetable patch. Ruth said it was okay. The kids decided what they wanted to grow and we went and bought the seeds and it's taken us all day to make this.' She held out her arm like a hostess on a game show. He was surprised that she didn't say taa-daa.

'Wow. That's great.' He knew his response was inadequate, but he could never be as enthusiastic as women seemed to need him to be.

'I've been reading about kids who don't eat,' Agatha was saying now, 'and there's this one doctor who suggested that you should get them to grow their own food as it makes it more appealing. I thought it might be good for Hal.'

'That's a great idea. Makes loads of sense.' Christian was genuinely impressed. 'Well done.'

She blushed and he noticed how with the sun on her hair it was much more auburn than brown. She ruffled Betty's hair. 'And she was so helpful I literally couldn't have done it without her.'

'I was so good Aggie bought me chocolate.'

'Anyway, you two, bath time,' said Agatha, taking them both by the hands.

Christian knew he should want to give his kids a bath after not having seen them all day, or at least offer, but they both looked so happy trailing after Aggie that it was too easy to let them get on with it. If you could get rid of the guilt, he felt as he opened a beer and took it into the evening sunlight in his garden, this would be perfect parenting.

The vegetable patch was undeniably ugly and it rankled him in a way he knew to be stupid. He dialled Ruth's number again, but it was still on voicemail.

'I just got home,' he said into the phone, 'to find that the kids have destroyed the garden. You could have told me before you agreed to let them dig up our lawn.' He pressed the red phone and immediately felt like his father.

Agatha appeared at the kitchen door. 'They both want you to say goodnight to them. I've made chicken for dinner, by the way.'

Christian stood up. 'Great. Oh, I forgot to say, Ruth's out at some awards do. So I'll probably eat in front of the telly. There's a match on I want to watch anyway.'

'Fine.' Agatha had to keep her voice cheery. She felt a surge of resentment. Didn't he realise how long it had taken to stuff that lemon-and-garlic mixture under the chicken's skin without breaking it?

Ruth hadn't been able to place the air of excitement in the office all morning. But then Sally had asked her if she thought the red or black heels were better and she had immediately remembered the awards ceremony that night. She had to rush out at lunch to buy a dress, which was infuriating because they couldn't afford it this month and she'd already decided on what she was going to wear. Recently everything was slipping out of her mind; she felt as though life was getting faster and leaving her behind. Maybe she should see a doctor. Maybe she should get a bigger diary or just write in the one she had. Which reminded her that she hadn't called the plumber about the fact that they kept on having to reset the boiler to get hot water.

The younger section of the magazine started raiding the fashion and beauty cupboards at four. By five they were drinking. Sally seemed to effortlessly be able to combine joining in with staying aloof, while Ruth remained glued to her computer, pretending she had some copy she had to finish. By the time she got into the loos to change it smelt like she presumed a brothel would. She didn't look good in the dress, she had chosen it too quickly and the blue didn't sit right on her olive skin. She tried tying her hair up, but felt she looked jowly. The expensive concealer did nothing to hide her bags.

They were getting a coach to Alexandra Palace where the awards were being held. The noise as she got on hit her like the sound generated by her children's parties, so loud it almost took you out of your body. She wondered if Betty and Hal were in bed yet. Nobody had answered the phone at home all afternoon, which had created a little knob of panic deep in her stomach. She hadn't been able to get hold of Christian either and now she had no reception on her phone, but Carol had assured her that she'd give him the message and, of course, Aggie was infinitely capable. She'd find a payphone when she got there if her signal hadn't come back.

Ruth sat next to Sally by the window near the front of the coach. Sally kept turning her back on her to listen and laugh at her team, as she called them all, which was fine with Ruth as a headache had settled round the top of her head, squeezing pain into her body. She rubbed her shoulders and could feel the tension nestling there like snarling dogs. It was going to be a long night.

Her signal had returned by the time they got there, so she hung back. She noticed Kate, the only other woman in the office with children, doing the same, a concerned frown on her face. She could hear her telling whoever was on the other end that the Calpol was on the top shelf of the third cupboard to the right of the cooker in the kitchen.

Ruth's message symbol was bleeping. Christian's voice came through, moaning about the garden. It stirred an immense anger in her that made her want to walk all the way home just to rub his smug face into the dirt he was complaining about. She jabbed a message out to him, not trusting herself to speak to him directly. *If you were ever available to take calls about vegetable patches from your kids you would probably have said yes as well and then it would have been a great idea.*

Christian received Ruth's message as Arsenal equalised and he was finishing his third bottle of beer. He'd meant to send Ruth a text saying sorry for sounding so pompous, but after reading Betty three Charlie and Lola books he'd lost the will to live. 'Did you know,' he'd said to the cat after returning downstairs from Betty's bedtime ritual, 'that Charlie has a little sister Lola. She is small and very funny. Except of course she isn't. She is annoying and precocious and due to total parental neglect has transferred all her negative attention complexes onto poor Charlie, who should get some sort of medal from Carol Vorderman.' His outburst surprised him so much he had completely forgotten about anything other than lying on the sofa, shouting abuse at eleven men on a grassy pitch.

Ruth's sanctimonious tone irritated him and made him glad he hadn't apologised. He texted back: *Get over yourself. It looks ugly.* His phone bleeped: *It's not all about aesthetics.* He wrote: *Have a good time at your party. I'm too tired to argue, having just got our daughter to sleep.* He nearly couldn't be bothered to read the next text: *Aren't you wonderful. Don't wait up.* Arsenal scored again, but Christian couldn't raise a cheer. Often his life felt pathetic.

Ruth knew she was drunk before she stumbled into the taxi and felt her head reeling. The jolts of corners taken too fast and a spicy smell she couldn't place were conspiring to make her feel sick. The driver had a small symbol of an Indian god on his dashboard; it was shameful that she didn't know its name, didn't even know which religion it represented. Still though it comforted her, reassured her in some indefinable way. She looked at the tiny icon, cheap in its fluorescent plastic, and envied its sense of stability, its ability to inspire wonder. So many hopes and dreams and wishes had been prayed into that image, it made Ruth smile.

Viva had won Best Design and Editor of the Year, so the champagne had been flowing all night. Sally had been in her element and Ruth had felt an unsisterly stab of jealousy watching her old friend so graciously accept her award and make a funny speech about Roger asking her whether she loved him or *Viva* more. 'I simply answered that he was my husband, but *Viva* was my baby. What I didn't add was that women always love their children more than their husbands, don't they.' Sally didn't have children.

Ruth's phone was vibrating, but the message she saw was an old one from Christian. *Did you call the plumber? There's no bloody hot water again.*

'No,' she said out loud. 'I bloody didn't.'

'Excuse me?' said the taxi driver.

'No, sorry, nothing.' Ruth threw the phone down next to her and stared out of the window at the grey streets, passing by like a dreary dream. She found it strange to think of all the sleeping bodies shielded behind all those front doors, encased in walls which felt so familiar and comforting to them, if they were lucky, but would be alien and frightening to her. It reminded her of going on holiday and how you walk into the apartment or cottage or room and feel so out of place you almost want to go home, but within days those new four walls suddenly feel cosy, like you've always lived there. Which in turn made her think about that old cliché, There's no place like home, which she pictured as an appliqué scene in a wooden frame, sitting in her granny's kitchen.

'Thirty-four sixty,' the driver was saying as they pulled up outside her front door. She shoved two twenties at him and only remembered her phone still lying on the back seat after she'd let herself in. She was too tired to feel upset.

Ruth went into the dark sitting room and saw Christian's plate and four empty bottles of beer by the sofa. It roused a fresh spasm of defeat in her. She picked them up and carried them into the kitchen, wondering who he thought was going to do it. Her husband had a habit of leaving cupboard doors flailing, drawers open at hip-hitting height, wet towels languishing on beds, dirty pants multiplying on the floor. What did your last slave die of? she'd shout, sounding like the sort of woman she had never wanted to be.

As Ruth stood up from putting Christian's plate in the dishwasher she caught sight of the tiny fence circling what must be the new vegetable patch. She felt a complete desire to see it rush at her heart, making her open the back door and step into her garden made yellow by the light pollution of night in the city. The patch was a perfect rectangle and she could see the grooves of the beds under a fine meshing. At the end of each bed was a white plastic stick with writing on it. She squatted in the grass and worked her hand inside the mesh to pull out one of the sticks. Betty's inexpert hand had written carrots and just below it Hal had scribbled something orange.

Her heart contracted so that she wondered if she might be about to die from all the alcohol and cigarettes she had uncharacteristically consumed. But really the problem lay with the image in her head; both her children as they had been as newborn babies, sucking at her breast. She would look down on them as they fed and marvel at the seriousness, the urgency, which accompanied their tugging. It used to feel like her breasts were attached to her heart by a series of thick ropes and that until that moment the ropes had lain slack and dormant. With each suck the ropes grew more taut, so that in the end her heart felt as though it had been pulled free, released like a sail on a ship. Both Betty and Hal had woken all night, every night, and when she had picked them out of their cribs, only half awake and smelling that indefinable scent only possessed by newborns, they had sighed with such contentment that she had sworn to never, ever let anything bad happen to either of them.

Then the wonder of it all. Watching a blank face smile for the first time must be more wonderful than the Hanging Gardens of Babylon or the pyramids; because don't all wonders occur only within your own world, really there's nothing else. Hearing a gurgle turn to a sound, feeling strength in limbs that only a day before had seemed so weak. You wait and wait as a mother at the start, wait for these minuscule miracles which make you writhe with excitement. But then those tiny bodies catch up with their whirling minds and all the things you've been searching for suddenly tumble out of them, so that you even miss some things. And then it stops being so precious and you forget, only for something like this to smack you right back to the impact of the beginning.

How had Ruth gone from falling so absolutely in love that she realised exactly where her heart was in her body, to missing the creation of something so fundamentally marvellous as this garden? Surely it was too mean of life to make her choose between herself and her children? The stick dropped from her hand and Ruth sat back heavily onto the already damp grass, covering her mouth with her hands to stop her sobs from waking anyone in the house.

Her crying didn't last long; self-indulgence never sat easily with Ruth, she became too aware of herself. Instead she made herself stand up and get upstairs to bed. She was drunker than she'd realised and she tripped as she pulled her clothes heavily over her head, worrying already about how she would feel in the morning. Her pillow was cool but her head spun when she closed her eyes.

Christian rolled towards her and draped a hand across her stomach, something she still hated him doing. 'Did you win?' he asked.

'Not personally. Sally did though.'

'So you celebrated.'

Ruth knew what he meant. 'Don't lecture me about drinking.'

'I'm not.' His hand moved down her body, stroking her thigh. 'I like it when you're drunk.'

Ruth knew how easy it would be to roll into him, to let go and feel good for a moment, but a sickness that existed both physically and mentally had taken hold of her. It seemed like too much of an effort; recently she'd even begun to see it as too much of a relinquishment, although she wasn't sure what it was that she was losing. She pushed his hand away. 'I'm knackered.'

Christian turned heavily from her and Ruth was sure she heard him sigh.

Christian had an early meeting so he was up and out before anyone had woken up. He found Ruth's mobile phone on the door mat with a card from a taxi firm. It didn't take a brain surgeon to work out what had happened and it annoyed him that she should always get away with her drunken nights out when he was made to feel like an alcoholic home-wrecker whenever he came in the worse for wear.

It was a beautiful spring morning but Christian had a headache and the sunlight glinting off all the expensive cars made him feel woozy. He'd been feeling peculiar since his disastrous interview with Sarah. The whole encounter had left him off balance. The difference in their circumstances had been so marked as to be grotesque. In the three years since they'd last seen each other he had a smart new job, a beautiful son to go with his amazing daughter and put a floundering marriage back on track. Sarah, on the other hand, was applying for a position beneath the one she'd had when he'd known her and looked as if she'd had some sort of breakdown. He'd checked her CV and it said single. He was not enough of a shit to feel good about any of it.

Then two days ago she'd phoned him. She'd sounded so faint and weak that when she'd asked if they could meet up, nothing serious, but it had been odd to see him in those circumstances and she didn't want to leave it like that, he had said yes. Christian had desperately wanted to decline as the whole situation seemed too dangerous, but he felt oddly responsible for how she had turned out and so had agreed. He was due to meet her the next day.

Christian was unused to feeling confused; normally he got on with things or asked Ruth what she thought. He texted Toby, the only school friend he still saw regularly and asked if they could meet for a drink that evening. He was relieved that the reply was yes and didn't even care that Toby suggested an impossibly trendy Notting Hill pub in which he'd feel completely out of place.

The day dragged. He had a long and boring phone conference with some stiff Americans, one of his staff called in sick for the third time that month, Carol was in a bad mood and the sushi he had for lunch was over-priced and tasteless. He called Ruth at four to say that Toby had rung because he was having a crisis with his latest girlfriend, so he was going to meet him for a drink, knowing she couldn't shout because of what she'd done the night before.

Toby was already at the bar when Christian arrived, looking like he owned the place and knew everyone there, which probably wasn't far off the mark. It was bad luck, Christian felt, that his best friend should make him feel so inadequate with his ridiculously glamorous lifestyle. He couldn't remember how or even when Toby had got into the music business or why he had made such a success of it. Either way, standing by the curved bend of the polished wooden bar, ordering two pints of Guinness from the barmaid, he felt wrong and out of place in his suit.

Toby was texting furiously on his iPhone. 'Fuck, I'm going to have to run in about an hour. We've got a band showcasing tonight and it's all gone tits-up.'

'Right.' Christian resisted an urge to ask himself along.
'Anyway, what's up? Why the urgency?'

Christian didn't know who Toby was sleeping with at the moment, but he'd lay money on her being as fit as a butcher's dog, as Toby would say. Life sometimes came too fast, you couldn't be sure if you were right or wrong, stupid or wily, pathetic or sophisticated.

'D'you remember Sarah?'

'Of course. Please don't tell me you're seeing her again.'

Christian waved from behind his pint. 'No. No. But this really weird thing happened ...'

'I need a fag for this,' said Toby, standing up. They shuffled onto the pavement, no longer pretending at what they were doing to their bodies. Christian helped himself to one. 'Thought you'd given up.'

'Only when Ruth's around.'

'So?' His friend leant against the grimy wall of the pub and Christian momentarily wondered what he was doing there.

'She came for an interview at my work.'

'Shit. What, you were interviewing her?'

'Yeah, and I hadn't bothered to check the CVs, so I was totally unprepared when she walked in and Carol was in the room and it was fucking awful. She looked terrible.' Christian flashed an image of Sarah in his mind. Sometimes he felt as though he was watching his life on TV and that nothing really mattered. 'No, she looked amazing. But, sort of, I don't know, wasted.'

'What, drugs?'

'No, more like life hadn't been good to her.'

'And I suppose you're thinking that's your fault? That she's been spending these last three years pining after you?'

'No, but you know, what with the baby and everything …'

Toby's phone bleeped again. 'Sorry, I have to get this.' He answered and walked to the kerb, balancing on the rubbish-strewn lip of the pavement as a child might. Christian checked his phone for something to do and saw that Ruth had texted, asking him to get milk on his way home.

'Sorry about that. Let's go back in,' Toby said as he returned.

They sat at the round table they had been at before, their own puddles of spilt beer still reflecting the lights from the bar. Christian hoped they would have been cleaned up.

'She called me a few days ago and I'm meeting her for lunch tomorrow.'

'Are you mad?' Christian was surprised to see anger on his friend's face, in the turn of his mouth before he could hide it. 'You know Ruth will leave if you do it to her again. Fuck knows how you got her to stay last time, but she's not going to take it a second time.'

'I'm not planning anything. But I couldn't say no. I feel guilty.'

Toby rubbed his eyes with the back of his hand. Christian wanted another cigarette. 'Look, it's not like she didn't know what she was doing. It was shit, but shit happens. People have miscarriages every day. I can't believe that three years on she's still upset about it. My guess is that she's seen a chance and decided to take it. And you, my friend, should politely decline.'

'I don't know. I don't think she's like that.'

'You don't want to think she's like that.'

Christian didn't know what he thought. It was possible Toby was right. 'Do you sometimes wonder if you are who you really are?'

'No. Yes.'

Christian felt angry, not necessarily with Toby, but he was there. 'You don't understand.'

'Please, don't start telling me how hard married life is. All that shitty love, friendship and children.'

Christian squeezed his hand round his glass. 'No sex, constant rows, massive mortgage.'

'It's not that bad.'

'What, and I suppose you'd swap your life for mine at the drop of a hat?'

'I'm not saying that, I'm just saying that Ruth and the kids are fantastic and sometimes I leave your house and feel a bit, I don't know, empty.' Christian laughed. 'Look, I'm not trying to say that my life's crap and all I've ever wanted is to settle down, but from where I'm sitting, yours doesn't look too bad either.'

Christian sat back. He felt battered. How could he and Toby be the same age, from the same background and yet at such different points in their lives? Everywhere there were all these choices, how could you possibly ever tell if you'd made the right one? 'D'you want another?'

'No, I've got to go.' Toby stood up. 'You were like this at school, always worried that so and so was doing better than you, or that the party you didn't go to was the best of the year. No one has it all. We're grown-ups now and grown-ups have it hard. None of us are out there having non-stop fun, in fact most of us are lucky if we're having even a bit of fun. I'd cancel Sarah and take Ruth out for dinner.'

Agatha had wanted to get Hal at least interested in the concept of eating before Ruth took him to see the stupid nutritionist on Friday. But half-term had been so busy with the vegetable garden and the trip to the museum and swimming that she hadn't done anything. Still, she doubted the doctor would have much effect anyway.

Ruth looked drawn and tired when she came down for breakfast on Friday, casual in jeans and a shirt, but she made a great play about how excited she was to have the day off. Agatha could have told her this was a stupid thing to say and, sure enough, Betty's lips were trembling over her Rice Pops.

'I want to come, Mummy.'

'But it'll be so boring. Hal and I are only going to the doctor's.'

'I like the doctor's.'

'No, you don't.'

'I do.'

Betty was crying now, working her way up to full-blown hysterics. 'It's not fair. Hal gets to spend a whole day with you. I never spend a day with you.'

Ruth put down her cup of coffee and for a moment Agatha wondered if she was going to cry. 'I'm sure Aggie's got something great planned for the two of you today.'

'I don't want Aggie. I want you.' Agatha told herself not to be offended by this as children always said things they didn't mean. She started to load the dishwasher and, even with her back turned, felt the atmosphere shift. Ruth was about to capitulate. As far as Agatha could see, situations like this were yet another reason not to work after you had children; you felt so guilty you never said no and your kids knew they could get away with anything if they moaned enough. If Ruth had been the one planting vegetables and looking at dinosaurs and marvelling at two strokes of doggy paddle swum without armbands she would now be able to say no.

Betty's screaming was becoming incessant, drilling into all of their heads, so that even Hal had covered his ears.

'Okay, okay,' Ruth shouted over the maelstrom. 'All right, you win, come with us.' Betty immediately stopped crying and climbed onto her mother's lap, planning their day with intricate precision.

Ruth looked over her head to Agatha. 'You could probably do with a day off, Aggie. And it would be lovely to spend some time with them both. We could go and have lunch in Hyde Park after the appointment, feed the ducks maybe.'

'I'll make supper for when you get back.' Agatha grabbed at strands of usefulness.

'No, please, I insist. Take the day, go and meet some friends. You've been working like a Trojan since you got here, you must think we're slave drivers.'

Agatha smiled, but she felt like crying. She had begun to allow herself to believe that the Donaldsons weren't ever going to notice that she never seemed to want a day off, never got a phone call, never met anyone. Now she would have to go through all the stupid pretence again of getting another mobile so she could ring herself, only to go and sit on her own in cinemas.

It wasn't that Agatha had never had friends. She'd had a couple of serious and intense relationships, friendships which she'd thought were the answer to her prayers and would never end. But she had always misjudged the other girls; they never understood her like she thought they had.

The best friend she'd ever had was a girl called Laura who she'd met at the cleaning agency she'd joined when she'd first got to London. From the moment she'd seen her in that spick and span office in Kensington she'd known they'd be friends for ever. There was something so sophisticated about her blonde highlighted hair and upturned collar and cut-glass accent that made Agatha want to possess her like some fabulous vase you'd put on a high shelf and never get down.

Agatha had managed to refine her Northern drawl in the time it took to cross the office and even she was impressed with the sound that came out of her mouth. She had steeled herself to seem super confident and gave a convincing story about needing money to fund her trip to Argentina which she was planning for the second half of her gap year. And wouldn't you know it, but Laura was also working for gap-year travel, except she was going to America. And with friends.

It was easy to find excuses to go into the office and even easier to make Laura laugh or exclaim over their similarities, when really you could read so much about a person just by looking at what book they were reading or what they ate for lunch or the magazine they read. *Pride and Prejudice*, Pret's no-bread tuna sandwich and *Heat*, respectively.

Agatha's mother and father were cruising in the Bahamas and her brother was at St Andrews and never came home. Agatha hated going to their house in Oxford without them and so she was sleeping on a friend's floor while earning some money. She would love to ask Laura round, but her friend's mother had depression and spent most of the time in bed and was really funny about dirt, so she couldn't risk it. In fact, she confided to Laura over coffee one day, her friend was starting to irritate her as she had a new boyfriend and seemed to have forgotten about everyone else's existence. Which was such a bummer as almost all her other friends were away.

Tell me about it, Laura had said, this summer was turning out to be so tedious she half wished she was going to Bristol in September. Bristol, that's funny, I'm off to Exeter, which is quite nearby, said Agatha. And at that moment she believed whole-heartedly that by next September she might have got herself into that very university because, when she stopped to think about it, that was what she had wanted to do all along.

Laura knew interesting people and went to amazing places and she started taking Agatha. Agatha was aware that to fit in properly she was going to have to be fun and available and always say the right thing. The problem was that it soon became clear that saying the right thing was knowing all the other people they were always talking about. Laura and her friends seemed to begin every conversation with the words, Do you know … or, As Connie was saying … or, When I was last at Tom's cottage … These phantom presences began to loom large around Agatha, they even invaded her dreams. It grew tiresome not knowing anybody and Agatha could feel people begin to lose interest in her as she showed her ignorance again and again. And it was almost like she was getting to know them all anyway, they all sounded the same and none of them ever materialised. So, one night, when maybe she'd had one glass of Chardonnay too many, she was amazed to find out that she did know Vicky, Vicky from Hammersmith who had been travelling round Europe all summer and whose parents lived in Hertfordshire. With the long blonde hair and amazing body, yes, how weird.

Except, wouldn't you know it, bloody Vicky turned up a week later, all bronzed and amazing, exactly as everyone had said. And she didn't know Agatha from Adam, had never even seen her. It was awful as Agatha had spent a whole evening telling anyone who would listen about their family holidays to Cornwall and their shared love of three-day eventing. Laura stopped calling after that.

It reminded Agatha of Sandra at school who had stopped talking to her when she'd asked Agatha's mum if she really did know Billie Piper. Her mother hadn't even known who Billie Piper was, which just about summed up the stupid woman. But even after she was found out, Agatha had wanted to scream that she did know her. She had read every single word ever written about her, she had followed her since before she was properly famous, certainly before stupid Sandra had heard of her. And then she'd had to listen to Sandra going on about Billie's eating disorder in the playground and she'd felt like she had to put her straight or hit her. But nobody would listen, so she'd said that Billie's mum was her mum's best friend and she'd known Billie since they were babies and she didn't have anorexia. And, you know what, even now she would be hard pushed to admit that it wasn't true.

Ruth began the day out with her children so positively. It had been a good idea of Betty's and Ruth was ashamed she hadn't thought of it herself. Unusually the monotony of grey which seemed to always sit over their heads had been replaced by a perfect sun resplendent in a baby blue sky. If you ignored the fact that they had to begin the day with a visit to a £120-an-hour nutritionist because her son wouldn't eat, you could imagine it was going to be perfect. And Ruth was going to make it perfect. She might have missed the vegetable garden, but surely special times could be found in lots of places.

On the way to the tube she thought it wise to remind Betty where they were going. 'You know you have to be really, really good in the doctor's office, don't you?'

'Of course I do, Mummy.'

'You have to sit completely still and let me talk to him. Do you understand? Absolutely no funny business.

Because it's very important that Mummy gets to hear everything he says. And then we can go to the park and if you've been an extra good girl I'll get you the biggest ice cream you've ever seen.'

Ruth always got a stab of anxiety going into the tube with her children. She ran through countless scenarios where a terrorist would let off a bomb or both her children would try to jump in front of a tube at the same time or someone would snatch Betty but to get her back she would have to leave Hal alone. Plus of course all the usual problems, like the fact that hardly any of the stations had lifts and no one ever helped with the buggy. She tried to visualise Christian in his day to calm these anxieties and then laughed at herself. It was odd how he still remained her constant, like a talisman that could be worried in her pocket.

The tube roared into the station with a rush of warm air which made Ruth want to shut her eyes and pretend she was standing on an African plain. The platform felt old and worn beneath her feet and there was an awful lot of day to get through before they could make their way back to this station. She worried that time with her children always going to be like this, a series of events that needed to be got through before you could legitimately put them to bed.

'Come on,' she was shouting now, pulling Betty onto the tube and in the process squeezing her hand too hard against the metal buggy handle and making her cry.

'My Brat,' screamed Betty as the doors whipped shut.

Ruth spun round in time to see the grotesque plastic doll fall under the train.

'We're going to kill my Brat,' wailed Betty as the train crunched off.

'Don't worry, sweetheart, I'll get you another one,' said Ruth, secretly pleased because those dolls could give women a complex all on their own and yet Ruth was sure she'd read they were the bestselling toys out there. They made Barbie and Sindy look like nuns, with their ridiculously provocative bodies that could only have been dreamt up by a fetishist. And their facial features were no more than an advert for plastic surgery, not to mention their clothes, which would make a street-walker blush. One day she would muster the energy to explain to Betty why it was neither clever nor cool to own such toys, why being a woman was about so much more than how you looked, why ... God, she couldn't think straight against the unrelenting screech of Betty's hysterics.

Christian knew Toby was right about Sarah, but he'd also known that he would find it impossible not to meet her for lunch. He arrived first at the Italian restaurant a few roads away from his office and chose a table at the back. The table was too small and intimate, with its depressing red-and-white checked plastic tablecloth and obligatory vase of breadsticks. Ruth would laugh at the framed photo of the Pope above the entrance to the toilets; he could imagine her saying that it didn't bode well for the food.

Sarah was an acceptable ten minutes late but she arrived looking embarrassed and flustered. She turned to the side as she squeezed into her seat opposite him and he could see how much weight she had lost, she almost looked like one of those models in Ruth's magazine. Today she was wearing black trousers with a black T-shirt and a leopard-print scarf tied round her neck. Her once blonde hair hung loose around her shoulders and there was only the faintest trace of make-up on her eyes. He knew it was wrong to find her as attractive as he did.

'I'm sorry to have called,' she said immediately. 'But it was all too weird.'

'No, it's nice. It was the right thing to do.' Christian pointed to the bottle of wine he wanted, it seemed unlikely that he could get through this without alcohol.

Sarah was nervous, he realised; she kept on re-adjusting her scarf and he noticed the red rash creeping up under her chin like some sort of rampant ivy.

'Anyway,' she said, breaking a breadstick but not eating it, 'new job?'

'Yeah, I've been there nearly two years now.'

'And it's okay?'

'Well, you know, as okay as jobs ever are.'

'But you've done well.'

Christian tried to hear a note of sarcasm in her voice, but couldn't find it there. He nodded and knew that he had to return like some semi-pro tennis player. 'And what about you, what have you been up to?'

'Well, I've mainly been living in Australia.' She looked down and crumbled more of the breadstick. Their wine arrived and Christian poured them both a glass.

'Australia. Wow.' He wanted to leave. He had always hated anyone who went to Australia for anything other than a holiday.

'Yeah, it was great.' He could tell she wanted to say something and so he let the silence build. Sarah tucked her hair behind her ears incessantly. 'After the, you know, miscarriage, I went back to my mum and dad's for a while and then I thought, fuck it, I'm going to get on a plane, and I ended up in Sydney and I met someone and stayed for two years.'

Christian liked the sound of someone, it had been foolish to imagine she'd been pining after him. 'Great. Did you work?'

'Only bar work and stuff. It's much easier to get by over there.'

Sarah chatted on about the weather and the standard of living and the beaches, stuff Christian had heard countless times before. It seemed implausible that he had nearly left Ruth for this woman. With the flip of a dice life took you on the oddest ride, up some ladders, down too many snakes. He could have had a whole life with Sarah, they'd have a two-year-old by now, probably living in some tiny flat somewhere because he had to give most of his money to Ruth, who would legitimately hate him. She could have even met someone else and he would feel lonely and jaded because of course most of their friends and relatives would have sided with her. He'd have two children he hardly knew, one who he'd never lived with, and he would have to take them on terrible days out to the zoo where they would all feel like crying. And then when Betty got older she would say to her future boyfriends that she didn't trust men much because her father had got some girl pregnant when she was three and left her mother to bring her and Hal up alone.

And nothing would have been different with Sarah. He could see that as clear as the sun shining through the window from the street. They would have spent the past two years arguing about whose turn it was to take out the rubbish, or why he watched so much football, or who was more tired. It was sad to realise that no one was unique and who you ended up with was more down to circumstances than design. He longed to be at home, sitting on one of the uncomfortable sofas he always teased Ruth for buying only because they'd looked good, with Betty and Hal fighting and him and Ruth looking at each other and feeling for one tiny second like they were in complete agreement.

'So what did you have?'

Christian hadn't been paying enough attention to what Sarah had been saying. His pasta was offputting; there was too much of it in too small a plate, making it seem sticky when really it was perfectly well cooked. 'Sorry, what did I have what?'

'Boy or girl?'

The question was appalling to him and Christian couldn't imagine why she would want to know. 'Oh, right. Sorry. Boy.'

'To go with your girl. How perfect.' The sarcasm was there this time. Should he apologise? Should he bring up everything that had gone on? Was that what she was expecting? He felt weary, it all seemed so pointless, nothing was going to be changed by ranting and raving, but maybe she needed to get something off her chest. Sarah, however, seemed to have had second thoughts and now she smiled. 'Sorry, I am pleased for you.'

Christian toyed with the idea of telling her that Betty still never slept through the night or that Hal had never eaten one morsel of food even though he was nearly three and existed on an average of about twenty bottles a day. But it seemed too much of a betrayal to his family, as if sitting with Sarah wasn't enough.

'Anyway,' he said, looking at his watch. 'It's been great, but I've got a meeting at three and, you know ...'

'Oh yes, okay.'

It was awkward leaving. Neither of them knew how to end it. Christian saw a pigeon with a broken leg in the gutter as they were saying goodbye and it looked so miserable he wanted to find a brick and bash it over the head. Its grey feathers were matted and it had a bald patch on its back and he worried that it had been abandoned by the other pigeons. As he watched Sarah walk away self-consciously he hoped she was leaving his life.

On his way back to his office Christian checked his phone and saw he had three missed calls from Ruth. There would be a certain irony to something bad happening to a member of his family while he was having a disastrous lunch with his old affair. He called her back immediately and she answered in two rings.

'Ruth, what's wrong?'

Her voice cracked as soon as she heard him. 'Oh God, it was awful. I've been trying to get hold of you for ages.'

'What was?' Panic rose like bile in his chest as he depicted terrible fates befalling his children, each racing heartbeat showing him a different image of terror.

'The nutritionist.'

He relaxed. 'Oh, of course, what did he say?'

'I can't talk now. You know, little ears and all that.' Her voice shook and he could almost see her trying to hold herself together for the sake of the kids. She'd done a lot of that when Hal was a newborn baby. 'I wish I hadn't gone, though. The whole day's been a disaster. I don't know if I can do this any more.'

'Do what?'

'Be a mother.'

'Come on, Ruth, calm down. Why don't we go out to dinner tonight and talk about this properly, see if Aggie can babysit?'

'I'm so tired, I don't know if I've got the energy.'

'Come on, just somewhere local. It'd be good for you.'

Ruth sniffed heavily down the phone. 'All right.'

The death of the Brat had been a bad omen. Betty's hysterics had only gathered momentum the further they got away from the scene of the crime. Nothing Ruth could say would calm her down so that by halfway there Ruth thought she might have a panic attack. The walls of the tube were too tight a fit and she was acutely aware of the bumps and grinds of the tracks. She wondered what she was doing, taking her children on this hurtling mass of metal deep underneath London. Everything seemed terrifying.

Betty had reduced herself to dull whimpering by the time they arrived in Oxford Circus but she was petulant and stroppy and hung off the buggy like a damp rag. The street was thronged with young girls waltzing carefree into Topshop, their skinny hips unscarred by child-bearing. Any of them could have been *Viva* models and yet the magazine was aimed at women like her. Well, not like her. *Viva* women juggled everything successfully, whilst also looking flawless.

The nutritionist's office was in a thin, tall building between Oxford and Regent Street and looked as imposing as a giant headmaster. Ruth had expected to press a buzzer and be shown up to a floor, but she was able to walk straight in and up to the reception desk because the nutritionist seemed to command the whole building. The receptionist gleamed, like a woman in a cosmetic surgery advert in the back of a magazine. Ruth felt grimy and under-nourished as she said Hal's name.

Dr Hackett's office was bigger than her sitting room and furnished in a parody of the image of a successful private doctor, with gilt-framed paintings, a large well-polished wooden desk and two deep leather armchairs positioned on either side. He sat in front of two floor-to-ceiling windows that looked out over a private garden which seemed an impossibility in the middle of the city. Ruth couldn't hear any traffic noise.

Ruth had fixed Dr Hackett in her mind as a friendly, slightly hippyish but very posh man with longish grey hair and gangly legs which he would cross and uncross incessantly. Never had he been a paunchy older man with spectacles on the end of his nose and a ludicrously expensive-looking three-piece tweed suit. He also shouldn't have been sitting on the other side of a heavy desk and he shouldn't have looked so bored by the whole encounter.

As she sat down, Ruth could see herself and her children through his eyes so exactly the recognition hurt. Betty's face was smeared and dirty and blotchy from the excess of tears; Hal looked nonplussed, stuck to her hip with a bottle in his mouth; and she looked too thin, with straggly hair and an air of neurosis resting on her like most women wore perfume. I'm not really this person, she wanted to say, you've just caught me on a bad day.

'So, Mrs Donaldson,' he said, 'what seems to be the problem with your son?'

Ruth immediately felt defensive. 'I don't know if it's a problem.'

The doctor sighed. 'If it's not a problem, then can I ask what you're doing here?' He made her feel stupid just as she supposed he'd meant to. She wondered how on earth he had ended up being a nutritionist.

'Sorry, I didn't mean that. I just meant we don't know what to think.'

'Please, put that down.' Ruth jumped, only then noticing that Betty was pushing an enormous glass paperweight perilously close to the edge of the desk.

'God, Betty, what are you doing?' she shouted. Betty's lip started to tremble. 'Sorry,' she said to the doctor. 'Hal has never eaten anything solid. Ever. He lives on bottles of milk.'

'How many does he have a day?'

The truth seemed suddenly untenable in this pristine office and so Ruth pointlessly lied. 'About ten.'

'At least they're sustaining.'

'Yes, but he's nearly three.'

The silence was broken by the sound of Hal's sucking. It could have been funny.

'Do you offer him food?'

'Every day. Every meal.'

'Do you eat with him?'

Ruth rubbed the side of her neck. 'No, not often.'

The doctor wrote something down. 'Do you work?'

'Yes, but my nanny is brilliant. She knows what to do. In fact, she's recently planted a vegetable garden which Hal helped with because she read that if you get kids to see the whole process of growing food, they're more likely to eat it.'

'That's not a theory I'm aware of.'

'It's not just Hal's garden. I helped too,' said Betty, slipping from her chair onto the floor and starting to cry. Ruth decided to ignore her.

'And how's the rest of his development?'

Ruth estimated she had about ten minutes before Betty launched into a full-scale tantrum. 'It's not great. He's well behind where Betty was at this age. His speech is still quite limited and he doesn't have many friends.' Ruth thought she might cry. Her stomach felt as though it had been clasped in a vice.

'Were you aware that refusal to eat can sometimes be a symptom of more serious physiological disorders?'

'No, I wasn't. Do you think Hal's got something like that?' She heard the pitch of her voice rising.

'I've no idea. I have no reason to suspect that at the moment, I'm just saying it might be something we should explore further down the line.'

'I want to go home,' said Betty, from under the chair.

'But are there any tests we can run?'

'Not yet, Mrs Donaldson. One step at a time.'

You can't do that, Ruth wanted to shout. You can't dangle a piece of information like that and not follow it up. She wanted to stand up and shake the stupid man until he told her every possibility.

'Have you tried not giving him bottles?'

'No. My husband did suggest that, but it seemed too cruel.'

Dr Hackett looked at her over his glasses and a look of pure contempt clouded his features. 'Cruel to be kind, I'd say.'

'Mummy, I want to go. You said I could get a new Brat.'

Ruth looked down at her daughter sprawled on the floor, her face turning red as she worked her way up to a howl and momentarily hated her. 'Not now, Betty, I'm talking. You won't get a new Brat unless you behave.'

'Do you work full time, Mrs Donaldson?'

'Yes.'

'Have you heard of separation anxiety?'

'Well, sort of.' Of course, of course. How stupid of her not to realise that this too was going to turn out to be her fault.

'When did you return to work after Hal was born?'

'He was about five months.' Ruth nearly apologised but managed to stop herself. She felt very hot.

'Five months is a bad age to be separated from the mother,' said Dr Hackett. 'There are lots of key developmental stages that can get missed.'

Ruth's mouth was dry. 'Really?' Why didn't he ask when Christian had gone back to work or how much he was at home? Or if he had fucked his secretary whilst she was pregnant?

Betty was wailing. Ruth had a terrible urge to kick her. It reminded her of how she had lain in bed next to them when they were tiny newborn babies and wondered how she would stop herself smothering them with a pillow or throwing them across the room. It wasn't that she had wanted to do it, in fact the opposite had been true. But it had seemed so unlikely that she was up to the responsibility it would take to sustain and nurture a whole life. Hal had fallen asleep on her shoulder and she could feel the sweat from his head seeping into her shirt.

'Are you going to do anything about her?' asked the doctor.

'I'm afraid she has these tantrums. There's not much you can do.'

She could see the doctor abandoning them to their fate. 'The best I can suggest for now is that you start limiting his bottles. Stop offering him food. Then, when he gets hungry, give him some things he'd like. Biscuits are good, or chocolate cereal. The important thing is to get him eating, we'll worry about the nutritional side later.' He was having to shout now to be heard.

Ruth stood up. She had received the same advice from her very understanding GP, but she couldn't take good advice even when it was given freely and without prejudice. Her limitations were stifling. She lugged Hal over to his buggy and strapped him in, then went to Betty and pulled her up by the arm, dragging her across the floor. It took all her energy to stop herself from smacking her daughter across the face.

'That sounds sensible. I'll get right on to it.'

Dr Hackett was open-mouthed and Ruth presumed he had never seen a family like hers.

'Come back and see me in a month,' he said, recovering his composure. 'Verity will make you an appointment.'

'Yes, fantastic.' Ruth was manoeuvring herself out of the door, one hand pushing the buggy and one dragging the hysterical Betty. 'And I'm so sorry about this.'

'Perhaps you'd be best advised to leave her with your amazing nanny next time,' said Dr Hackett as she shut the door.

Ruth didn't bother to speak to the gleaming Verity as she left. Betty was by now screaming for a Brat. Ruth bent down next to her daughter and hissed, 'You are not getting a Brat. I told you to behave and you didn't. We are going home.'

Betty wailed harder. 'I hate you, Mummy. I hate you.'

White specks danced in front of Ruth's eyes and she was painfully aware of her own heartbeat. I hate you too, she wanted to scream at her daughter, as she'd once seen a mother say to her child in the playground. Big red buses roared past her and glass shop doors swished to and fro as customers ebbed and flowed. People bustled past, tutting at the woman unable to control her children on the pavement. A thin man with a massive placard reading

'Golf Sale' brushed past her and she caught the pity in his eyes. The ground vibrated beneath her feet, sound coming at her from above, below and the side. She was acutely aware of herself as if on a map, a tiny speck on a rabbit warren of grey streets. She could imagine all the boilers burning in all the houses, all the wheels of all the cars turning relentlessly on the tarmac, all the voices shouting to be heard, all the babies crying, all the bins that needed emptying, all the lives that had to be lived. Ruth stepped into the road and stuck out her hand, willing a taxi to stop.

By the time they reached their house, Ruth felt as if her shoulders were locked tight. Betty had quietened to a whimper and Hal was still asleep in his buggy. They made it through their front door in one piece, which was, Ruth felt, as much as you could say about their day.

Agatha was sitting at the kitchen table with a cup of coffee and a magazine and she looked shocked to see them. 'I thought you were going to feed the ducks,' she said. 'I was just on my way out.' Ruth looked at the clock, it was ten past one. She probably hadn't used up more than fifteen minutes of her hour's appointment.

'Could you put on a DVD for Betty,' she said, slumping at the table. She wanted a cup of coffee but found she couldn't move. Agatha had been reading a story about a well-known TV presenter's stalker nightmare. It seemed refreshingly tame to Ruth.

Agatha bustled back into the kitchen. 'She says she's hungry. Haven't you had any lunch?' Ruth shook her head. 'I'll make her some cheese on toast. Do you want some?'

Ruth looked at the capable young girl standing in her kitchen, still ready to take on the world. Maybe they should go back to having children at sixteen, it was about the only time in your life you felt optimistic enough and had the energy.

'No thanks, Aggie,' she said, and then she started to cry.

Agatha came and sat next to her. 'What's wrong, Ruth? What's the matter?'

The urgency in Aggie's voice was especially touching to Ruth; it was as if she cared. It made her momentarily aware of how child-like Aggie was. 'Everything,' she managed to say. 'I'm a terrible mother.'

'Don't be silly.' Agatha put her hand over Ruth's. 'You're great. What's made you say that?'

'The nutritionist blamed me for Hal. He didn't even ask me about Christian. Why does it all have to be my fault?'

'Don't listen to him. He doesn't know anything. Come on, Ruth, the kids love you.'

'But why doesn't Hal eat? And why does Betty cry all the time? Why won't she bloody sleep?'

Ruth looked up and saw some starlings playing in the blue sky out of her kitchen window. She felt jealous of their freedom, their lack of responsibility. She turned her attention back to Aggie, who she could tell was trying to say the right thing.

'You can tell me to butt out if you like, Ruth, but I've listened to you and Betty at night. And I'm not saying you're wrong or anything, but you know, sometimes when you've been in a situation too long it's hard to see a way out ...'

Ruth's heart clenched. 'Go on.'

'Well, it's only a theory, but you could try taking her into bed with you.'

'She used to sleep with us every night,' said Ruth. 'She didn't even have a cot for the first year. But then Christian insisted we move her.'

Aggie blushed. 'Yes, but she never wakes up till midnight. You could start her in her bed and then let her come in to you in the middle of the night. I think she's scared. That's what it sounds like when I listen to you.'

'Scared?' Ruth tried to remember her daughter's cries in the night, tried to make sense of them the way Aggie seemed able to do.

'Yes, it's like she's got herself into this cycle and she knows she makes you angry and now she's scared. I don't know, it might be worth a try.'

'Anything's worth a try,' said Ruth.

'I hope you don't mind me saying anything,' said Aggie.

Ruth put her hand over the girl's. She felt ashamed for bitching about her to Sally, ashamed for ever having thought badly of her. She was a sweet young girl wanting the best for them. 'Don't be silly, Aggie. It's so kind of you to be thinking about us. I'm the one who should be apologising for keeping you awake.'

Aggie shook her head. 'So you'll try it?'

Ruth smiled. 'I will. Tonight. We'll do it tonight.' She moved her hand and laughed. 'So, now we've sorted out Betty, what are we going to do about Hal? He's going to be three in a few weeks and he doesn't eat.'

'It's his birthday soon?'

'Yes, and I haven't organised anything.'

'Oh, would you let me, Ruth? I'd love to organise him a party.'

'Oh no, Aggie, you've done enough. I couldn't possibly.'

But she looked so keen, like a puppy. 'Oh, but I'd love to. I love organising parties. I once had a job as a party planner.'

'Really?'

'Yes, I did loads of kids' parties. I love them. I'd love to do that for you.'

Ruth laughed, pushing the hair out of her eyes. She felt tired to her bones and the offer sounded as sweet as nectar. 'Is there no end to your talents, Aggie? What would we do without you?'

By the time Christian got home Ruth looked as though she had been beaten up. In the low half-light he could see her reading to Betty, who wasn't listening but instead complaining that she didn't want them to go out. Ruth soldiered on with the tale of the Princess who could feel a pea through twenty-four mattresses; it was one of Christian's least favourite stories. He peeked in on Hal, who was sucking silently in his dream. He found that he loved his children so much more when they were asleep. He would gaze on their little faces, so earnest and content, and feel the emotions coursing through his body. Christian had believed this to be the most profound type of love, when you loved someone even at the moment they needed nothing from you. But as he stood over his son's cot he wondered if he had got it the wrong way round.

He went into their bedroom to get changed and saw the towel he had used that morning lying damply on his side of the bed. His side of the bed had felt soggy for weeks and he wondered if Ruth was trying to tell him something. But before he could properly articulate the thought Ruth was standing in the doorway saying she felt too tired to go out.

He looked over at her and saw the black circles gouged under her eyes, her hair awry on her head, her pale and gaunt face, her bedraggled clothes. She made him feel momentarily worried. She was starting to look like she had at the end of that first year with Betty. Ruth was so complicated, she made his head spin. Part of her wonderfulness, he knew, lay in that complexity, but it interfered so constantly with everyday life, he also hated her for it. He wondered how she could be bothered with all the worry and anxiety which seemed to accompany her every waking moment.

'Come on,' he said. 'It'll do you good. We can just go to Lemonas.'

She sat on the side of the bed and he saw she was going to cry. There was no doubting where Betty got her trembling bottom lip. 'I think I've fucked everything up.'

Christian sat next to her. 'What do you mean "everything"?' Although he knew.

Now the tears came. 'The kids, mainly. How do we have a child who doesn't eat? We're like some terrible BBC Three documentary.'

'Don't be silly. We'll look back on all of this in a few years and wonder why we got so worked up.'

'But do you think it's all my fault?' Ruth looked up at him and the desperation in her eyes made him want to protect her for ever, to stop the bad thoughts and take the pain away. He considered telling her that he feared it was his fault, but he didn't want to bring Sarah into her head.

'Of course it isn't. Why would it be?'

'Because I work.'

'Because you work? What are you talking about? Where did that come from? Millions of women work.'

Ruth ran her hands through her hair. 'God, I don't know. The bloody nutritionist, for a start.'

Christian stood up. 'Come on. Let's go to the restaurant and talk about it there. I'm hungry.'

He was amazed that Ruth stood up and opened her closet door.

The restaurant didn't look anything special from the outside and Ruth and Christian had nearly walked past it when they'd first moved in. Now they went there as often as they could and it felt like a little home from home. There was so much comfort to be found in the wonky wooden tables, the tea lights in old jam jars, the standard issue metal knives and forks, even the strings of plastic lemons criss-crossing the ceiling. The food was like the best sort of picnic: warm pittas, freshly made hummus and taramasalata, feta that was neither too sharp nor too salty, olives so juicy that you couldn't stop the oil running down your chin.

On the way there Ruth told him that Aggie had suggested taking Betty into bed with them to try to make her sleep. He heard the desperation in his wife's voice and felt surprised with himself for not thinking of this solution himself, it was so obvious. But it had always been such a contentious subject; it had taken him so long to persuade Ruth to move Betty out of their bed in the first place. A whole year without sex, it sounded like something you might read in an advice column. Now, though, it seemed less important and, as Ruth pointed out, Betty didn't usually wake until midnight. It's a good idea, he heard himself saying, let's try it tonight. Anything to break this misery which seemed to enshroud their lives.

With a glass of red wine in her and another one waiting, Christian saw his wife relax. Her shoulders dropped and her mouth turned up into a half smile. She looked pretty if wan in the flickering light of the candles.

'So tell me about this nutritionist,' he said, wanting to take her hand across the table, but as the thought flittered into his brain like a starling in a church roof, she used her hands to wrap her shawl closer to her slight body.

'I guess he was just old school. I don't know why I let him get to me so much. It was a shit day. Betty dropped her fucking Brat onto the track on the tube and then had hysterics all the way there. I think the people in the carriage would have preferred me to have a bomb rather than Betty, you should have seen the looks I got.' Christian laughed. Ruth smiled back at him. 'Then I was expecting some nice Alan Rickman type of doctor and I got fucking Dr Crippen.' Christian laughed again. 'Seriously, he was like a parody of a posh doctor. And all he could ask was when had I gone back to work and then he said that five months was a critical time and had I heard of separation anxiety. I wanted to ask him why he wasn't asking when you went back to work or anything like that, but instead I kept apologising. And then Betty started freaking out and so we had to go before our hour was up and as I left he said some snide remark like, Why don't you leave her at home with your fabulous nanny next time?'

'We should complain.'

'Don't be silly. He didn't do anything wrong. In fact, he was probably right.'

'What do you mean?'

Ruth tucked her hair behind her ears. She couldn't force any more of the food down, even though it was delicious and she'd hardly eaten anything. 'Well, I waited a year before I went back with Betty, and she eats. And I looked up everything he said on the Internet this afternoon and there is research on it.'

'There's research on everything.'

'Yes, but did I go back to work for me or for Hal?'

'Does it matter?'

'Of course it does. That year after Betty I nearly went mad, and so I rushed back to work after Hal, saying that we needed the money and everything, but we could have stayed in our old house.'

'It was tiny.'

'Yeah, but we could have, and then I wouldn't have had to work.'

Christian was becoming confused by the turns in the conversation. He felt as if he'd been led too far into a maze. 'But you wanted to go back.'

'I know, that's what I'm saying. Why did I want to go back? Why can't I look after my kids? Am I a bad mother?'

And there was the exit. Of course, this was what it was all about. 'Why does working make you a bad mother and not the millions of other women who do it?'

'Maybe they are too.'

'Yes, and maybe so are all the women who stay at home and go silently mad or build up a head of resentment. I think you'll find there are bad mothers everywhere, as well as good mothers.'

'But ...' Ruth was drawing a pattern on the table with a drop of red wine.

'Staying at home and baking cookies doesn't make you a good mother, Ruth.'

She looked up at him, her eyes glistening. 'Well, what does then? Because I'm all out of ideas.'

Agatha did not want Ruth's life. Let's just get that straight, she said to herself as she looked up cake recipes the next day. But it did give her a warm feeling of superiority to see Ruth falling apart while she coped so well. The woman was nothing more than a mess. Sometimes when she was breezing through the house tidying and sorting, she would have conversations in her head with Ruth's mother, a woman she had never met and someone whom Ruth rarely spoke about. All of which was fine by Agatha because it was one less person to interfere in her new life. But surely you couldn't have a daughter like Ruth and not worry about her, and surely, if the errant grandmother met Agatha, she would be reassured that life was as it should be. Yes, it is quite worrying, Agatha would say to the woman as she mended another broken toy or plumped cushions which were fatally sagged, but I'm coping fine, you stay where you are. Don't be silly, it's nothing, I want to help.

She had decided on a menu of egg or ham sandwiches, biscuits, little sausages on sticks, chocolate crispy cakes and, of course, the all-important birthday cake. Everything was going to be home made. She couldn't decide if she should put a bit of orange into the biscuits or make one of those lemon drizzle cakes that Betty liked. But, it was Hal's birthday and shouldn't you always make children a chocolate cake? She was trying to find the perfect icing because everything like butter or vanilla seemed too boring.

The food was only a small part of the whole thing. She wanted a theme, but it was difficult with Hal because he was only interested in his plastic house and Thomas the Tank Engine. And every boy of his age liked Thomas, so what would be the big wow about theming a party along those lines? In her mind she was going to amaze all the guests, make Ruth never want to let her go and the children love her forever. The idea must be there in her mind, but for now it was still out of focus and she couldn't make out all the details.

She had been trying to get a guest list out of Ruth for days now, but she was always too busy and there were only twelve days to go and you had to give people some notice. Don't worry about invitations, Ruth had said, I'll just telephone everyone. Which annoyed Agatha, who had spent three whole nights in her room making twenty invitations which shimmered and sparkled like proper works of art. But how many people do you think will come? Agatha had tried. Ruth had frowned in that way she had when she was trying to remember something: wrinkling up her forehead and contracting her eyebrows so she almost looked ugly. Agatha had once had a job in the bowels of some massive medical school in central London in which she'd had to spend eight hours a day filing endless pieces of paper in the dark. There were whole rows for each letter, and whole trolleys of papers for each row. Agatha had started diligently, but by the end she had begun haphazardly stuffing the paper anywhere she fancied, revelling in the mess that would probably never be undone. As she stood talking to Ruth now she was reminded of that room.

'God,' said Ruth, which, Agatha had noticed, was how she began most sentences, as if appealing to a saviour for help. 'Well … Toby, as he's Hal's godfather, and I guess I'll invite Sally … and it's a good excuse to get some friends round who've got kids because we never have parties and then we can kill about five birds with one stone. And of course I'll ring my parents. Christian's are away, so don't worry about them. I'll write you a list, but I guess it'll end up about twenty grown-ups and twenty kids. Is that all right? Can you manage that many, Aggie?'

It was no surprise that a list had never been forthcoming, but Agatha had worked on the assumption that there would be more rather than fewer guests and had added smoked salmon to her list of sandwiches. She'd been woken in the middle of the night by the thought that maybe she should get some wine, but when she'd mentioned this to Ruth she'd been told that Christian would deal with that. There was just one other thing, something she'd had to steel herself to ask Ruth: could she invite the little boy from the toddler group she'd been taking Hal to, as they seemed to get along so well. Of course, Ruth had chimed as she'd been rushing out the door, the more the merrier.

The toddler group was on a Tuesday in a draughty church hall across the park from where Agatha dropped Betty at school. Children's activities were often stuck underground, out of sight, Agatha had noticed. Often in rooms with no natural light and no heating and occasionally ominous smells. They were invariably run by harassed-looking women who were always begging things off the people who came in the form of money or favours. Someone had to lead the art activity, and so far Agatha had done this three times. She still felt her first art group had been the most successful. She had saved egg boxes for weeks, cutting them in two so they looked like caterpillars before the group began. Then she'd bought some pipe cleaners and made tiny pom-poms out of left-over wool and used the glue and paint at the hall. Everyone had congratulated her. One woman had even written down her number in case she ever wanted to change jobs.

It was the same woman whom Agatha had overheard talking to a friend as they sat in a circle waiting to sing songs before the group ended.

'These songs give me an out-of-body experience,' she had said. 'It's like I'm floating above myself and I look down and I think, What am I doing, jumping around a room pretending to be marching up a hill? I used to save people's lives on the operating table and now I'm singing about sick bunnies.'

Her friend had laughed and said, 'You can't think about it too much or it'll drive you mad. You just have to remember that it'll be over soon.'

'Not if you have another one.'

'Yes, but then you really are mad.'

'But do you want Barney to be an only child?'

'Basically it's a choice between Barney being an only child or a motherless child, because if I had another I would end up hospitalised.'

And then they had both laughed as if they got the joke, but Agatha couldn't see for one second what was funny about what they had said. She hugged Hal's chubby body more tightly to her and smoothed his blond hair against his head, sucking in his sweet scent. She could not understand how anyone didn't marvel at this, didn't want to consume their child with love. It made Agatha want to cry when she looked around and saw all these amazing children with such unworthy mothers. Images reared up before her of Barney and his friends stuck in front of whirring televisions, being fed cheap pizzas and going to bed without kisses whilst their mothers sat in kitchens drinking wine and bitching about how much they hated it all. Ruth, she realised, was one of those women and it made her wonder if perhaps working was the kinder choice.

It is very odd how sometimes the phone can ring and you know with absolute certainty who it is before you pick up. People whom Christian generally hated would claim to be psychic because of this. Christian wasn't psychic but he still knew that his vibrating mobile would deliver Sarah to him as soon as it started to buzz face-down on his desk. Ignoring it was still an option at that moment. She wouldn't leave a message and probably would never call back. But his hand twitched and he answered.

'Christian.'

He tried to sound surprised. 'Sarah. Hello.'

'I'm sorry to call again. It's just that …' she hesitated and in the hesitation Christian felt time loosen. Choices and decisions whirred around him as if he was on a brightly lit fairground ride. He shouldn't have picked up, but now he had, he felt sunk, as if free will had been taken away. 'I didn't say what I wanted to when we met up. I wondered if I could see you again.'

'Do you think that's a good idea?'

'Probably not. But … look, to tell you the truth I've been having therapy, and my counsellor thinks it would be good for me.'

'Okay.' The floor felt like sand under his feet.

'It's not as scary as it sounds.'

There was no way he could refuse now. This, he realised, was it. 'Right. When's good for you?'

'Anytime.'

'Okay.' Christian flicked through his diary, looking for an evening he could tell Ruth he was working late. And so it started again. 'I could do Friday after work. About seven.'

'Fine. How about The Ram?'

It was where they used to meet. 'Great. See you then.'

What if he lost his family without meaning to? Without even wanting to?

Ruth was looking out of her window at work watching a shadow float across the building opposite her. The shape was mesmerising and totally inexplicable. Her office was high up in the sky and yet something fluid was dancing like a feather across the concrete mass opposite her. Ruth's mind couldn't find an explanation for it and she wondered if life as she knew it was about to dissolve and a new order take its place. She willed this to be true. She would have liked to shed her skin like a snake and start again. But then a plastic bag floated into view and she realised that a gust of wind had simply caught a piece of rubbish and thrown it into her eyeline to tip her slightly off balance.

Ruth dialled her mother's number. It was lunchtime, the office was only half full and her plastic box of limp salad was inedible. As the rings sounded into her ear she imagined her mother's neat and ordered house in Gloucestershire. She imagined her immaculate mother hearing the sound from her well-manicured garden and starting the walk up the path so she could hear who wanted something from her now. Ruth liked to make it a rule never to want anything from her mother.

'Hello.' Her mother sounded out of breath.

'Sorry, Mum, it's just me. Did I get you in from the garden?'

'Yes, I always forget to take the phone out with me. It drives Dad mad.'

'How is he?'

'Fine. At golf.'

'And how are you?'

'Splendid, darling. In fact, you're lucky to catch me, this week has been hectic. It's the fête on Saturday.'

'God, is it that time of year already?'

'We were hoping you might come down for it. I did tell you about it last time we spoke.'

'Oh shit, yes you did. I'm sorry, I forgot. I'll talk to Christian, let you know.'

Ruth wondered when her real life would start. When she would become like her mother and remember things, have time for things, make things, grow things, have a bit of fun. The idea tugged on her arms.

'Anyway, are you okay, Ruth?'

No, Ruth wanted to say, I'm slowly turning to jelly and I'm frightened that I might soon dissolve. I'm losing my grip on life but I've got a great nanny who'll take over if I do slip away. Do you think that's enough? Do you think

my kids would even notice if I wasn't there any more?
I'm not sure Christian would.

'I'm all right, apart from terminal tiredness.'

'You work too hard.'

'It's not that bad.'

'And you expect too much.'

Ruth found her mother so direct and clipped she never
knew if she was making a generalised comment or telling
her something useful.

'Don't we all?'

'No. In fact, I think the secret of life is to expect as little
as possible.'

Ruth laughed. Only her mother could claim to know
the secret of life.

'Anyway, I was ringing to ask you to Hal's birthday
party. It's going to be the Saturday after next at our house.
Stay the night, if you like.'

'How lovely. Do you want a hand? I could come early,
bake something.'

'Aggie's got everything under control.'

'Aggie?'

Ruth heard the disapproval in her mother's voice but
tried to shut her mind to it because it chimed too deeply
with her own feelings. 'She's amazing, Mum. I don't
know what I did without her.'

'You seemed fine to me.'

Conversations with her mother always left Ruth feeling
soiled, as though she'd committed a sin that she could
never amend, as though she'd got it all wrong. Ruth's
mother had an unshakeable belief in her own rightness
and, annoyingly, it was not an assumption Ruth had been

able to ignore. Were all children plagued by a fear that perhaps their parents were right? Ruth found it hard to imagine an adult Betty so troubled.

After speaking to her mother, Ruth would wonder if complete self-belief was the answer to life and whether imagining something to be so was all it took. Occasionally she tried it, but she irritated herself too much. Hearing know-it-all tones coming out of her mouth made her want to lie under a duvet and admit defeat.

Articulating panic to someone who had never felt it was very hard. It was true that when she had had her breakdown after Betty her mother had been non-judgemental, but Ruth had still been left with the sense that she had let her down, that Stella Douglas' daughter should have inherited her own steely determination.

And surely her mother's disapproval was well founded this time. Surely you should organise your own child's third birthday party. Or at least want to. But Ruth found it so easy to hand everything over to Aggie. She could imagine asking the girl to buy Hal's presents; she would no doubt make a better job of it than Ruth could. And while it was comforting to feel so confident about the person looking after your children, was there something wrong with a mother who let this all happen?

Kirsty materialised next to Ruth's desk, making her realise that she'd been lost in another world for too long.

'Ruth, I need to ask you a favour. You know I wouldn't ask if I wasn't desperate, but I've literally exhausted all other possibilities and, like, I can't think of anyone else.'

'Don't worry. What?' Ruth had lost the ability to say no outside her home a few years ago.

'You know all these interviews we've got to do for the next issue – the women who are living their dream?'

'Yes.' The idea made her feel weary.

'Well, that woman, Margo Lansford, who gave up some job on the stockmarket to move to a farm and breed pigs or whatever –'

'Make soap. Yes.'

'Well, she can absolutely only do the interview this Saturday, and I'm going to my friend Emma's wedding in Scotland and there's, like, no way I can miss it. And I've asked, literally, everyone else I could think of, but no one can do it. And, I mean, I could ring a freelancer, but I thought I'd better check with you first, especially after that bollocking Sally gave us all about budgets.'

'You want me to do it?'

'Well, I mean, only if you can. Or I'll get a freelancer in.'

'No, no. That's fine.'

'She's only in Surrey and she's got four kids. Maybe you could take yours?'

Life was refreshingly simple in Kirsty's world.

Much, much later, Ruth was lying next to Christian in bed. The day had seemed relentless and she'd longed for this moment for too much of it. Her body sank into the mattress, her limbs lifeless beneath the sheets. They had been letting Betty come into their bed for a few days now and a miracle did seem to be occurring. Their daughter was waking later and later each night, padding the few feet from her room into theirs, where she would climb over their sleeping bodies and crawl between them. That morning Ruth had woken with the alarm and been unable to remember Betty even arriving in bed between them.

'I can't believe we didn't think of letting Betty sleep with us before,' she said now, staring upwards at their cracked ceiling.

'I know,' said Christian. He was reading a document for work and he let it drop onto the floor.

'Thank God for Aggie,' said Ruth.

'I suppose we'd have figured it out on our own.'

Ruth laughed. 'I doubt that.'

Christian smoothed some hair off her face. 'Do you feel any better for it?'

'Not yet, but I read on the Internet that it takes a few days for a sleep-deprived body to get used to rest. You can feel worse before you feel better.'

'Makes sense.' Christian kissed the tip of her nose. Ruth wished all moments between them could be this calm. 'In a few years they'll both be at school and it'll be much easier. This is only a little bit of time.'

And it was true that when Ruth remembered time it had raced by her, like a greyhound chasing a hare round a track. 'You're right,' she said, 'I must remember that more.'

Christian lay down and turned off the light. 'Got to get some sleep, big day tomorrow at work.'

'Oh, I forgot to say,' Ruth ventured into the darkness, 'I've got to go and interview some woman who makes soap in Surrey on Saturday. She's got four kids and a big farm. She said we were all welcome. Do you want to come?'

'Yeah,' said Christian lazily, 'don't mind, whatever you think.'

The vegetable patch was growing vegetables. Agatha knew it was ridiculous to be impressed by something doing what it had promised, but it had seemed a bit far-fetched when they'd planted those tiny seeds all those weeks ago. Over the course of the past couple of months she had taken Betty and Hal to the bottom of the garden every day for signs of life. At first they'd had to squat close to the ground and Betty had been petulant when there was nothing to see. But then, one day, even from the kitchen door Agatha could see what looked like a fine film of green covering their patch. They had rushed across the lawn, the excitement beating in their chests, and been rewarded with tiny sprouts of plants emerging from the ground. At that tender stage they all looked the same, one tiny delicate stem with two oval-shaped leaves opening on either side. Some were still in the act of breaking through the soil and Agatha wanted to sit by the patch all day in the hope of seeing life growing before them.

Now the little seedlings had developed into fully fledged plants. The potatoes were tall and threatening, the carrots wispy and ethereal, and the tomatoes were just losing their flowers and budding small round nuggets of green. Agatha taught the children to touch them to release their scents, smells which would waft around them in a haze of delicious goodness that made Agatha want to cry.

But best, best of all, Hal was as interested as Agatha had ever dared to hope. He had been transfixed by the sight of the miniature plants and could spend hours playing by the vegetable patch waiting for them to grow. His fascination when Betty had first pulled a potato out of the ground was so sweet that Agatha had let Betty try a few carrots, even though she'd known they weren't ready. Hal had even asked to touch them, when usually he'd have cried if he was too close to a vegetable. He'd stroked the hard skin and brushed it clean of the earth and then held the potato up to the light like he was examining a precious stone.

'You can eat that,' said Agatha. 'Betty's going to have it for her lunch with fish fingers.'

'And the carrots,' said Betty.

'Of course, the carrots as well.'

'If you want, you could try some,' said Agatha nonchalantly over her shoulder as she carried it all into the kitchen, belying the fact that her heart was beating as fast as if someone had said they loved her.

Agatha and Hal had a secret. Even Betty didn't know about it. Agatha had told Hal not to tell anyone, but she wasn't sure if he understood this or if he forgot most things that happened to him. Agatha had stopped offering Hal food from almost her first day. She couldn't bear the look of terror on his face as soon as he saw her opening the fridge or getting out the tiny jewel-coloured plastic plates and cups. So one day she'd told him that she didn't care if he ate or not, that as far as she was concerned bottles were fine and he could have as many as he wanted, whenever he wanted them. Sometimes she even let him stay sitting in his plastic house, watching Thomas on the telly through the window whilst she fed Betty.

But then a few weeks ago she had bought a packet of chocolate buttons. She opened them when Hal was sitting next to her on the sofa, sucking intently on a bottle, his eyes fixed on the screen. She had made sure that they were warm, so their sweet smell rushed out of the packet and into the air as soon as she broke the seal. Sure enough, Hal looked round and watched as she popped them into her mouth. After a while she pretended he had surprised her.

'Oh, Hal,' she'd said, 'you made me jump, looking at me like that. Don't tell anyone, but these are my favourite sweets.'

Hal let the bottle fall from his mouth.

'Do you want to touch one?' Agatha had asked, holding her hand steady between them. 'They feel a bit like velvet.'

She was sure Hal didn't know what velvet was, but he reached out and poked the soft round circle.

'The best thing about chocolate buttons,' Agatha went on, 'is that you don't have to eat them. You just put them on your tongue and they melt. Do you want to try?'

And to Agatha's amazement, Hal had picked up a button and put it into his mouth. He now ate buttons with gusto and had licked a chocolate digestive and taken a spoonful of jelly. Agatha planned to try a yoghurt soon, but then the potato fell into her lap.

Agatha cooked the potatoes for longer than necessary and then mashed them with lots of butter and milk. She spooned most of them onto Betty's plate, along with the fish fingers and carrots, and then called Betty in. The little girl was naturally overcome with joy at the thought of eating vegetables from the garden and kept exclaiming at their deliciousness. Soon Hal was at the door.

'Has your DVD finished?' asked Agatha.

He sidled up to her, nudging her legs in one of their unwritten conversations that only they knew the language to. She picked him up and cuddled him onto her lap.

'Betty's eating the potatoes from the garden,' she said. Agatha waited a beat. The moment had to be perfect and she was waiting for Hal's body to relax into hers and Betty to leave the table. When everything was in place she whispered to him, 'You could try some, they're quite like buttons.'

Hal didn't say anything, so Agatha passed him a tiny spoonful, the smallest offering to the smallest god. The spoon hovered by Hal's mouth; for a second Agatha thought she might have read him wrong and a fine sweat broke out along her top lip and her leg began to quiver. But then Hal opened his mouth, she put the spoon in and he swallowed. She didn't offer him any more and he didn't say anything. He got down from her knee and went back to his house.

By the time Ruth arrived home Agatha was bursting to share her triumph, but Ruth was in a terrible mood. She was complaining of a migraine and moaning about an interview she had to do the next day, even though it was Saturday. She barely listened to Betty telling her about the vegetables and then claimed she was too tired to give them a bath. Agatha wanted to slap her across the face, but instead punished her by not telling her about Hal and the potato. More and more she was starting to think that Ruth didn't deserve her children.

'Do you want me to have the kids tomorrow if you have to work? I don't mind,' Agatha volunteered when Ruth came downstairs from putting the children to bed.

Ruth was already getting the wine out of the fridge. 'No, no. Christian and the kids are coming with me. The woman I'm interviewing has four and she said it would be fine.'

Agatha had become increasingly concerned about leaving Hal with Ruth or Christian. They were still offering him food, making him sit at the table in front of a plate piled high which they would then spend half an hour pleading and cajoling with him over, until he was finally released, crying and snotty, to find Aggie and curl into her lap. She couldn't bear the thought of a whole day without him, not being there to wipe away his tears and whisper in his ear that it would be all right, soon it would be Monday and he could go back to normal.

'Do you really want to do that? I mean, won't they get in the way? I don't mind having them.'

'Don't be silly, Aggie, you need a day off. Go out, have a bit of fun.' Ruth walked into the sitting room and Agatha could hear the telly being turned on.

Agatha stayed in the kitchen to clear up the mess from supper, as well as to hide the tears building at the corners of her eyes. It seemed unfair that she should be the one bringing these children up and yet have so little say over what they did. One day she would become disposable to the Donaldsons, she suddenly realised, opening a great big gaping hole in her stomach, and then she would have to leave and Hal would be given over to someone who could never begin to understand him like she did.

The Ram brought back memories which Christian knew should be left alone. Once he had fucked Sarah in the loos. He was incredulous with himself for agreeing to meet her there, but something close to excitement twitched in him as he walked into the pub. It had changed during the past three years; it was more sophisticated with grey walls and large comfy sofas looking over low tables on which little tea lights flickered. Sarah was already there, sitting in a corner with a drink, looking stunningly pretty in a simple summer dress.

'I'm sorry about last time,' she said as soon as he sat down. She had regained some of the youthful confidence which he'd found so attractive before and he felt unnerved. Or rather he felt old, like a stupid, middle-aged man having his head turned by a promise from the past. He might have recently renewed his third passport, but it didn't have to be over yet.

'There's nothing to be sorry for.'

'Come on, I was a bag of nerves.'

'I wasn't much better.'

'I could do with a fag. D'you want to go outside?'

'No, thanks.'

'Have you given up?' The question was too knowing.

'Sort of. You know.' He would not be drawn into criticising Ruth this time. He still worried that this had been his worst betrayal of his wife, something which he felt sure she would never be able to forgive. But Sarah had made all the disdain he felt for Ruth pour out of him like a wave crashing onto a beach. Sarah only had to ask the most innocent-sounding question and he could hold forth for hours about his wife's lack of awareness, the way she stifled him, how she had let herself go while pregnant, the fact that she never found anything funny any more, their lack of a sex life.

'Anyway, I'm just going to say it this time,' said Sarah now. 'If we get it out of the way early on, then maybe we could have a nice evening, you know, for old times' sake.'

'Okay.' Christian drained his glass.

'I think you were a shit. You treated me badly. And Ruth, for that matter.'

'You've got me there.' Christian felt relieved, if that was it then he'd said much worse to himself already.

'I've thought about it all a lot and what made me most angry is that I protected you from everything, when you should have gone through it with me.'

'Protected me?'

'I didn't miscarry, Christian. I had an abortion.'

Christian was shocked, both by his naivety at not working this out and by the act itself. Sarah had done him a favour, but, shit ... something primal in him felt revolted by the information.

'Aren't you going to say anything?'

'Sorry. I didn't guess, which makes me very stupid. I'm sorry you had to go through that alone.'

'It's okay. I had a tough time afterwards. It's why I went to Australia and, of course, I hooked up with the first totally unsuitable man I met and then it took me ages to get out of that relationship because my confidence was so shot. Eventually my parents had to come over to get me and bring me home and I've spent the last year in therapy.'

'Shit, I thought you said you'd just got back.'

'You're not the only one who can lie, Christian.'

'Can I get you another drink? I need one.'

Christian tried to clear his head at the bar, but the walls seemed to be closing in on him. He felt as though he owed Sarah something, but he couldn't work out what it was. He knew what he owed Ruth. Or more than that he knew what he wanted from Ruth. He could feel her body next to his in their bed, the smell of her skin when he'd kissed the top of her nose the night before. By the time he got back, Sarah was smiling.

'Sorry to spring that on you. It's become important to me that you knew. Don't ask me why. But I do feel better for having told you.'

'Look, I'm sorry too. I was so selfish, I was only thinking about myself at the time. If it helps, it hasn't exactly been a bed of roses for me.'

'But it's worked out with Ruth?'

'Yes. She's been very gracious.' The word sounded strangely like a criticism.

'And you're happy?'

'As happy as anybody else.'

Sarah looked at him over her glass. 'That's always been your problem, Christian. You never expected to be happy. You don't mind settling for content.' Christian noted how diametrically opposite Toby's assessment of him had been. He wondered who was right.

'Are you happy?' He knew this was the wrong response and that he should have defended Ruth, because of course that's what they were really talking about. But he couldn't do it.

'I'm getting there.' She crossed her legs so that her skirt rode up and Christian had to lean forward to curb his desire. He didn't want this to be happening again, but he felt drunk, almost drugged.

'I'm going to have to go, Sarah,' he said, ridiculously, giving everything away.

'But it's only nine thirty. You haven't even finished your drink.'

'I know, but I can't do this. I'm glad I came and you got a chance to tell me everything. But I should go home now.'

She smiled. 'I'll walk to the tube with you.'

The air was still warm when they got outside and the streets were full of beautiful young bodies. Christian felt separated from them by himself, but knew Sarah offered him a passport into their world. In a not too distant future they would be Betty's people, but surely he could make one last claim on them.

Halfway to the tube Sarah turned off. 'Actually, I'm going to get a bus. The stop's here and it's more direct.'

'Where are you living now?' He wanted to put her into some sort of context.

'With my parents in Islington. My dad would kill you if he knew I was with you now.' She laughed and he was reminded how many years separated them.

'It was great to see you again. You look fantastic.'

'So do you.'

Sarah leaned into Christian and brushed her mouth against his. They held the position for a second longer than necessary and he felt her arm encircle his waist so that her breasts flattened against him. He could taste the hollowness of his desire at the back of his throat.

She pulled away. 'Bye then.'

When he got home Ruth was asleep on the sofa in front of *Newsnight* with three-quarters of a bottle of wine in her and no food. She looked pretty from where he stood in the doorway and, even though he knew he was a sad and pathetic man, he wanted to take her to bed. She woke up as he switched off the telly.

'You're drunk.'

'Is that a statement or a question?' He suspected that Ruth believed she owned him in some indefinable way, giving her the right to tell him how to live.

'I can smell it on you. I thought it was a business dinner.'

'They're the worst ones, Ruth.'

'Doesn't it ever occur to you to say no?'

'Not really. You look knackered, why don't you go to bed?'

'Don't patronise me.'

'I'm not. I'm just saying ...'

'That I'm not as attractive as all those twenty-four-year-old childless girls in your office.'

They had slipped, like Alice, into that place between reality and absurdity.

'I don't know what you're on, Ruth, but it isn't pleasant.'

'Oh, and I live to be pleasant for you. In fact, why don't I give up work and become some sort of domestic goddess with a little pinny and cookies baking in the oven and the children all tucked up in bed so that you can go out and be important and not worry about anything other than the next secretary you're going to fuck?'

'Ruth, you need to stop this before you say something you'll regret. I don't know where any of this has come from, but you're talking nonsense. When have I ever asked you to give up work?'

Ruth started to cry. Great big heaving sobs which shook her body so that she looked like a drowning kitten. Christian felt a surge of emotion for her that he couldn't place. She was so complicated it seemed impossible to comfort her and it made him feel hot and trapped.

'What's wrong, Ruth? Do you need to see a doctor or something?'

She sank down onto the sofa. 'I don't know what I need. I don't even know what I want. I'm lost, Christian.'

Ruth woke at four in the morning, which was always a bad sign. In the worst times she had woken at four every morning, her body shredded by exhaustion but her mind spinning in ever-decreasing circles. It was the same start which got her now, as if her heart had been given an electric shock. Christian was snoring next to her and she regretted their stupid row. Her last words to him were playing pinball in her mind. She shouldn't have revealed so much of herself. You should never tell men the depths of your despair because then they thought you mad and wished they could still get away with locking you in the attic. If only they shared the same language, she found herself thinking, she could tell him how she was feeling, he'd give her a hug and they'd move on.

She gave it half an hour and then got up, knowing it was better to pass these hours with a cup of tea in the kitchen rather than lying in bed. Betty had, as was now usual, found her way into their bed at some indeterminable time in the night; she vaguely remembered her small form at the door, her warm body crawling over hers before squeezing herself between them. She was now wedged against Christian, stuck with sweat to his back. Ruth nearly moved her, but couldn't bear the thought of waking her. Instead she gazed at her tiny daughter and, for a second, felt that she fully understood Betty's anger; she was after all nothing more than a miniature woman. Ruth resolved to be much nicer to Betty when she woke up.

The kitchen always felt so different at this time of day. She saw it for what it was and was thankful that it expected nothing more of her. Since the advent of Aggie it was also always so clean, even the supper from the night before was washed up and ready to go again.

Once she was sitting at the table, watching the sky break an uncomfortable dawn, Ruth allowed her thoughts to acknowledge themselves within the tangles of her mind. She looked up and caught herself in the mirror which was propped against a wall at the far end of the table. She stared into it, trying to see herself. But it was as if she had selective glaucoma; however hard she looked her face was blurred. As a teenager and even in her twenties, she had been confident in how she looked, had known that her face was pretty and her body taut. But now ... now, she could see age creeping over her features, announcing itself with lines and bumps, red patches on her cheeks and thick bags under her eyes. Her skin looked worn away so it was almost translucent, like the wings of a butterfly, and her hair was as insipid as over-cooked spaghetti. She even had a mole on her cheek which sprouted dark hairs if she didn't keep it in check.

And her body was not her real body, of that she was sure. One day she would reclaim the clear, toned skin of her youth which allowed her to wear shorts and bikinis and tight dresses. Not the mottled, dimpled covering which made her look like she had been soaked in tea for too long. At least she was thin, but it wasn't the right kind of thin. It was so easy for women to be either too fat or too thin. The perfection everyone sought was so small a space as to be invisible; even the obscenely beautiful models on the pages of *Viva* had to be photoshopped to achieve a perfection which was fake. And these were women who inspired clichés amongst men, in open mouths and shortness of breath and babbling words. Could this all still be true? Ruth wondered, as she ran her hands over her face; it felt like her bones were trying to force themselves out of her skin, as if bored by having to support the insubstantial person she had become.

Christian claimed not to have fucked Sarah because she was prettier than her; although Ruth was sure she had been and that must have been a bit of a bonus. It was interesting to note that men rarely had affairs with women if they were older than their wives, with a plumper body and greyer hair. And anyway, she only had his word for the fact that he hadn't found Sarah more attractive and when you considered the amount of lying he'd done, it hardly gave her confidence. But more insidious was, why did this fact matter so much? Why did it eat away at her image of herself like maggots on a decaying corpse? It's not about looks, he'd said at the time, that never came into it. You're the only person I want to talk to and surely that means something. And yes, she saw his point, but there was still something terrible about being exchanged for a younger model. About knowing that only recently he had run his hands over smoother, fresher flesh.

She fretted that forgiving him made her constantly and unspokenly somehow subservient to him for ever more. Was there now some terrible acknowledgment between them that she was weaker, that she would keep him at any cost? Before she had got married and had children, Ruth had been certain that she'd never forgive an affair and yet, him leaving had seemed impossible at a time when she was barely able to get out of a bath without help. Sometimes she wondered if that was why he had done it then, simply because he knew he would get away with it, even if he was found out. And why was it that the definitiveness of youth always, always had to give way to the compromise of age?

Christian claimed to have had a mild nervous breakdown. He'd even gone to therapy for six months to try to understand why he'd done it, but Ruth suspected that had only been to placate her, to show he was serious about being sorry. Not that she'd doubted his sincerity, that he'd genuinely wanted to stay, that the whole affair had no doubt been a mistake. But often she wondered if they'd papered over the cracks in their desperation not to fuck up too much and that maybe they would be better off apart. All those old sayings kept reverberating round her head; sometimes rows of old women would rear up at her, telling her that men didn't stray for no reason, that there was no smoke without fire, that a woman's place was in the home.

In the end, the best reason Christian could come up with for his behaviour had been that he felt pushed out of his own marriage. That since Betty's birth he had felt sidelined, that Ruth had fallen so completely in love with their daughter she hadn't even bought a cot for the first year. And then there'd been the depression, which he'd found terrifying, and once she'd gone back to work she was either feeling guilty or exhausted and they never had any fun any more. So, to comfort himself in her second pregnancy, he'd decided to sleep with someone else. Except of course he hadn't gone so far as to articulate the last bit to her, that was something he only said within the confines of her mind.

It isn't the same for men, she had wanted to say, but never managed to spit out. Women grow them, we give up years of our lives, we distort ourselves, we flood our bodies with alien hormones. Of course we don't go back to normal. Christ, you men don't know the half of it. Once we've had a baby, that's it, we don't ever become a single entity again, even after the cord is cut. But for Christian to have understood this he would have had to transcend himself, something which no one is capable of doing.

Ruth could remember him saying all these things as they had sat at this very table after Betty was in bed and just before Hal forced himself out of her. She mostly remembered that time for all the bottling up; for not screaming obscenities at him, for not turning up at his work and hitting Sarah, for not sending him more than ten defamatory texts a day. By the time she got to speak to Christian in the evening she would feel as though she'd eaten too much fast food which was now stuck in her throat. But as soon as they were able to speak she would feel starving, desperate to go over and over the details, devouring every last morsel of information in the hope that she could somehow make sense of the mess.

Worst of all, Ruth had known, she still knew, that Christian had a point; everything he said had been true. She knew she had to accept responsibility, but she didn't see why she should shoulder all the blame or that he had needed to make his point in such a way. Just be careful, Sally had said to her one day when Ruth had decided to let him stay, don't do it because you're feeling vulnerable, do it because you want him to stay. But Ruth hadn't been able to make a judgement on that, she couldn't separate her need for help from her love for her husband.

The other thing that Sally had said could have come straight out of the pages of *Viva*: If he's capable of doing it once, he might do it again. Christian, of course, swore this wasn't true, that he didn't want to be unfaithful to her, that he'd never done it before. And Ruth believed him; she knew that at heart he was a decent man who was, when it came down to it, honest and trustworthy.

She didn't worry about whether it had happened before or start to wonder if he secretly visited lap-dancing clubs or even if he would look for it again. But she also knew he was weak and now, sitting at her kitchen table, she realised they had slipped back into their old patterns and this was a dangerous moment.

I love you, he'd said to her a few nights after telling her that he'd been sleeping with a girl at work who was now pregnant, even though Ruth herself was due to give birth in three weeks. I've never stopped loving you. I loved you from the first moment I saw you and it's never gone away. And Ruth knew that to be true. She could clearly remember the rush of emotion which had enveloped them both when they'd first met. All sense of decency and decorum had seemed irrelevant and they had spent the first few weeks pouring their souls into each other, mingling everything, sleeping rarely. There had never been a doubt that they would spend the rest of their lives together. If they could just get back to that moment. If only they could spend one more night on her thin student-issue bed, holding the nylon curtain away from the window as they lay beautiful and naked, looking out at the dawn, wishing for every day like it was the most exciting time of their lives.

Sometimes Agatha found you needed to write things down in order to sort them in your mind. Her head often felt crowded out with all the stories. Not that she was a liar as the stupid woman at the hospital had insinuated, but she was aware that we all tell ourselves stories to make life easier to deal with. It is hard to get by unless you sometimes tell people what they need to hear. And, to be clear, this is not lying. Lying is mean. Lying is something that people do to get their own way when it would probably be better if they didn't. Liar, liar, the children at school used to chant. But I'm not, she wanted to shout back, I tell you what you want to hear and you are too stupid to realise that.

It's not a lie if you don't tell your mum and dad, Uncle Harry had said. Although in fact, everything about him had been a lie, he wasn't even her uncle. He didn't drive her to girl guides every Saturday to give her mum a break. Instead he drove her to the top of Eccles Hill and told her that what they did was fine, everyone did it and there was nothing wrong in it. It had taken her years to realise that he was lying, even though she had somehow known from the start that he was right and she could never tell her parents.

Hal was definitely real and Agatha had undoubtedly been sent to save him. She wrote some simple facts in her notebook.

Hal finds eating hard.
I make Hal eat.
Hal loves me.
I love Hal.
Ruth and Christian do not understand him.
He is happier with me than he is with them.

The simplicity of it all made Agatha want to sing. This was what she had been waiting for all her life. This was surely what love was, the sureness of a give and take which hurt no one, that was unspoken, that existed on its own in its own time and space, that was neither messy nor dirty, that did what it said.

Hal now ate yoghurts, biscuits, chocolate buttons, bananas and Marmite sandwiches. Agatha had wanted to unveil his amazing development at his birthday, making Ruth and Christian so grateful they would let her stay forever. But now this didn't seem enough. They were both so distant and distracted, Agatha wasn't even sure they would be as thrilled as they should have been. Since handing over Hal's party to her, Ruth hadn't asked one question about it. Agatha still didn't even have a guest list and it was happening in only ten days' time.

Over the last few days it had dawned on Agatha that Ruth was not dissimilar to her own mother. They were both scatty and tired and disorganised and left too much to chance. As a child she had longed to shake her mother as she flapped around the kitchen, failing to put anything away or complete any tasks, always too sleepy to listen to her reading or too busy to help with homework. It was when you got to this stage that you let other people take responsibility for your child and then bad things happened. Agatha did not ever want a situation where bad things could happen to Hal.

Agatha was worried Hal might eat something on the stupid trip to the farm that Ruth had planned for the next day, which presented her with a dilemma. If she asked Hal not to eat then she might not only put him back in terms of eating, but she would also be asking him to lie for her, something she could never imagine doing. She didn't want her and Hal to have a secret which they couldn't share with his parents, but what were her options if those parents didn't understand? In the end she told Hal that they were planning a surprise for his mum and dad and that on his birthday they were going to show them what a big grown-up boy he was now he could eat. So, it was very important that he didn't eat anything at the farm because then the surprise would be ruined. Hal nodded in his serious way, but Agatha wasn't convinced he understood. If someone offered him a chocolate button she couldn't be certain that he wouldn't eat it. The thought made her itch, as did the thought of letting Ruth and Christian in on the knowledge of his eating.

'I cannot believe you talked me into this,' said Christian as Ruth began passing him the multitude of bags they needed for a day-trip to Surrey. 'Why don't you go alone? I'll take the kids swimming.'

'Don't be annoying, you agreed to it. The kids are excited.' Ruth made up the bit about the kids. She had no idea what they would like to do today.

'But some bloody hippy commune? I mean, please.'

'Why do you have to make everything sound so shit. It's not a commune.'

'You know what I mean. They'll be all holier than thou with their organic kids. I bet they don't even have a TV.'

Christian's words echoed Ruth's own thoughts, but she wasn't going to let him know. Instead she wondered how many bottles Hal would need. 'Can you get Betty into the car? We're going to be late.' Ruth stood at the bottom of the stairs and shouted up, 'Aggie, we're going.' There was no response. 'Hal! Come on. I don't want to be late.' She could hear rustling and laughter from Hal's room. A minute passed, but they didn't appear. A surge of exasperation knotted unhealthily in Ruth's bowels. Her foot went to the bottom step but she didn't move forward and, in her failure to move, she realised that she felt embarrassed, that she would feel like she was intruding if she broke up their game.

But then Aggie appeared with Hal on her hip. 'Sorry, we were playing dress up, I was just getting him changed again.'

Ruth thought she could hear an edge to the girl's voice. 'It's okay, but we really do need to get going now.'

Still Aggie didn't move. Instead she put her hand on Hal's forehead. 'He seems hot and tired. Are you sure you don't want to leave him?' As Aggie spoke Ruth saw Hal nestle his head onto her shoulder, her hand involuntarily stroking his cheek.

Ruth held out her own arms. 'No. I want him to come. Thanks.'

'But if he's ill …'

'Aggie, I think I can manage. I've been dealing with children's illnesses for years.' Ruth could feel a shift in the air which she couldn't place, but at least her words made the girl move. Aggie reached the bottom step and tried to hand Hal over, but the little boy stayed stuck to her side, his legs wrapped tightly round her waist. Ruth watched the scene in amazement as she tried to coax her own child out of another woman's arms. She was shaking, her voice rising shrilly as she told Hal not to be so silly. He used to do that to me, Ruth wanted to scream, I know what that feels like, I know what it is to wrench a small body off you and walk away. But I do not know what it is to be the wrencher, to walk away with the small body.

'Don't worry, sweetheart,' Aggie was saying now. 'You're going to have a lovely day with Mummy. I'll see you later.'

Reluctantly Hal let Ruth take him, but she knew he was looking at Aggie over her shoulder as she carried him out to the car.

'Are you okay?' asked Christian as they drove off. 'You look very pale.'

'No, I'm not okay. Hal didn't want to come.'

'I don't blame him.'

'No, Christian, I'm not joking. I had to pull him off Aggie just now. It was like he wanted to be with her more than me.'

Christian cut up a woman in front of them. 'Don't be ridiculous. He was probably tired or something.'

'No.' Ruth looked out of the window and tried to make sense of what she had seen. 'No, it was more than that. It wasn't right.'

'You can't have it all, Ruth. You can't leave them all week and then not want them to get attached to the nanny. You should be pleased they like her so much. Think of Mark and Susan who found out that girl had been sitting Poppy in front of CBeebies for eight hours a day and feeding her chocolate spread. At least we know Aggie's doing a good job.'

Ruth looked back at her two children strapped into their seats as they sped along the dirty London streets. Stop the car, she wanted to shout, it's so much more likely that we'll crash than get there unharmed. The air vibrated around them and everything seemed painfully fragile.

It had started to be that Agatha felt scared when Hal wasn't near her. And not only scared that something might happen to him, but scared for herself. She recognised it as a return to the restless anxiety which had accompanied so much of her childhood. After they had left for the farm Agatha went into Hal's bedroom and sat next to his cot. She pressed her face against the cold wooden bars so she could draw in the scent of him, but it wasn't enough. She pulled the bedding out of the cot and lay with her head on his soft pillow and the covers over her head. But even Hal couldn't stop the memories.

'Just touch it,' Harry had said. 'You don't have to do anything more than touch it.'

But of course that had been a lie. Over time touching had not been enough. In the end it had filled her up so she felt sure it had passed through every organ in her body. It was too big. Everything about Harry was too big. From his lips to his fingers to his stomach. Sometimes he would forget himself and then she would feel like he was going to crush her to death and all the air would be pushed out of her as surely as a deflated balloon.

At night she would sit with her parents and Louise, her sister and will one of them to notice her, to see that she was not normal. But no one had ever looked up from themselves and so she had begun to tell herself stories to make it better. Harry died many, many times. His deaths were violent and painful but never caused by Agatha herself or even a member of her family. Eventually her family started to die as well, less violently and less painfully, but with pathos and sympathy. Agatha told their teacher that her dad had leukaemia and only a few weeks to live. And that same teacher had taken Louise aside to tell her how sorry she was and from her reaction they'd guessed she didn't know and so they'd taken her to the school office and called up their mother and she had rushed over and again failed to back up Agatha's story. The school's counsellor had tried to get to the bottom of it, but her questions had been so standard that Agatha had been able to give her answers without saying anything real.

Tell us why you did it, her parents had pleaded as they'd sat round the kitchen table that night. It's such a wicked thing to say and so obvious that you were going to be found out. Did you really think you could say that and the school wouldn't mention anything to Louise, or us? And so Agatha learnt a lesson: stories had to be based in reality or they were lies, and they had to be told to the right people.

The farm was exactly as Ruth had imagined it would be. A perfectly proportioned house surrounded by muddy fields up a bumpy track. The front door was open and smoke was puffing artfully from the chimney. Children's bikes were scattered in front of the door and chickens were pecking in a corner. Even a sheepdog lay asleep on a flat stone. She was surprised that Channel Four hadn't snapped them up for a sanctimonious lifestyle documentary.

'God,' sighed Christian. 'This looks like hell.'

An overly thin man sauntered out of the door, a young boy hanging off his leg as another, slightly older, hit him with a stick.

'Cut it out, Jasper,' snapped the man. 'Those people are here now. Mummy wouldn't want them to see you doing that.' Ruth noticed that he had a glint in his eye as he spoke and he had raised his voice, making sure they heard.

She got out of the car, taking charge of the situation as she knew she had to, even though every fibre of her body wanted to run and hide. She didn't dare even look at Christian, his anger would be too terrifying. 'Mr Lansford?'

'Charlie.' He wasn't smiling.

'I'm Ruth, from *Viva*. Thanks so much for having us all out here. Letting us intrude on your weekend.' Her voice sounded ridiculously jolly, like she was trying to keep them all upright with the force of her goodwill.

'Margo insisted,' he replied, peeling his older son off his younger one. 'Fuck knows where she is though. Probably baking some bread to impress you. Really we live off economy white sliced.'

Ruth started to attempt a laugh, although the whole situation lacked any humour. Christian had been right, she should have come alone.

'I heard that,' sang a woman's voice from inside the house and then Margo appeared and everything went back to normal because she was completely and exactly as she should be. She was tall, thin to the point of wiry, with long, straggly hair that probably always lived bunched up on top of her head. She was dressed in an odd assortment of silky, ethnic clothes that did nothing for the near concave nature of her body. A baby of indeterminate sex rested on her hip whilst a toddler clutched her free hand. 'We never eat white bread, do we, Sammy?' Sammy stopped thumping his brother for a second and looked at his mother with utter disdain.

'Of course we don't,' shouted Charlie, hugging his wife too tightly. 'That would never do, would it?'

Ruth realised they had gate-crashed a row and were going to be used as some sort of disenfranchised referee unless she checked the situation. She also realised that the Lansfords were enjoying it. 'Anyway, thanks for agreeing to be interviewed,' she said to Margo. 'And for letting us all descend on you like this at the weekend.' Christ, she sounded as though she was at a demented drinks party. 'This is Christian.' She turned to see Christian still sitting scowling in the car, the kids fighting in the back. He got out as he saw them all looking at him and Ruth wondered if Charlie and Margo could see how much he hated her at that moment or if only she could read his face so precisely.

Margo took charge as she no doubt always did. 'I thought you boys could take the children round the farm. Why don't you let them play on the hay? Then Ruth and I can have our little chat.' No one wanted to do what Margo had suggested, but no one raised any objections. Ruth decided not to even look at Christian, to go into the house and deal with all the shit on the drive home.

The house was as beautiful on the inside as the outside, which somehow sunk Ruth further. Margo had perfected the look of disorganised mess which looked comfy and inviting and flowed together and, even though Ruth knew it took a whole lot of effort, she was still charmed. They went into the white kitchen plastered with shelves and cupboards overflowing with often cracked but still beautiful bits of crockery. Margo gestured for her to sit at the obligatory long wooden table with a bunch of flowers in the centre which Ruth feared had been picked somewhere on the farm.

'What can I get you to drink?' asked Margo.

'I'd love some coffee,' answered Ruth.

Margo frowned. 'Oh, sorry, we don't do caffeine in this house. I've got all kinds of herbal tea though.'

Ruth hated herbal tea. 'Oh, right, don't worry. I'll have whatever you're having.'

As the kettle whistled, Ruth tried to remember why she was there. She struggled to think up some good questions to ask this vision of perfection before her, but she couldn't think of anything she wanted to know the answer to.

'So,' she began, hoping something would follow as Margo handed her a steaming cup of purple liquid. 'What a beautiful house.'

Margo was obviously used to hearing this. 'It was a complete wreck when we found it, but we saw the potential and we love a challenge.'

'How long have you been here?'

'Four years.'

'So you did all this with the children?'

'With some of them. Two came during.' Margo laughed; she was used to being told she was wonderful, but Ruth couldn't force the words out.

'So, Vicky, our Features Editor, who you've been speaking to, she tells me that you and Charlie worked in the City before all this.'

'We did, that's true. We were both investment bankers, for our sins.'

'That's a bit of a change then, from the City to this.'

'Yes, it is, isn't it.'

'What prompted it?' Speaking to Margo was a bit like reading *OK!* magazine. It made Ruth feel dirty and unworthy, yet fascinatingly jealous.

'I suppose it was one of those eureka moments. We were on holiday in Greece and Charlie and I suddenly realised that the nanny had put Jasper and Sammy to bed every night since we'd got there. And I said to him, Haven't we earnt enough money? Don't you think we could just bloody stop? And I expected some huge row or something, but he looked up at me and said, Yes, I think we probably could. We both resigned the day we got back from holiday and put our house on the market and found this one, all within a month.'

Did people have eureka moments? Had that particular cliché moved out of language and into experience? Ruth doubted it, but she laughed, trying to sound jolly, 'That's a very supportive husband.'

'We've a strong bond, Charlie and I,' answered Margo. 'We know intuitively when the other needs something.'

Ruth wanted to throw her disgusting tea in Margo's face. Her hand vibrated on the mug and she wondered what would happen if she did, if that would be the signal that she had gone mad, if she'd be carted away and labelled forever more. Instead she said, 'But did you have any idea what you were going to do?'

'Not at that time.'

'So I take it you had enough money not to do anything?'

'Not really. We had about a year's grace.'

'That was very brave.'

'It felt more like necessity. Bravery didn't come into it.'

'What do you mean?'

Margo looked a little irritated. 'I mean, sometimes you reach a point in your life when you know it's not working and you know you're going to have to change or go under.'

Ruth wondered if anything Margo ever said was real. She could imagine her screaming at Charlie or weeping when she thought no one was looking, but she doubted she would ever let her mask slip in public. It was tiring talking to someone who didn't say anything other than what they thought you wanted to hear, or maybe what they wanted you to hear. But it was also terrifying to hear herself in Margo, to hear a woman she knew she hated articulating her own desires. She tried another question. 'Have you ever regretted it?'

The baby started to cry and so Margo picked her up and began to feed her. Ruth remembered the feeling and it surprised her with an internal tug. 'No, I don't believe we have. It's been tough, but most things that are worth achieving are tough, don't you find?'

'Tough how?'

'Oh, you know, renovating a house this size is a nightmare. And then starting a business has so little to do with what you're making and so much to do with banks and loans and scary men telling you you're mad.' Margo laughed and Ruth realised she was being conned again.

Ruth looked at her notes. She could write this article with her eyes closed. She probably didn't even need to interview Margo. 'So how did you come up with the idea for the soap then?'

And there you had it. Give up, give in, get back onto dry land. Ruth sat back and let Margo educate her on the finer details of plant condensing and sustainable packaging.

By the end of an hour Ruth was desperate to leave, but she was also dreading seeing Christian, so it was a nice surprise to see him laughing with Charlie as she left the house. She didn't let her guard down though as you could never tell with Christian, his moods could flick like a light switch so she wasn't sure exactly what she was in for as they drove out of the farm. But his smile stayed in place.

'God that was classic,' said Christian.

'Classic how?' Ruth was rooting in her bag for Hal's bottle as she spoke.

'I don't know what Margo told you, but her husband is one fucked-up man. He hates her.'

'Don't be ridiculous.'

'I'm not, I swear I'm telling you the truth. It was hilarious. He's got fags and whisky hidden all over that farm. He's angry as hell.'

'Angry at what?' Betty was kicking the back of Ruth's seat.

'At her self-satisfied crap, most likely.'

'You didn't even talk to her.'

'I didn't have to. Christ, she looked vile.'

Ruth knew this was a moment in which she could agree with her husband, they could have a good laugh and that would be that. But that was never that with them. Something about his judgemental attitude or maybe his pleasure at someone else's distress caught at her. 'She wasn't that bad. God, at least she's having a go at making it better.'

Christian snorted. 'At making what better?'

'Life.'

'You do know that her father bought them that farm, don't you? She's loaded. She made him give up his job and jack it all in to live on a farm and make shit soaps that will never make any money.'

'You talk as if he's got no free will. He could have said no.'

'No, he couldn't. You know what it's like.'

Ruth turned to look at her husband's strong profile. 'What are you saying? That all you poor men have to do everything to keep us women happy because we're all so deranged?'

'No, Ruth. I was talking about Charlie and Margo. He said they went on holiday a few years ago and she cried every day and refused to get out of bed until he agreed to leave London with her.'

'So you think it would have been better for them to stay in London, working hard, never seeing their kids?'

'Not necessarily, but I don't think they have to go and play at being the perfect Swiss Family Robinson when they obviously aren't.'

'Unlike us.' Ruth could hear the pitch of her voice rising like a scale. Christian, she realised, was sure that he had heard the right story. More than sure; he hadn't even questioned it. Ruth on the other hand was always painfully aware of what was going on behind the words. She sometimes conducted entire conversations feeling like a puppet talking to another puppet, imagining what the other person was really thinking about as they showed their public face. Christian believed people were as they seemed. He hadn't yet worked out that everyone had a front, that they all wept at their kitchen tables and picked their noses in front of the telly.

'Fuck, what's eating you?'

'Daddy said fuck,' said Betty from the back.

'You're eating me,' said Ruth. 'With your sanctimonious crap.'

'Bollocks. You're angry because you didn't get the real story.'

Ruth always felt there was a tipping point in every argument: at one moment she was sitting on the edge of a cliff and in the next Christian was dangling her over it. Her face flushed and her heart beat faster. 'Don't you dare tell me whether or not I got the story.'

'Oh, come on, Ruth, don't tell me she told you anything more than a few soap recipes?'

Tears scratched at Ruth's eyes, she could feel them forming inside her. 'That is so patronising.'

Christian laughed. 'But true, right?'

'If you must know,' she said, 'I got the story our readers want. They don't want to know about her failing marriage or the fact that Daddy pays for everything, they just want to hear about a plucky woman who's done what they all dream of. They'll only half read it anyway, sitting at their desks during some depressing lunch hour or with one eye on the kids in the park. They want to feel that things are possible, not that they aren't.'

Christian tried to take her hand. 'I'm sorry, I didn't mean to make out that what you do isn't good.'

She shook him away. 'Well, you did and anyway you're right. What I do is shit, like what you do is. All you and I do is feed meaningless crap into people's lives. Moving pictures and easy words to take away the pain.'

'Bloody hell, you think about things too much.'

'Don't be absurd. You can't think about anything too much.'

Betty started to whimper in the back. 'I need a wee, Mummy.'

Ruth ignored her. 'And I don't know why we bother anyway. I doubt it's worth all the bloody sacrifice.'

'Shit,' said Christian, pulling the car into a service station. 'You're asking some big questions.'

Ruth turned to see a wet patch appearing on her daughter's trousers as they came to a stop. She felt so tired with the way they interacted she could have lain down in the car park and slept. Even breathing seemed a chore. 'Yes, maybe I am,' she said. 'I just can't find any answers.'

Agatha hated days on her own. Really hated. She became too aware of herself and the fact that she was capable of anything, that she was not necessarily in control of her actions. Her head felt bigger or maybe just fuller when she was alone. Like someone had emptied a pint of water into it, shifting her off balance and blurring her senses. She would watch herself doing something and feel disconnected to the experience. As she buttered her toast she realised that it was entirely possible for her to use the innocent-looking knife to cut deeply into her wrists, letting the blood spill onto the clean kitchen floor.

Agatha had often wondered how hard it would be to pierce human flesh. When the children fell over their skin seemed to peel away so easily, exposing their inner selves so red and raw. But Agatha knew enough about the human body to know that these wounds were mostly superficial, that to really get into the body you had to get through seven more layers of skin and then you'd only reach muscle and fat which in turn could be hiding a bone before you came into contact with any of the life-giving vital organs.

Harry had been fat; Agatha reckoned that even a very sharp knife would have taken a lot of cutting. He would have screamed out in pain. The children screamed out in pain when they just grazed their knees and Agatha had noticed how this letting of tears seemed to somehow take away the pain, like it released something inside them. The Victorians had believed in making you bleed to take away illness. Harry had never used a knife on her, although his weapon of choice had often felt sharp. He had made her bleed many times but he had never made her cry. At the time it had felt like one important victory she had won against him, but now standing in the Donaldsons' kitchen with the blunt kitchen knife clasped so tightly, she wasn't sure if it had been.

Christian called Sarah on his way to work on Monday morning. He told himself that he needed to speak to her again to find out more about the abortion, but he doubted this was true. He had thought a lot about the abortion, but he couldn't comprehend what it had been like for her. He felt sorry for her and saddened by a loss which wasn't his to feel, but it wasn't any of this that made him pick up the phone. It wasn't the awful visit to the farm or the madness of Ruth's over-reaction on the way home. They'd even had sex that night which had been loving and giving and made him feel warm towards her for the whole of Sunday. It wasn't really anything.

Sarah sounded too knowing when she answered the phone, like he was predictable and it had only been a matter of time before he rang. But he'd gone too far now and he felt he didn't have any other choice than to get on with whatever it was he was doing. Which was what exactly? After the phone call, as Christian reached his gleaming office and said his easy hellos, he wondered what he was after. He didn't want another affair, really he didn't. But somehow he wasn't prepared to let Sarah go yet either.

He turned on his computer and the screensaver of his wife and kids popped up as it always did. His own face was reflected over theirs asking too many questions. In trying not to become some sad married man had he simply become some sad shitty married man? He couldn't put his finger on what it was that was missing or even what would make it better. He had tried drinking too much or having the odd line of coke, but the kids made hangovers pretty much impossible. He had tried fucking a young woman but the pain he'd caused Ruth had been too hard to bear. He supposed that he could still buy a motorbike and kill himself going too fast down a motorway, but that seemed pretty pointless.

Christian had nothing but contempt for people who talked about giving it all up and moving to Cornwall to open a café. Their visit to the farm on Saturday had only confirmed his suspicions about these types of people and yet it had also left a nasty taste in his mouth. He wouldn't want to be Charlie, so seething in his own anger that Christian wouldn't be surprised to one day read in the paper that he'd killed his whole family. But still he remembered exactly what the man had said and the sentiment chimed uncomfortably close to what he thought himself.

'They're never happy, women,' Charlie had said as they'd sat in the barn, taking turns to swig from one of his many hidden whisky bottles, both sucking on fags.

'When Margo flipped out, I tried to see the bright side. I told myself that it was pretty pointless going into work every day when we didn't need the money, leaving the kids with all these ghastly girls who hardly spoke English, and I thought, Yeah, why not? Let's give it a go. But then we get down here and within bloody seconds Margo's all like, So what shall we do now? She was pregnant again then, by the way, and the house was a tip so we were supervising builders and dealing with planning and everything, but still she was like, What next? And I thought, What next? What bloody next is that we might relax and live a bit. I said to her, For God's sake, we've both made enough money, you're going to inherit a fortune, why don't we kick back for a bit and see what happens? But she couldn't. Oh no. What would everyone think? she actually said that. What, I said, all those fucking tossers who boast about their cars and Spanish villas who we've left behind in London? Who cares what they fucking think? And she was all outraged. I hadn't realised, but she liked those people, she still wanted them to be our friends. So she set up the stupid soap business that costs us more to run than we make, but still inane magazines like your wife's come and interview her about it and take photos of her with all four kids and everyone's, like, God she's so amazing, look at her perfect life. It makes me fucking sick. Doesn't anyone tell it like it is any more?'

Sarah told it like it was this time. They met in a café which overlooked the big lake in Hyde Park and she had tiny red spots high up on her cheeks. 'I am not going to be fucked around by you again, Christian,' she said as she played with her cappuccino.

'No, you've got it wrong ...' he started.

'Got it wrong how?' He noticed that her eyes flicked with anger in the same way Ruth's did and he was floored again by the sensation that nothing was ever going to be different and he was never going to escape himself. 'Got it wrong that you want an easy affair?'

'I don't want another affair.' Which was true, but about as far as he could get.

'Oh, so you're going to leave Ruth and the kids and set up home with me then?'

'Is that what you want?' Christian felt as though he had lost his footings and that the lake had somehow flooded the café. He hadn't meant to say any of this, but he hadn't bargained on anyone else being in control.

'My God, are you serious? I've spent the past three years trying to get you out of my head and then I walk into that stupid interview and I see you sitting there and I realised that not one fucking thing I'd done had worked.'

'I'm sorry.' He tried to take her hand, but she wouldn't let him. 'I'm so sorry about the abortion. I can't believe I let any of that happen last time.' Did he only want absolution? He couldn't be that much of a shit. Surely he wasn't putting this girl through all of this only to make her say it was okay, he wasn't that bad?

'Have you got me here to apologise? Is that it?' she asked, as if he had spoken out loud.

'I don't know why I've got you here. I don't know why I'm here.'

Sarah sat back in her chair. 'You're here because you've got a shit marriage but you haven't got the balls to leave.'

'No. Please, don't bring Ruth into this.'

Sarah snorted. 'It's a bit late to start defending your wife, don't you think?'

'Honestly, Sarah, don't. Ruth has nothing to do with this.' He was angry but he didn't get up and walk away.

Sarah stood up for him. 'Tell you what, Christian, you figure out what you want from me and then let me know, okay?' She turned and left without looking round and he didn't call her back. He sat at the round white table and let his eyes stare out over the lake. The surface was so calm it was as if someone had covered it with a giant roll of clingfilm. Boats waited and ducks swam. He breathed deeply and realised how good it felt to be alone.

Hal's birthday was next Saturday, which was only six days away and really only five, because you couldn't count on doing anything useful on the day itself. And still Ruth hadn't given Agatha a definite guest list. She was starting to find Ruth pathetic, even a bit disgusting. The children had returned from their day out in a state. Betty was soaked in wee and Hal was starving; Agatha had worried he might be sick from all the bottles he'd been given.

'I forgot to take a change of clothes,' Ruth had said as she carried Betty in, crying and cold. 'Could you run her a bath, please?'

Hal was in his father's arms and they were laughing together at something, but Agatha could tell he needed a Marmite sandwich. 'Shall I put both of them in?' she asked as gaily as she could manage.

'No, don't worry,' said Christian. 'Hal and I are going to have a game of Thomas. I'll bath him in a bit.'

Agatha's arms pricked. She couldn't be sure that Hal wouldn't ask for food and then all her waiting would be discovered and it would be taken the wrong way, or maybe the right way, and she'd be asked to leave. 'But it's school tomorrow. Don't you think ...?'

Christian looked at her in a way that told her the discussion was over. 'Hal doesn't go to school, Aggie. I think he's got time for a game with his dad, don't you?'

And so that was that; Agatha had to give Betty a bath and wait another whole hour before she got Hal on his own and could give him some food. Christian and Ruth had jumped at her offer to read him a bedtime story, shutting the door as they left the room, their voices already rising through the floorboards. Hal lay against her, munching on his sandwich as she read to him, stroking his hair. She wondered how she ever could have doubted the trustworthiness of this wonderful little boy. He would never give her away or betray her and that knowledge was like a warm blanket over her cold mind.

Events were moving too fast now and she couldn't go on feeding Hal in secret, away even from Betty, who would be bound to tell her mother. Something drastic was going to have to change, but Agatha felt like it was too much to accomplish before the party. They had to get through that day and then she could make a few decisions.

The next day she rang Ruth at work, something she almost never did, and asked outright how many people were coming. Ruth sounded like she'd forgotten about the party, but then she said, 'Sorry, Aggie, I know I haven't been on top of this. I promise I'll make some calls today and let you know this evening.'

Sally was leaning over Ruth's desk when she took the call from Aggie. 'All okay?'

Ruth shook herself. 'Yes, fine. That was Aggie being super-efficient again, asking me for a final head count for Hal's party on Saturday.'

'That's good, isn't it?'

'Yes, of course it is.'

Sally sat down in the chair next to Ruth. 'Except …?'

'I don't know. I'm probably inventing problems because I can't bear that she's so much better at it than me, but, well, do you think someone can be too perfect?'

'Like how?'

'Like there are no cracks in her at all. She never lets anything slip, everything's always done perfectly. Every base covered. It's like she's a … I don't know, robot or something.'

Sally let the copy drop onto the desk and Ruth remembered that Sally was also her friend. 'But do you think she's good with the kids?'

'Yes, but that's part of it. She's almost too good. The other day when we were going out I literally had to pull Hal off her. He wanted to stay with her more than he wanted to come with me.'

'It's hard for me to say,' said Sally. 'Not having my own kids, it sounds like an ideal situation. But I can see it must be hard.' She looked down and pretended to pick a thread off her skirt. 'Ruth, are you sure you're talking about Aggie?'

'What do you mean?' Ruth could taste chalk.

'I mean, are you maybe talking about how it makes you feel? You've got a great nanny by the sounds of it, and I can see how that might not be as fantastic as it sounds. Maybe you feel a bit redundant at home.'

Ruth was worried she might cry. 'That's just how I feel. But Christian thinks I'm being stupid and I probably am. It's like I'm so selfish I want the nanny to be a bit crap so I can feel better about it. That's mad, isn't it?'

'Not really. It's like when I go away on holiday I never want you to do too good a job running *Viva*. I'd say it was pretty natural.'

Everything felt disjointed to Ruth, as though reality existed apart from her and she wasn't sure what was going to happen next. 'You're right, it is about me, not Aggie. She's amazing really. She's got Betty sleeping and it's like a miracle. But I don't have time for anything any more. God knows what's going to happen to Christian and me. We never speak and if we do it's just organising shit. There doesn't seem enough room for everything inside me.'

Sally put her hand on top of Ruth's. 'Do you need some time off?'

'No. Do you want me to take time off?' Her voice sounded panicked.

'No, I want you to be happy. You're a good friend, Ruth, and you seem a bit lost.'

'I'm fine. I mean, I'll be fine, I'm just being stupid.' Ruth wasn't sure why she was clinging so desperately to her job, but the idea of losing it was terrifying. Surely it would be too much of an erosion of herself to discard what had been her public face for so long. I'm a journalist, she would say to people she met. Yes, I work on *Viva*, I'm the deputy editor, and instantly she was more interesting. It was all wrong, but Ruth didn't feel strong enough to put it right.

Sally stood up. 'Okay, but the offer's there. And if not, hey, it'll make a great feature.'

After Sally was back in her office Ruth dialled Christian's number and he answered immediately. 'Where are you?' she asked.

'Sitting in a café in Hyde Park.'

'Really? Why?'

'I had a meeting and I walked back through the park and it looked lovely. It's really quiet here, Ruth, I could sit here for hours.'

They sat in silence for a while as Ruth tried to make out what he meant, but she couldn't place him just sitting, it seemed too still.

'Are you okay?' she tried this time.

'Yeah, fine. You?'

'Not really.'

'What's up?'

'I don't know. Sort of everything and nothing. You know.'

'Can't say I do. You'll have to be a bit clearer, Ruth.'

'Do you think Aggie's okay?'

'Yes, I think she's great and the kids love her.'

'Exactly.'

'Ruth, it's not about you or me. If we're going to do this it's better they have a nanny they love.'

Tears, snot and sadness mingled in her throat. 'I know, I know, it's just … I don't know. Have we made the right decision?'

Christian sighed and for a moment she thought he wasn't going to answer or maybe get angry, but he was calm when he spoke. 'I don't know, Ruth, I really don't know.' And it was only after they'd said goodbye that Ruth realised he hadn't even asked her what decision she was talking about.

What is the point at which you realise a marriage has broken? Now that Betty slept better and Ruth was less tired, thoughts other than plain survival were beginning to re-emerge inside her. Ruth often thought of weddings as tying an intricate series of knots around a couple, like one of the cat's cradles she used to make at school. At first you are comfortable in the binds, but as time drags on and you both put on a bit of weight they start to chafe. And then someone wants to go in a different direction and they become not just uncomfortable but irritating. Except of course no one can find the scissors and so you both hack away on your side, unpicking, getting tangled up and maybe one day finally releasing yourself. Then as you reach the moment of release you are consumed by panic, wondering how you're going to stand up without all those ties, and so you wrap a few thin threads back around your body in a desperate attempt to keep upright. If Ruth imagined her and Christian in this web she saw very clearly that they only had one real knot left amidst all the broken string and shredded wool. The kids in the centre and a mess all around.

Ruth still hadn't called anyone about the party when it came time to leave so she took the bus and squeezed her personal business into travelling time. She hated thinking she was becoming the sort of person who had a use for every second. Most people were on answerphone, which was always the best result when you made a call, but a couple of her friends picked up. As she spoke to these women who once had been an intricate part of her exist-ence, she imagined what they were doing. She heard them running up streets to child minders or talking over shouting children and frying suppers. Ruth saw them as they stood in their days, she even saw their beginnings and ends, saw them pulling themselves from sleep in the morning, collapsing back into bed at night. They were all the same, she wasn't alone. Legions of people existed as she did, which meant maybe she wasn't entirely wrong; a thought almost as sweet as sherbet popping on her tongue. Good friendships made you realise that you weren't going mad. They were like a massive vitamin injection straight into your arm, re-invigorating you and giving you the energy to keep going for another couple of months. She mustn't let it slide like this again. Christian was right, she should get out more and stop saying she was so tired. One night out with her friends would probably be the equivalent of six months' worth of therapy. The answers seemed momentarily simple; she needed to look around a bit more, to get back to herself, to remember what made her happy.

'I've got a list, finally,' said Ruth as she walked through the door. Betty ran at her, nearly knocking her over.

'Let Mummy take off her coat,' said Aggie. Hal was sitting on her lap and they were watching *In the Night Garden*.

'Don't worry,' said Ruth, picking up Betty. 'Have you had a good day?'

'It's been great,' said Betty. 'Aggie took us to the park after school and I played on the slide with Megan.'

Ruth shot a glance at Agatha. It rang a bell but not loud enough.

'You know, that girl in her class who wasn't being too nice,' said Aggie.

'Oh God, yes, of course. Shit, I was going to speak to her mother, wasn't I.'

'Don't worry, I did,' said Aggie. 'She was really nice and Betty's going there for tea next week. I think it'll all blow over.'

Ruth was gripped by panic as the young girl in front of her dealt with their life. The ground shifted beneath her and her breath came short and sharp. 'I should have done that,' she managed to say.

Aggie blushed. 'Oh, I'm sorry, it's just I was there, I didn't realise ...'

Ruth sat in the chair by the window, Betty on her lap and her breathing slowed. Aggie was of course right. She had just been there. Ruth had to stop doing this to herself, she had to stop thinking that only she could handle everything, that it was only the right thing if she was in control. 'It's okay,' she said. 'Thanks.'

'I was wondering if it might have had some bearing on her not sleeping,' said Aggie now. 'You know, being scared at school isn't the best way to sleep well at night.'

Ruth was filled with love for Aggie, it was as if she had a light shining around her. 'I expect you're right, again,' she said. She leant forward with her piece of paper. 'Anyway, I've got your list.'

Agatha had seen the panic in Ruth's face when she'd told her about Megan, but the woman was so daffy she didn't deserve to be spared her own failings. She looked at the scruffy piece of paper Ruth had given her with names and numbers scrawled across it. Only a couple had ticks next to them. 'I've put the amount of people coming next to each person. As you can see, I haven't managed to get hold of everyone, but at least you'll know what to expect if everyone comes, which they won't, of course.'

Why 'of course'? wondered Agatha. What would stop you coming to a child's birthday party anyway? Her mother had never got it together to give Agatha a proper party. There'd been a celebration on the day, a few children and friends of their parents all holding paper cups filled with warm liquids and eating sandwiches which had been made too early and left uncovered so they tasted slightly stale. Mum, Louise had shouted in the middle of one of these tepid affairs, Agatha says you've got her a pony and you're keeping it at the stables in Langley and I'm never allowed to see it or touch it and anyway that's not fair 'cause you wouldn't even get me a rabbit for my birthday. Agatha had watched her mother's smile go from real to frozen without really changing. My goodness, that's generous, Aunt Kate had said. A pony, Agatha, what a lucky girl. And then her mother had laughed. Can we talk about this later please, Louise, she'd said, much too gaily.

If everyone came to Hal's party there would be thirty-one guests, twenty-one adults and ten children. There would be no warm liquids, stale sandwiches or make-believe presents. I had to lie, she'd shouted at her mother later, because what you gave me was so rubbish. You're just ungrateful, her mother had shouted back; we do our best, your dad and I, we do our best. Well, try harder, Agatha had wanted to say, because your best sure isn't good enough.

Ruth moved next to her and stroked Hal's face. 'And how are you, sweetie?'

Agatha could feel Hal flinch. 'He's fine, a bit sleepy, it's been a busy day.'

'What are you planning for the party? Can I help?'

'Oh no, no, you're fine,' answered Agatha, the very thought of Ruth's help making her feel sick. 'It's nothing special. Well, of course, it'll be special, but you know, I'm not planning anything over the top.'

Ruth looked at her for a beat too long and Agatha felt her cheeks growing hot. 'Okay, well, don't go mad and wear yourself out, Aggie. We really appreciate this, you know, you've been amazing.'

Hal wouldn't let Ruth take him to bed so she went up with only Betty and for a moment Agatha felt sorry for the woman. To be so inept that even your nearly three-year-old son sees you for what you are must be heartbreaking. She smoothed Hal's hair against his perfect head and hugged him closer to her chest. Slowly a kernel of an idea was forming itself in her heart.

Christian tried very hard to work out what he wanted, but nothing concrete formed in his mind. He thought about calling Toby a couple of times but not only did his Facebook status crushingly reveal that he was in Ibiza, he realised that he didn't want to hear what Toby would say. Instead he sent him a message about Hal's party, as Ruth kept badgering him to do. He'd be back on Friday. Maybe they could find a quiet corner and Christian could ask his advice. After that there was no one. He had drifted from all his university friends and now if they did go out with other couples it was mainly just the husbands of women whom Ruth knew. His brother lived in Australia and they knew precisely nothing about each other's lives. And his father was ex-army, poker straight, eminently shockable and of the put-up-and-shut-up generation.

Really it had always been Ruth. Ruth had been his best friend for as long as he'd known her. She was quick and bright and funny and knew him better than he knew himself. He longed for her now so he could ask her advice. But she'd got lost along the way. It was like he'd been on a long car journey with all the windows open, so that his head felt full and his ears buzzed with unrecognisable sounds. And yet she was still indefatigably there. Christian could feel her presence in a way he had never felt anybody else. She seemed so physical and solid next to him it gave him a rush of comfort, as though she had a force field around her which was strong enough for both of them.

Christian wondered if this was what love is. The basic knowledge that someone was looking out for you, that there was one person out there in this sea of bodies who understood what you meant and why you had said it. Who wasn't scared to shout at you, who loved you enough to be bothered to try and change you. Christian remembered one of the very few times he had been rude to his mother, a woman who was so steely as to appear cold. Why are you always so mean to me, you're always getting at me, he'd wailed at her, aged ten, maybe eleven. And he had been shocked by her answer as she'd turned from the stove, steam reddening her cheeks and moistening her eyes. I am mean because I love you so much. The easy option would be for me to let you eat with your mouth open or not say thank you, because then we wouldn't have a row and my life would be peaceful. But I tell you these things to help you in the world, because people who eat with their mouths open or forget to say thank you are never much liked. And I want you to be liked. I love you and I want the best for you. He wasn't sure if Ruth still cared that much about him.

Christian knew that he wanted to be liked and loved, probably by as many people as possible, but mainly and most importantly by Ruth and his children. But it was so hard to let go of everything else, to admit to yourself that you were never going to be more than you.

Ideas were forming round Christian, not so as he could grab them yet, but he felt their presence. Then Sarah called him two days after she'd walked away from him in the park. She sounded tearful and asked him to meet her after work and he couldn't refuse because he'd asked exactly the same of her only days before. The water from the lake flooded back but this time he was sitting at his desk and soon it had covered his head.

He rang Ruth at work to say Giles had asked him to take his place at a boring function. Okay, Ruth said, what do you think we should get Hal for his birthday? I don't know, Christian had answered, I wouldn't bother, he's still very little and he'll get heaps from everyone else. That's nice, Ruth replied, too busy to even consider your son's birthday. You will be able to come, won't you? I mean, you won't suddenly have some important function you have to attend because you are of course so important. And then she'd put the phone down and Christian couldn't face ringing her back.

Sarah was sitting outside the pub when he arrived, a faceless one this time that neither of them had been to before. He thought he saw one of Ruth's friends at the next table and his heart leapt in his chest like a demented rabbit. He went inside to get them a drink and tried not to think about Sarah sniffling at their table.

'D'you want one?' she asked, her hand shaking as she lit her cigarette.

Christian shook his head.

'I'm sorry I said all that to you last time,' said Sarah. 'I don't know what came over me. Sometimes you make me so angry, I just want to give you a taste of your own medicine.'

'Please don't apologise. The truth is that both you and Ruth are way too good for me.'

Sarah drew deeply on the cigarette. 'I don't really blame you. I mean, what could you have done, left your wife when she was about to give birth?'

'I could have not got into it in the first place. We could have been more careful. I could have been more careful.'

'Because then you could have walked away, right?'

'No. No, that's not what I meant.'

'What was it anyway?'

Someone was surely going to save him. 'What was what?'

'Us. You know, what was I to you? Be honest, if I was just a cheap fuck, you can say it.'

The words made him physically recoil, like she'd hit him. 'It was never that straightforward, Sarah. I didn't get into it thinking I was going to leave Ruth, but it became more than it should have been. Christ, I don't really know.'

'Why did you choose Ruth?' And she said it so bluntly he momentarily thought he must have misheard.

'Oh God.' The need to run made his legs twitch under the table.

'No, Christian, God can't help you now,' said Sarah, her eyes shrinking to half their size. Christian wondered if she might be mad. He decided the quicker he answered her questions the quicker he could leave.

'I chose Ruth because she's my wife and she was about to have my child and,' he didn't know if he should go on, but something about this young girl sitting here judging his relationship made him feel angry, 'and because I love her. You know, we fight and often we don't understand each other, but I do love her.' And the presence of the words given life by his warm breath momentarily comforted Christian, made him sure of his choice. But Sarah looked shattered. Christian worried he had broken her. 'I'm sorry, you asked, that's the truth.'

'You wouldn't know the truth if it fucking hit you, Christian. Did you ever give me a moment's thought?'

'Of course I did. I do. That's why I rang. I'll never be able to say sorry enough for what happened, but what's the point of this?'

Sarah picked up her glass and for a second Christian thought she was going to throw it at him. He saw it leave her hands and felt the thin shards break the skin on his face. He wondered how he would explain it to Ruth. But she put it back on the table without drinking. 'The point of this is that it's my turn.'

'Your turn? Your turn for what?'

'Don't play thick, Christian, it doesn't suit you. It's my turn for you.'

Christian wondered if he had entered some parallel universe where people bargained with each other's lives as though they were pieces on a chessboard. But Sarah looked serious. 'What are you talking about? It doesn't work that way.'

'You had your chance, Christian. I killed our baby for you. You're not going to get away with this again.'

'Get away with what? We haven't done anything.'

'Oh, and Ruth would see it that way, of course.'

His head was spinning, he couldn't see clearly, like some cliché. 'What are you saying?'

'I'm saying it's game over. She's not going to forgive you again.'

'So, let me get this straight. You think you can blackmail me into being with you? Sounds like a healthy start to a relationship.'

Sarah laughed and this time she did sound mad. 'A healthy relationship? Yeah right, like anyone's got one of those.'

Christian had a migraine about once a year and he knew what was coming when the sweat started to trickle down his back and he got flashes at the corner of his vision. He had to get to a dark room and lie very still with lots of strong painkillers inside him that would do nothing more than take the edge off a pain so intense he felt sure it was going to kill him. 'I'm going to go now,' he said. 'This is mad and I have to get home.' He stood up and Sarah grabbed at his leg.

'Please, don't leave me. Come home with me tonight. Just one night, I didn't mean all that stuff about telling Ruth.'

Soon he was going to be sick. 'Sarah, I've got to go. I don't feel good. We'll talk later in the week. I promise.' It was as easy as breathing.

'Really? Will you call me tomorrow?'

A clamp had fastened itself around his head, squeezing his brain out the top, shooting arrows across his shoulders. 'Yes, I will.' He stumbled out of the pub, simply grateful to be released, unable to focus on anything other than his need to get home. He began trying to flag down a taxi, longing for the moment when he could sit in the back and count down the minutes until it might start to get a little better.

Agatha ordered the food on Tesco Direct; it had made shopping a whole lot easier since Ruth had showed her the password, and she absolutely never bought anything that wasn't to be used by the family. Some nannies would get themselves their own shower gel or their favourite biscuits or little things like that, but Agatha would never steal from anyone.

Except that one time, of course, and that had been a necessity, so you couldn't call it stealing. The way Agatha saw it, she had been at war, and what's that saying, something like anything goes in love and war. Yes, it had been more a case of survival.

Agatha had been fourteen when she'd realised that she had to get away from the vileness of Harry and the apathy of her family else she would either die or kill someone.

Either way, her life would be over and that seemed unfair, considering she wasn't the one who'd done anything wrong. She'd worked out by then that what Harry did to her was wrong. And not only wrong in that it made her feel ill and sick, but literally wrong in the eyes of the law. Somehow though she had never been able to communicate this to Harry himself. It was true that their meetings had become far less regular and they often went for months without seeing each other, but if ever he did get her on his own, it didn't take him long to get her naked and vulnerable.

One of the things Agatha hated most about herself was that she never screamed or lashed out or told him to fuck off, that she was going to call the police. He constantly rendered her speechless and powerless, every time took her right back to the first time and for the minutes that it took, she was once again nothing more than a shaking nine-year-old, not even sure if this was just another awful part of growing up.

He rolled off her and said, 'My God, girly, I think we're getting somewhere, I'd hazard a guess you enjoyed that.' And all in a flash she had seen her future, she had realised that she would never be free of him unless he died or she got too far away for him to ever find her again. Because if at this point right now she was unable to set him straight, then when would the time ever come? She might be able to limit his chances to twice a year, but the fact that he was always there, leering over her shoulder like a character from a Grimm fairy tale made it impossible for her to get on with anything else. It had taken eighteen months' planning and much pilfering from her mother's purse to save enough to leave, but days after her sixteenth birthday she'd left home and never gone back.

It had been so easy to watch herself walk away, to realise that she was going to do it at last. Her parents didn't know whether she was alive or dead and sometimes she imagined ringing them and explaining everything. But what was everything? Where did it start, had it even ended? She wondered now if she would ever tell them, if she saw them again, or if the tale had got somehow lost in the tunnels of time. Either way, she could never forgive them. They'd had the most precious thing in the world, a child, and they'd let their own neuroses and bad temper and stupidity get in the way of keeping that child safe.

Ruth reminded Agatha a lot of her own mother. They weren't bad women and they loved their children, but they didn't seem to realise that wasn't enough. Betty, Agatha had decided, would be fine. She was just like Louise, all pretty and headstrong and opinionated. She would definitely shout and when she did Ruth would do her best to make everything better. But Hal. Little Hal. He would never shout in a million years and Agatha shuddered when she thought of all the things that could happen to him.

Hal had kept quiet and nobody had fed him. Can you imagine that? If anyone ever found out and asked her why she had done it, that would be the first thing she would say. They just stuffed bottles into his mouth because he didn't ask for food and that was the easiest option. Yes, she imagined saying, it was shocking. I don't know what would have happened if I hadn't come along.

Hal now ate eggs, cheese, cake and those organic puffs that all the mothers in the park seemed so fond of, as well as everything else that Agatha had already got him to try. In fact, he was pretty much eating like a normal three-year-old now, except of course for the fact that you had to mash everything up because his mouth was so unused to chewing. It had become a bit of a trial in the evening, waiting for moments when no one was looking and sneaking him food. So far Agatha had told him that they were saving his eating as a big surprise for his party, but with the day now only forty-eight small hours away, anxiety was taking hold of her. Hal had become too much her own to share him with anyone else. Hal would soon eat something in front of one of his parents and then they would know his secret and he would become theirs again. The thought made her contract inside herself so her stomach felt squeezed.

When Ruth arrived at work on Thursday morning everyone except Sally was huddled round Bev the Fashion Editor's desk. They were all crying, some more overtly than others.

'What's happened?' asked Ruth, her mind already taking her to far darker places than was probably necessary.

Kirsty answered, 'Paul Rogers died last night.'

'Paul Rogers the photographer?'

'Yes, he was killed in a car crash.'

'Oh my God, Bev, I'm so sorry.'

Bev didn't hear and Ruth reckoned she had enough consoling shoulders so she went into Sally's office. Sally was tapping at her computer. 'Shit, I just heard about Paul.'

'I know. Crappy, isn't it? But to be honest, Bev was the only one who knew him well. If it wasn't politically incorrect, I'd tell them all to get back to their desks.'

Ruth felt light-headed. 'Didn't he have kids?'

'Yeah, two.' Sally stopped writing and looked up. 'Sorry, I know I'm being a hard-nosed bitch, but I can't stand the way when anyone dies they immediately become a saint. I never saw Paul when he wasn't off his face. I'm surprised he didn't drive his car into a tree years ago.'

The ground shifted from beneath Ruth's feet, as if a black hole had opened up. 'I better get on,' she said, making her way to her desk.

Ruth had probably met Paul Rogers twice, maybe three times, but he was often in the office, bounding around, calling everyone 'love', a camera round his neck, rolls of film in his hand, T-shirts with stupid slogans on his chest. And yes, he probably was a bit of prick and mostly coked up, but still he had seemed very vital to Ruth. She couldn't believe that solid presence of a man had simply gone, here one second and not the next. She imagined his body, all white and lifeless, lying on a mortuary table, with everything that made him Paul evaporated. One of her friends had been with her father when he died and she'd told Ruth that it had made her believe in the spirit. It was different from watching someone fall asleep, she had said; he took his last breath and then he reared up, as if something was pulling him forward, before he flopped back down and shrank into himself. There was no mistaking that something had gone, something had left his body.

Death, Ruth realised sitting at her desk, was the great equaliser. No matter how successful or clever or pretty or popular we were, we are all reduced to the same flesh and bones in the end. And when you understood that, then what was the point in trying to do or be anything? It made Ruth feel empty, hollow almost, as if someone was slowly deflating a balloon in her stomach so that all she could taste was stale air. Thoughts danced about her head like children playing a game of hide and seek. Stop, she wanted to shout, slow down so I can catch you and get to the bottom of what you are about.

The only thing you can be sure of in death is the one thing no one is sure of in life. Once you are dead, people realise how much they loved you. Maybe in the moment of death you realise who you love. Ruth began to wonder if she was wasting her time and in that thought she had to hold onto the edge of her desk to stop herself from toppling off her chair. What was happening to her and why did she feel like she was falling?

She tried to get a grip on herself but her age kept floating into her head. In eighteen months she would be forty; she was now closer to fifty than twenty, her life probably nearly half lived, if she was lucky. She might go beyond eighty, but from watching her grandmothers she knew these years would disintegrate into nothing more than constant rounds of frustration and pain and confusion and anger and tiny, meaningless tasks.

There had to be time for everything and everyone in all the long years that most of us lived. And yet, it appeared that there wasn't. Betty and Hal refused to leave Ruth's thoughts. She imagined them at home, saw them as clearly as if she was there with them, hearing their chatter, feeling their little hands in hers. She longed for them as desperately as if she hadn't seen them for a year, a devastating emptiness spreading through her body and a foul taste of nothing refusing to leave the back of her throat.

Kirsty came snivelling back to her desk. 'I can't believe that, can you?'

'I know, it's horrid.'

'And his wife's so nice and his girls are only young.' She sniffed again, then passed Ruth a wedge of papers. 'The proof's in. Sally wants it signed off by the end of the day.'

Ruth tried to bring herself back by opening the mock-up of the magazine. She flicked desultorily through its manicured pages. Even in black and white you could see how many lies all the photographs told. It depressed her unduly today. It made her wonder if they were peddling pornography. Because what was the point of all these glossy, inflated, unsubstantiated and ultimately false images? Surely they were only there to excite an uncontrollable desire in the reader, to render them helpless, to get them salivating, to look at what they had with loathing, to make them want to go out and possess things beyond their reach. To make them buy the magazine again next month.

A photo of Margo and her children stopped her. They'd been given the title page of the story, called unimaginatively, *The Good Life.* A sickening strapline ran across their feet, framing the picture: *If you've ever thought about giving it all up, read this with caution or you could find yourself resigning, putting your house on the market and looking into organic farming.* She hated the jaunty tone of every single piece they put into the magazine. There's enough shit out there, Sally had said to them all in an editorial meeting a few months ago, it is now officially our job to cheer everybody up.

Margo Lansford is a woman with a plan, except it's not a plan that most of us would ever dare put into action. But Margo's not like the rest of us. She's got the courage of her convictions and the willpower to see it through. Ruth wanted to put a red line through the word willpower and replace it with money. *Margo was an investment banker earning a six-figure salary, with two young children at home, when she and her husband decided to jack it all in for a life of bucolic idealism in rural Essex.* Jane, the sub editor, had crossed out bucolic idealism and written blissful soap-making. She'd then written in brackets, 'Let's not confuse the readers with too many long words'. Ruth's red pen twitched in her hands but she didn't write anything onto the page; she wasn't sure what the real story was or what words she might use to convey it. *'We went on holiday to Greece,' Margo said as she poured more Chamomile tea in her beautifully shabby chic kitchen, 'and one night I looked at Charlie and said, "What on earth are we doing. We never see the kids, we have a house we're never in and we have to schedule time for a conversation. Let's just stop." And he looked at me and said, "Yes, what a wonderful idea." We haven't looked back since.'*

Kirsty reappeared. 'Sorry, I forgot to give you this note. It was handed into reception this morning.'

Ruth took the fragile envelope and saw her name written in a rounded girlish hand. Something caught in her throat and she allowed herself a minute before opening it.

Ruth, we need to talk. None of us can go on like this. I am in the café opposite your office and I'll wait here all day. Sarah.

The tipping and the flipping gathered pace, a bird fluttered helplessly in her throat, her eyes stung, her palms sweated.

Ruth had never even seen Sarah and something close to excitement accompanied her frenzied race down the stairs. This was it then, this was the moment when she surrendered her life as she knew it and watched someone else take control. Because of course Christian must be seeing her again, maybe he'd never stopped. Whatever it was, she would be unable to forgive him a second time.

Ruth saw the person who could only be Sarah from the door of the café. She was nothing more than Ruth had expected, which depressed her in some unfathomable way. She walked towards her with the advantage of being the one approaching, so she could stand over the girl for a few minutes, which was a small victory but still surely worth something.

When she had found out about the affair the first time, Ruth had fantasised about meeting Sarah. All the things she would tell her about sisterhood and respect and karma and how Sarah's life was never going to be fulfilling and happy until she stopped taking what didn't belong to her. But sitting opposite her now, all those thoughts slunk away like a hissing cat. She was nothing more than a girl, thin and white and dressed in black, no make-up, bags under her eyes, scruffy hair. She didn't look like a winner, or maybe it was that what she had won had been too hard fought for and Ruth felt an unexpected jab of sympathy for her.

'I'm glad you came,' said Sarah. 'Thanks for that.'

'I was hardly going to ignore that note, was I?' Now she was still, Ruth realised her whole body was shaking.

'I'm sorry it's had to come to this. I was hoping Christian would have the guts to tell you, but I don't think he ever will.'

Don't use his name. Don't fucking use his name. And in the thought Ruth wondered if she could still not want to lose him. Her speech was slow, she had to dredge for every word. 'I'm afraid you're going to have to fill me in. I don't know what we're talking about here.'

Ruth noticed that Sarah was clutching the table so hard her knuckles were white. 'I'm not prepared to go on waiting any longer. I told him that, I even said I was going to tell you, but it's made no difference.'

'Yes, but tell me what? Are you having an affair again? Christ, did it ever stop?'

'Yes, it stopped. When he wouldn't leave you because you were about to have your son, it stopped. I went to Australia and had a pretty shit time and then I came back to England and I applied for a job at Christian's work – by coincidence, I didn't know he worked there – and we met again and, well …'

There were so many questions Ruth wanted to ask they had jumbled her brain so she could barely remember her own name. 'When was this?'

'A couple of months ago.'

'And you've been seeing each other since then?'

Sarah nodded. 'I'm sorry, I really am.'

Ruth was vaguely aware that Sarah was playing a game and she felt like a mother, like the person she was, not prepared to put up with the shit. 'No, don't apologise to me. I think I might hit you if you do that. I just need the facts then I'll move out the way and let you and Christian get on with it.'

What was she, twenty-three or -four? What did he see in her? The whole thing was preposterous. Betty and Hal were right there as Ruth tried to imagine the effects of her new life.

'What exactly has he promised you, Sarah?'

'He wants to leave but he feels like he can't. He says he loves the kids and he still loves you, but not in that way. He's told me you always row and you don't have sex.'

'We had sex at the weekend.' Even as she said the words Ruth knew you should never have conversations like this. 'In fact, we have sex all the time. But then, you can't ever trust a liar, can you, Sarah?'

The girl looked down and Ruth realised she was trying to be graceful and demure. 'I don't care what you say. You're bound to want to fight for him.'

Ruth laughed. 'Are you joking? You honestly think I'd want anything to do with him after this? You're welcome to him.'

Sarah smiled, like a child, like Betty would if you told her she could have two ice creams in a row. 'Am I?' Her voice was chirpy. 'Are you sure? You won't stand in our way?'

Ruth was never going to let Betty meet this monstrosity of womanhood. She felt that she had to say something; a desire to protect Christian washed through her. 'We're not talking about a dress, you know, we are talking about a person.'

'I know, I'm sorry.' Sarah leant forward, Ruth wondered if she was going to take her hand. 'It's just that I've waited so long to hear those words, I can't believe it's happening. I can't believe it's been this easy and you've been so reasonable and I could have done this all along and everything would have been sorted and we could try again.'

'Try again?'

'For a baby. You know we lost the last one.'

Bile and sickness flushed through Ruth's guts. 'Oh my God, are you serious?'

'Of course.' Sarah's hands were now folded protectively across her tummy.

'Are you pregnant?'

'Not yet, but I'm hoping it'll happen soon.'

It was as if someone had told her she was living with a murderer. Her husband was going to discard one family and start another just like that. Like he'd painted a room the wrong colour and thought, Fuck it, I'll buy another pot of paint and spend another day painting it. 'I've got to go,' she said, standing up.

Sarah looked up at her, all doe-eyed again. It seemed far-fetched to think that look had entranced her husband. 'I'm sorry I had to do this, Ruth, but you know Christian, he's just so useless.'

And that was too much. Ruth leant over the table so that Sarah winced. 'Actually, I do not know Christian.

Which is quite scary because I've lived with him for the past ten years and I've only just discovered that I have no idea who he is. And I cannot imagine why you or anyone else would want to be with someone as totally vile as he is. And as for being reasonable, you can tell Christian I intend to make his life a fucking misery.'

Ruth left. The day was much, much too bright and too many people were ambling along as though they had nothing particular to do and it was going to be another of those enjoyable days which you roll through so they become nothing more than a fuzzy impression of what your life is like, rather than a proper memory. Ruth felt insulted as well as sure that she was going to faint and she didn't want to do it in public. She hailed a taxi and gave her home address. On the journey she had the presence of mind to ring the office and say she had been suddenly struck down by a terrible headache. The woman who made the call was quite impressive, a calm ordered voice which so belied the crashing ocean in her mind.

She hadn't let herself cry in the taxi so by the time she was putting her key into her front door her eyes were aching with the effort of holding back the tears. Betty would still be at school and she hoped Hal wouldn't see her. There was laughter coming from the kitchen but the door was nearly closed, so Ruth couldn't see what was going on. She contemplated going straight upstairs but knew that was too weird so instead she called out to Aggie. The laughing stopped instantly.

Aggie's red face appeared round the door. 'Ruth, are you okay?'

'No. I've got a monstrous headache. I just wanted to let you know that I'm at home, but I'm going to bed. Would you mind not telling Betty I'm here and not letting Hal up? Sorry, but I've got to sleep.'

'Of course, that's fine. Can I get you anything?'

'No, no.' Ruth had her hand on the banisters, she was maybe only a few words away from her bed. 'I've got stuff upstairs. I need to sleep. Oh, and if Christian calls, tell him I can't talk, I'm asleep.'

'Okay, well, shout if you want anything.' And then she pulled her head back behind the door and Ruth wondered why she hadn't properly come out or why Hal hadn't tried to see her.

Ruth's bedroom looked different already and not only because it was so neat and clean when she'd left it such a pit that morning; she was used to that. Aggie had asked Ruth a few weeks before if it would be all right if she made their bed and cleaned their room. Why would I mind? Ruth had asked, but also why would you want to do it? Aggie had laughed, I hate walking through the house and knowing there's a mess anywhere, she'd said. I know it's odd, but I've always been the same, I used to tidy up after my mum when I was little. So now Ruth lived in almost hotel cleanliness and perfection, which was of course wonderful, yet at the same time somehow … what was the word, strange, disconcerting, wrong? It made her feel beholden to Aggie, made her feel that the girl knew too much about her, that she'd got too far in.

She dropped her bag where she stood and kicked off her shoes, allowing herself to fall onto her bed. She wept with an abandon that would have put Betty to shame.

I just need to get this out, she thought to herself, and then I can think about all of this properly. Except the tears didn't stop and the self-indulgence felt right this time. Every thought was a new and painful experience which pushed salty water out of her surely by now swollen tear ducts. She felt miserable that Christian could have thought so little of her that he could allow this to happen again, that he didn't even feel the need to tell her of his plans. She hated the thought that her children were going to grow up only seeing their father every other weekend, that they would have to watch him living with brothers and sisters to whom they felt disconnected, that they would always feel second best and that this would in some way influence their future relationships. She didn't want to share them out like a box of chocolates at Christmas and birthdays and in the summer holidays. She never wanted to hear them tell her about the food Sarah cooked or what colour their bedrooms were in her husband and his new wife's home. She mourned the loss of love in her life. She couldn't face the thought of pulling herself together and re-packaging herself on a dating website and then all the plucking and waxing and low lighting that it would take to get her naked in front of anyone ever again. Or getting to know another man's body so that it felt warm and comfortable. She didn't want to know about someone else's past, she didn't want to meet any more parents or sets of friends, listen to more moans about jobs that weren't perfect.

Her phone rang from her bag and she raced for it. Christian's name flashed on the screen and she itched to answer, but she wasn't ready yet. If she spoke to him now she would want to hurl abuse when she needed to get a handle on why he had done this. She would probably only have the right to speak to him like he was her husband a few more times and she needed to find out as much as possible in those conversations. She did not want to be left with those nagging, gnawing questions which would eat away at her, giving her an ulcer or something more serious. Because, once he had left, that would be it, they would have to resort to clipped pleasantries as he stood in the hall waiting for the kids to be ready. She would watch his body through his clothes, knowing how it felt, yet with no right to remember any more. She dialled the number for his message.

'Ruth, where are you? She's mad, I promise you. I had no idea she was coming to see you. It's all bullshit, we haven't been seeing each other. Ruth, I love you, I'm not going anywhere. Please call me so we can talk. We have to talk.'

At first Christian's words were like a balm, like a hand rubbing her back so that her tears reduced themselves to a short catch of breath in her throat. She started to dial his number, but then began to wonder. He must have spoken to Sarah to know she had come to see her. Which meant that they were at the very least in contact. He had hidden all this from her, he had betrayed her simply by uttering one word to that girl again. So it couldn't all be bullshit. They had been seeing each other, even if it wasn't in the way she had imagined. And of course the physicality of anything was important for Christian, but it didn't mean that much to her. It was the fact that he had been able to forget her for long enough to have a conversation with Sarah, to maybe meet her for a drink, to lie and lie and lie again. She heard his pompous voice shouting into her phone that he loved her and wasn't leaving and she wanted to scratch his eyes out. It was not enough to say those words, to state what he was going to do as if she had no say or she'd be so grateful he hadn't been fucking his secretary again she'd lie down and let him trample all over her for a second time. Now she knew what she wanted to say.

He picked up in one ring. 'Ruth, where are you? I've been worried sick.'

'I'm at home. You didn't look too hard.'

'I'm on my way back now.'

'No. Betty will be home soon. I'll meet you somewhere. How about St James's Park? It's right by your work.'

'Okay, if you want to come over here.'

'I don't want to be anywhere near home. I don't want to ever be reminded of the conversation we're about to have.'

'Ruth, nothing's happened, she's mad.'

'Seriously, Christian, shut up. This isn't up to you any more. I'll be there as quick as I can.'

Aggie had been shocked when she'd heard Ruth's voice from the hall. It had been a physical sensation, like someone had dropped a stone into her stomach, sending little rings of panic through her body. She hadn't felt like that for a long time and it wasn't nice. Hal had just started eating his lunch; fish fingers and carrots from the garden, even a spoonful of peas, which was a new taste she was road-testing. They were laughing at the fact that a green, round pea had the same name as what you did after you'd drunk too much. Then she'd heard Ruth calling her and for a second she'd wondered if she'd gone back to hearing things when they weren't there, but no, Ruth called again. Aggie's immediate reaction was to hide Hal's plate in a cupboard but that would be too confusing for him and could put his eating right back. Should she go into the hall and shut the door behind her or would that make Ruth suspicious and Hal nervous? In the end she motioned to Hal to keep quiet and stuck her head round the door, like she was in the middle of something important. As soon as she saw Ruth though she realised she needn't have worried as the woman was obviously ill; she was as pale as snow, her eyes were red and raw and her shoulders were hunched as though she was trying to fight off a deep pain. Do you need anything? Agatha had asked. But all Ruth had wanted was to be left alone. Don't tell Betty I'm at home, she'd said, and don't let Hal upstairs.

Agatha shut the kitchen door on her and gathered Hal onto her lap, helping him spoon his food into his mouth.

'Mummy,' he said, looking up at her.

She kissed the top of his head. 'Yes, my love, that was Mummy. But she's gone to lie down, she's not feeling well.'

'Mummy,' said Hal again, burrowing his head into her neck.

You didn't realise that breaking hearts existed outside of songs until you had children. Memories rushed at her of her own mother lying in her bed, the thick curtains drawn against the day, telling Agatha to keep the noise down, she had one of her heads. But I want to show you my picture from school. This must never happen to Hal. Agatha felt this like a round boulder in her stomach. He was too kind and trusting and tender, he would not be able to cope with all the disappointments and rejections.

'Hal,' said Agatha now, 'what if you call me Mummy? Just as a joke and only when we're alone. But we could pretend I'm your mummy and then you wouldn't have to ever miss her again.'

'Mummy,' said Hal again, looking up at her and smiling. It was obviously what he'd meant all along. She smiled at this. They understood each other, her and Hal, like no one else in the world.

He looks just like you, a woman in the park had said last week, and Agatha had smiled and pushed Hal a bit higher in the swing. It was easy if you remained calm and polite and didn't tell an outright lie or try to strike up a conversation with anyone which could tie you in knots. It would have to be only her and Hal, there wouldn't be room for anyone else, anyone to wheedle out the truth and disapprove. But that was okay. It had been only Agatha for so long now it would be a pleasure to share her life with someone and she couldn't think of anyone she'd rather be with than Hal. Which was not something she could imagine Ruth ever thinking.

Sarah rang Christian at eleven thirty, as he was about to go into a meeting about whether or not to sack the presenter who couldn't seem to speak properly. He let it go to answer and didn't remember to listen to the message until lunchtime.

'I've done it, Christian, and Ruth was fine. She did seem a bit shocked and she said she's going to make your life a fucking misery, but you couldn't expect much else I suppose. But anyway, none of that matters, 'cos she said she's not going to stand in our way. Isn't that amazing? Call me as soon as you get this.'

Ruth often said inexplicable things to Christian like, I feel dizzy or The world is spinning too fast or I can't seem to get a grip on life. But in that moment he not only understood what she meant but experienced all of those shape-shifting feelings that make you realise life is never going to be the same again. He immediately rang Ruth but Kirsty told him she'd gone home sick. He was about to call there when he thought he'd better find out what he was going into.

He left the office to call Sarah.

'Christian, did you get my message?'

'Yes. What did you say to my wife?' He wanted to punch her. The sensation rose up in him so violently and yet so unexpectedly that he stumbled.

'Why do you sound like that?' she asked.

'Tell me what you said, Sarah.'

Her voice was unsure. 'I said what we'd agreed. You know, about how this couldn't go on and you felt too guilty to leave, but that it was my turn now.'

He couldn't keep the shout down. 'What we agreed? When the fuck did we agree that?'

'Last time we met.' She was crying now and she disgusted him. 'I said I couldn't wait any longer, Christian, I said I was going to tell Ruth and you said you'd call the next day but you didn't, so I did what I said I would.'

Christian pulled at his hair. The madness was all around him, palpable, fucking everywhere. 'How dare you come into my life and think you can turn it upside down. We haven't even done anything. This is fucking mad.'

She was weeping now. 'But you promised. You said.'

'I didn't promise anything. Shit, this is such a mess.'

'She's going to leave you and then what will you do?'

Christian's head loosened. 'I'm not going to let her leave, and even if she did I would never end up with you.' He put the phone down but it was without conviction. He knew he had handled everything wrong. Some of the things he'd said to Sarah swirled in his body like the cigarette you smoke at the end of the night which refuses to leave your lungs. Something was not ringing true. His righteous indignation did not feel righteous.

He left Ruth a message and she eventually rang him back and agreed to meet him, but something about her tone told him that he had a long, long battle ahead. He was starting to believe he'd got it all wrong and his life was going to slip through his fingers like nothing more than a bucket of sand. Something had tricked him, some malevolent external force had made him believe he wanted things that were as flimsy as the tail on a firework. He had been blinded by bright lights and tripped up by misconceptions, none of which were true.

As he sat on a bench waiting for his wife he remembered making a phone call when he was a young teenager and being connected to a call that was entirely not his. Two women talking. He had been mesmerised by them. He had sat and listened to their conversation which had drifted over so many subjects he'd wondered how they knew such things. A recipe for a cake for a daughter's birthday, news on the other's piles, an update on a brother's heart attack, the worry of a husband who found it harder and harder to get out of bed … Christian had been let into their private world, had been allowed for a few minutes to share in their innermost being, to be part of someone else. But then one of them had said, Can you hear something? And the other had said, Yes, like someone breathing on the line. And he'd lost his nerve and put the phone down. And then they were gone and he hadn't asked them anything, they would never even know he existed. Those women had stayed with him all his life and yet it was only now, in the middle of watching his life being sucked down a black hole, that he realised why he had never forgotten them. If only he had understood before this moment. If only he had been clever enough to learn their lesson. If only he had realised what they taught him: that life is lived in the minutest details. That every emotion is within touching distance, hiding under the sink or in the garden or round the corner. He'd spent all this time looking off into the distance while happiness eluded him right under his nose.

Sarah kept ringing but he couldn't turn his phone off in case Ruth tried to get hold of him. He would ring Sarah eventually and apologise for the way he'd spoken to her. He would make it clear that he loved Ruth and that he didn't want to be with Sarah, but he would also say that he had treated her badly and had been a coward and he hoped she would be happy. He was sorry he had shouted. Sorry he had called her mad.

Ruth appeared out of nowhere. He had been scanning the park for her but then suddenly she was there. Next to him on the bench, looking like she'd been in a fight. They sat silently for a while, neither wanting to dive into the shit piled at their feet.

'I am so sorry,' Christian said finally.

'Sorry for what? For what you've done, or being found out?' Her voice was too hard.

'For what I've done. Not that I have done anything this time.'

She laughed. 'You know, once I might have believed you. But having your girlfriend sitting in front of me telling me how you're going to start trying for a baby sort of put the kibosh on that one.'

'She's not my girlfriend.'

'Yes, but you've obviously been seeing her.'

'I've seen her, but not in that way.'

She flashed her eyes at him. 'Any way is unacceptable, Christian. Do you not get that?'

He felt desperate. 'Of course I get that. That's why I didn't mention it.'

'Not mentioning it is worse than meeting her. Fuck, you are so stupid.'

'I thought I could deal with it.'

'No, you thought you could get away with it.' And possibly she was right. He felt pathetic.

'Ruth, nothing happened. I love you.'

'It doesn't matter what happened and you don't love me. When you love someone you respect them.' She had an answer for everything and they were all probably right. He felt defeated, like he'd never win, and what was he trying to win anyway, what was the prize here?

'She came for an interview at work, for an admin assistant role. Carol had set it all up, I had no idea she was coming in until she walked through the door. And then she rang the next day and asked to meet up.'

'There wasn't a moment in which you thought maybe you shouldn't?' He heard a catch in her voice and it gave him hope that she still retained a tiny bit of feeling for him. He imagined her love like an electric light bulb, which at this moment had one tiny filament attaching the working parts.

'I'm sorry, Ruth. I didn't meet her because I wanted to start anything up again. But it was odd seeing her, and she sounded desperate on the phone and, I know I shouldn't have, but I thought it would be one last drink.'

'What, for old times' sake?'

'I know. It was stupid.'

'And then what happened? It was so great to see her you had to do it again and again?'

'No, it was complicated. She told me she hadn't lost the baby, but that she'd had an abortion and then had a breakdown and gone to Australia. Fuck, it sounds lame now, but I felt sorry for her. I felt responsible.'

'For the first time in your life.'

'What?' Christian tried to look at his wife but her face was set so hard he barely recognised her and she scared him.

'Responsibility is not your forte, Christian. Sure, you have a good job and you're a good dad, as far as it goes, but you've no idea what really goes on with the kids. You don't worry about things like I do. You sail through life, taking care of yourself. And I'm not saying you'd let us starve or anything, or if something bad happened you wouldn't worry, but you don't premeditate anything. It's like you're you on the surface, but just under your skin you're still eighteen. Sometimes it's like you resent us.'

'I'm not, but that's not …' Christian searched for what he wanted to say but Ruth's words stung him as if she was throwing pins at him.

'I was stupid to take you back last time. You never properly changed, so this was always going to happen again.'

'But nothing happened.'

'Stop saying that, it makes you sound stupid. You met her, you were no doubt nice to her, nice enough that she thought you were going to leave me …'

'She's mad.'

'And stop saying that. Take responsibility for that as well.'

Christian sat back on the bench. 'Ruth, I'll do anything. Please give me one more chance.'

She laughed at him again, a horrid sound that was not a description of mirth. 'You sound like Betty. And no, the answer is no.'

'I know I've got it wrong.'

'Do you want a medal?'

'No, I don't mean just Sarah. There were two women once …'

'What, more fucking women?'

'No, when I was younger, on the phone.'

'I don't want to hear about your teenage phone sex, Christian.'

'Ruth, stop it. Listen to me. I think I get what's wrong with me. I don't think I've ever realised, before right now, what we had.'

Ruth held her hand up. 'Please stop. I've heard enough of your bullshit for one day.'

He held his head in his hands in a gesture which seemed false but which he felt so keenly, desperately searching for something, anything. He'd take Ruth any way, he realised, it didn't even have to be that she loved him. 'But what about the kids?'

'Like you were thinking about them.'

'Ruth, I'll change, I promise. I'll never make you sad again.'

She gave him a look she usually reserved for Betty's wilder claims. 'At least stay in the realms of reality. We're married, it's our job to make each other sad.'

He wanted to grab her, to shake her and look deep into her eyes so she could see how much he meant this. They did it in films and it worked, why couldn't the same apply in real life? Because that was what this was, Christian realised, maybe ten years too late. It felt as real as a newborn baby or a car crash or the death of a friend; a moment which sucks you so completely into the here and now you are for once certain. 'No, you know what I mean, please, Ruth, please don't do this.'

'I'm not doing anything, I'm responding. And I want you to leave, as soon as possible.'

'No, please, really.'

'God, you are so arrogant!' Her face was flushed and her voice was rising. 'You really thought you could get away with this, didn't you?'

'I wasn't thinking like that at all.'

She stood up. 'I've had enough of this. You've ruined my life enough for one day. I should be getting back to the kids.'

He stood up as well and put his hands on her shoulders. For a tiny moment they looked at each other and they both longed for things they couldn't have. 'Ruth, it's Hal's birthday on Saturday. Please give me till the end of the weekend. It's not fair on him.' There, he'd played dirty, but he meant it and he was desperate.

Ruth looked as though she knew she'd been had. 'Okay,' she said, 'till the end of the weekend, and just because of Hal.' She shook his hands off. 'I'm going to get a taxi home but don't follow me. I can't bear to sit in the same space as you.'

He watched her walk away and realised his son had saved him for the second time in his short life. He felt dirty and unworthy, ashamed and guilty. Totally undeserving of a family who only a few days ago had seemed a burden. Could he admit that to himself and were you allowed to think thoughts like that?

Christian looked across the landscape of his life and realised he didn't bring much joy. He didn't even have many meaningful relationships. Of course there was Ruth and the kids, but she was right, he floated with them, he didn't interact. And Toby, of course Toby. But how much was that to do with history and how much to do with what Christian did for him? He never spoke to his parents beyond pleasantries, had no idea who his brother even was. There were lots of faces at work who were good for going to the pub with for a quick one after work, which pissed Ruth off because it meant he never got home in time to put the kids to bed. But when you looked at it they were all nearly ten years younger than him, he was their boss, they probably only relaxed after he'd left. A sickness washed over him like a shroud.

Ruth only just made it to the street and into a taxi. A fatigue so pure had descended on her she wondered, absentmindedly, if she really was sick, rather than emotionally bludgeoned. The brief respite from Betty sleeping better had evaporated as quickly as steam from a boiling pot. She wondered if this was what her tiredness had always been about, a deep sense of despair in a life which she feared was wrong.

Her body was strung out like washing on a line, she felt as see-through and inconsequential as a lace nightdress. The next few days stretched out before her like one of those never-ending American roads and she wasn't sure if she could make it. She wasn't sure if she could keep up the hard front which she would now need forever more to protect her against Christian. Because one moment of weakness, one day of PMT, one sleepless night, one glass of wine too many and she'd be weeping and wishing for him to put his arms around her.

One day she'd let herself mourn for all the lost moments and days that she had foolishly presumed would belong to her and her children. She saw herself on all the endless weekends that lay ahead: another drawn-looking woman in a park with two children fighting, an ill-conceived picnic at her feet, waiting ... waiting for what? For time to run out, the kids to grow up and then ...? Then the loneliness of dinner for one, of trying to find something for herself, of taking up a hobby that was more of a chore, of accepting invitations from kind friends for holidays in which you always felt you were in the way.

Ruth could remember every detail of the first time Christian had shattered her world. She'd started her maternity leave the day before and had spent her first full day with Betty in a state of contentment. She'd got her to bed and the house was relatively tidy and she had been making a salad, feeling strangely pleased with herself, as if the world had an order and she was part of it. Then Christian arrived home.

Ruth had known he was drunk from how he shut the door. She could tell from text messages as well. Sometimes she didn't mind that much and sometimes it seemed like a crime against humanity. Tonight was a crime night. She was shocked that he hadn't realised it was a special day; what if she went into labour and he was too drunk to drive her to the hospital? Ruth had all these arguments on the tip of her tongue, ready to go, when he stumbled into the kitchen and she knew something was very wrong.

'Shit, what's the matter?' she'd asked, and at that moment she'd only been thinking along the lines of a lost job or a crashed car, which had seemed bad enough until he'd spoken.

'I'm leaving,' Christian had answered.

'Leaving? Where?' The baby was wedged under her ribs and it made coherent thought a struggle.

Christian wouldn't look at her, he kept shuffling his feet like a child. 'I'm leaving you. This house.'

'You what?' She'd had to sit down, her legs had given way, like you see happen in films.

'I'm sorry, Ruth. I can't go on. We're living a lie, we don't love each other, we don't like the same things, we never do anything together, you're always exhausted, we never have sex.'

'But I'm eight months pregnant.' The words sounded as helpless as the baby she was about to give birth to.

'I know, but it's not only that. This has been going on for years.'

'Years? Why didn't you say something then? Why did you get me bloody pregnant?' There was anger in there, but for now she felt as if she was sinking.

'I don't know. I'm not saying I don't love you. Or that it's always bad. But, you can't tell me you're really happy, can you?' He flopped into the chair opposite her.

'Christian, are you on drugs? I'm due to give birth in three weeks. Do you think now is when we should be having this conversation?' And then she had seen what the real problem was, as clearly as if she had been standing next to him. 'Oh my God, there's someone else, isn't there?'

He had started crying then, crying in a way she doubted he had done since he was a child, and she had felt disgusted with him. 'She's called Sarah and she's pregnant as well.'

The air was sucked out of the room. 'You're joking.'

'No. It wasn't planned, she only told me today.'

'You fucking shit.' It wasn't enough, but it was all she had.

'I know,' he'd said, and that had almost been the worst admission.

They had sat at the kitchen table in silence, both trying to absorb what had happened. Ruth wasn't sure she could give birth and care for a newborn on her own. She knew that lots of women did it, but she didn't think she was strong enough. But then Christian was by her feet, kneeling, trying to put his arms around her belly which was as round as the world. 'Ruth, I'm sorry. I don't really want to leave. You've got to help me, I don't know what's happened. How did this happen?'

And even as she was scratching his face as if only the feel of flesh under her fingernails was going to be enough, she had already relented. She knew she was going to forgive him from that second. If he hadn't asked for it she would have probably begged. Now was the first time she had admitted that feeling to herself, as she sat in the taxi on her way home and the memory forced more tears out of her stinging eyes. She was weak and pathetic and maybe only had herself to blame.

Agatha knew something was going on. Ruth was in bed one minute, too ill to see the kids, and the next she was racing out the door, saying she was meeting Christian. It was very confusing for the children, especially as she hadn't even told Betty that Ruth was upstairs. Agatha felt annoyed with Ruth and hoped she wouldn't take another day off tomorrow as she had everything she needed to do for the party arranged into very specific timelines and Ruth didn't do specific.

Betty's bottom lip quivered as she watched her mother rushing away from her again and Agatha pulled her onto her lap, knowing too well the feeling of having a confusing mother. She wished she could take the girl with her, but in reality Betty was too far gone; she would miss her mother and ask too many questions, possibly give them all away. Besides, Agatha could already see very strong traces of Ruth in her which weren't all to do with how she looked. She refused to brush her dolls' hair and was happy to chuck them all into their box after playing with them without worrying whether or not they were comfy. In the morning she'd try on three different outfits, pulling all her clothes out of the drawer and then stuffing them back in without concern for Agatha's neat folding. Once, only once, Agatha had looked into Ruth's drawers. Not because she wanted to take anything, but to see if she was right. And of course she had been. Nothing was properly folded or colour co-ordinated. There didn't even seem to be a system and in her underwear drawer there were old broken bits of jewellery and a leaking biro.

Hal would grow to look more like her over time, Agatha was sure of it. Genetics, she had decided, were not important. Life was about who loved you, not who had made you. Surely that was true. She imagined a day when Hal and her would be like two peas in a pod, identical in thought and body.

She already had his passport, which hadn't been hard to find. Ruth and Christian had a room they called an office, which was nothing more than a large cupboard forced out of the space under the stairs. They had a badly organised free-standing filing cabinet in there and all the passports were in one of its drawers. Agatha didn't worry that they might notice Hal's was missing, and even if they did they would blame each other. Hal's clothes were nearly all washed, folded neatly and calmly in his drawers.

What they were going to do when they left was more problematic. Agatha had to admit that. In a year or so it would be fine and she could enrol him in school and then she'd be able to work while he was there, but at first it was going to be very tight. She wouldn't be able to apply for benefits as she suspected Hal would be front-page news. She wouldn't be able to work and she'd have to disguise him somehow. She had bought a box of brown hair dye, which she planned to use on them both first thing, before they even got on a train. But she worried that wouldn't be enough. She'd used Ruth's laptop to investigate communes and they sounded interesting. As she'd read about them she'd convinced herself that she'd been brought up in one, because she had, hadn't she, when you thought about it. She'd integrate into everything so well, she could use all her organisational skills to make a real difference, to make everything run smoothly so that soon her and Hal would become an indispensable part of the group. She just hoped that it was as easy as walking up to a commune and asking if you could be part of it. Surely that was how it worked, wasn't it?

Ruth was surprised to find herself waking up the next morning at five o'clock because it didn't feel as though she'd slept at all. Her whole body ached, but especially her eyes and her head. It felt like she had a hangover when really she hadn't drunk the night before, simply coming home and shutting herself in the bedroom. She'd heard Christian come in about an hour later, but he'd had more sense than to try to see her. She had no idea where he'd slept and didn't care.

The night had been painful, as nights often are. If you have problems, Ruth found, they multiplied like bacteria in the dark hours, looming over your head like a cartoon monster. In her mind she had already calmed a weeping Betty as they watched Christian leave, attended his wedding to Sarah for the sake of the children, argued with him over money and, at one point, hit him round the face. It seemed too cruel to realise that all of this had been nothing more than a series of malevolent fantasies and that the reality still had to be lived through. Lying in her bed, in an already bright bedroom, she felt incapable. She felt like pulling the covers over her head and admitting defeat. Signing the kids over to Aggie, resigning her job, never speaking to Christian again. It was a choice, she realised, to get up and keep going.

But it was Hal's birthday tomorrow and there was always something. There would be a reason to get up for the rest of her life and the thought made her feel exhausted. Don't wish your life away, a teacher had said to her once when he'd caught her clock watching and she'd had no idea what he'd meant. He'd dropped down dead a year later, just as she'd been about to start her A levels. The problem was not in her body, she was now sure of that.

Christian had broken her heart. As good as if he'd taken it out of her body and stamped on it in front of her. It seemed too teenage, too romantic, to think that about her own husband. And yet it was the truth.

But the truth was also deeper than that. Deeper than her thoughts in the taxi the night before, deeper than her dreams, deeper even than her anger. In the cold light of dawn, Ruth knew that she'd played a part this. She realised that she had always seen herself as the victim, but that life was rarely that simple. She was not excusing Christian, that was maybe something she could never do, but she thought it was time to admit she'd fucked up as well. Sometimes she felt like she couldn't help it that she found life so hard and at others she thought maybe she could. Since the children, she'd built a wall around herself and her feelings. She loved them too intensely to let anyone else in and she worried so incessantly about all her choices that she was constantly guilty and distracted. The year after Betty's birth had taught her how fragile all our minds are, how easily and quickly they can shatter so you hardly recognise yourself or anyone around you. Since then it had become of extreme importance to her that she remained in control; there was no letting go because look where that got you. And somewhere along the way she had lost her ability to have fun. Her anxiety had trickled irrevocably into their lives so that now she feared her mind was like a blender, processing all information with the same murderous intensity.

Life ate away at her like a caterpillar on a leaf. She held her arm up now and the light from the window showed her how translucent she'd become, how she was almost disappearing. It would be hard to love someone who found themselves so consistently wrong, she realised. Her marriage was probably salvageable, but Ruth couldn't decide if it was too late for her. She wondered if she would ever be able to articulate all these thoughts to Christian, if he'd understand them, if they'd be able to act on them, if, in the end, their love was enough.

She was crying again so she decided to have a shower as a counter attack. The water felt warm and soothing on her skin and it had the desired effect for the few minutes it took her to remember that her parents would be arriving in a couple of hours. Her head felt too heavy to sit upright on her neck.

When Christian heard Ruth moving about overhead he got up off the sofa. He didn't want the kids or Aggie finding him there so he went to their bedroom to at least remove his clothes. The bed looked hardly slept in, just a small neat indentation where Ruth had lain. It surprised him, this lack of turmoil, and he worried that his wife had already disposed of him. It was nothing more than he deserved, he supposed, but it also seemed unfair.

Christian had lain awake most of the night, trying to think of something to say to persuade Ruth to let him stay. There was not much that he couldn't talk his way out of and yet for the most important deal of his life he was all out of ideas. Christian had once over-heard himself being described as a character, which had sounded as fatuous as something a reality show contestant would say because, without a character, surely you were no more than a shell. But now he wondered if perhaps a character was all he was; that all his meaning had vanished or maybe never even been there in the first place.

When he'd first met Ruth he'd been amazed at her seriousness. He realised that he'd been attracted by something in Ruth which he had expected her to discard when their lives linked together. Could it come as a great shock that a woman who thought as much as she did would find motherhood so overwhelming? He realised that he'd failed to understand or love her properly. What Ruth needed was reassurance and what she got was worry.

What time are you leaving work? she'd ask him most days at about three and he'd sometimes purposefully lie to teach her a lesson. Who's that? she'd say when his BlackBerry bleeped on the weekend and he'd shrug enigmatically and say, No one, even though he knew this would make her paranoid. It wasn't that he wanted to be mean, but sometimes she made him feel he was nothing more than another naughty child in her life. Get out of my face, he'd want to shout, go and fret about something else. But of course this had been wrong, he realised now, as he sat nervously on the edge of a bed that might soon not belong to him. If he'd come home when he'd said, refused the second drink, told her it was just a spam message on his phone, she would have relaxed and probably not asked him next time.

Ruth jumped when she saw him and he felt responsible for how bad she looked.

'Sorry,' he said, 'I didn't want the kids or Aggie finding me on the sofa.'

She shrugged, not able to meet his eyes.

'Are you going to work today?' he asked.

'No. I'm calling in sick.'

'I will too.'

'No, don't. My parents are coming in a few hours and I don't think I can bear to play happy families for a second longer than I have to.'

What Christian would have liked to do was pull Ruth towards him, while she was still wet from the shower. For them to lie on the bed and make love, properly, as they never seemed to do. His words were not ever going to be enough and he wanted to show her what he meant. But there was a force field around her; he felt he might get an electric shock if he even tried to touch her.

'D'you think we'll get a chance to talk at all this weekend?' he ventured.

'I doubt it. I haven't got anything more to say.'

'Please, Ruth. Whatever happens, we have to talk.'

She spun round at this, a hairbrush extended out to him like a weapon. 'Why didn't you fucking tell me you'd seen her again?'

'I don't know, I wish I knew the answer to that. I was knocked off guard seeing her and then she called and told me about the abortion and I got sucked in. But nothing happened, nothing was ever going to happen.'

Betty appeared in the doorway, dishevelled from sleep.

'Hey, princess,' he said, picking her up. 'You're up early.'

'I'm hungry,' she answered. 'Mummy.'

'Mummy's still getting dressed. I'll take you down-stairs.' They all seemed surprised by his offer so he left with his tiny daughter, wondering if all parents sucked up their emotions, waiting for a more appropriate time.

There is a song, who the hell was it by? Christian racked his brains, he couldn't even remember the exact line. Something about how the singer regretted all those wasted breakfasts feeling tired, when they could have been spending time with their daughter. Shame washed through him as he realised it was Abba. It could have even been from Betty's *Mamma Mia* DVD. He tried not to cry at his ridiculous new-found pathos and instead tried to shock himself into submission. Betty and Hal had never been properly real to him. Or maybe that was too harsh, but it could be true that he had loved them abstractedly, loved the thought of them more than the actuality of them. But here they were, little people, growing and changing and being. He didn't want to miss another second. Which was another terrible song, wasn't it?

Maybe this was when you knew it was bad, when your life dissolved into nothing more than terrible cliché-riven lines from songs you wished you'd never heard.

Agatha was not amused when she got into the kitchen to find Christian sitting with Betty as she ate her cereal while Ruth stood leaning against the sink, drinking a cup of tea and wearing jeans. Please let her not be staying home today.

'Aggie,' she said, much too brightly, 'I'm not going to work today, so you can put me to good use for the party.'

'Are you still ill?' Agatha was clutching at straws, she didn't want Ruth having anything to do with Hal's party.

'I'm not too bad. But I can't face the thought of the tube and everything. Oh, and my parents will be arriving at lunchtime, so you know.'

'I didn't realise they were coming today.' Agatha went to the kettle in order to give her frustration some activity. Surely you couldn't be as forgetful and downright stupid as Ruth. Earlier in the week they'd discussed Ruth's parents' attendance of the party and Agatha had very kindly, in her opinion, insisted they sleep in her room rather than the ridiculously too small box room. She'd assumed they would be arriving on Saturday and staying one night. Now she'd have to get all her stuff together and still make it look like she wasn't doing a runner in the next four hours. Not to mention everything she had to do for the party.

'Sorry,' Ruth was saying now, 'I'm sure I said. Anyway, Mum's super organised, she's not a bit like me, she'll be a great help.'

Tears stung Agatha's eyes at this new information. A fussy grandmother as well as a useless mother, all fucking up her neatly laid plans. Hal started calling from upstairs and so she responded.

Ruth put a hand on her arm. 'Don't worry, Aggie, I'll go. It's not often I get to give the kids breakfast.'

Agatha's mouth flailed like a fish drowning in oxygen, but what could she say?

Ruth made her way up the stairs to the sound of her son. It had been an effort to be jolly for those few short minutes and she wondered how she was going to survive the day. She looked at her watch, it was only just after seven. Why was Aggie up? But then again, she must always be, Ruth realised. When she flew into the kitchen at seven thirty everything was always neatly laid out, Betty already eating, tea in the pot. How quickly she'd let this happen. She'd never asked Aggie to do breakfast or to get the kids up, but somehow this had become something which she did every day. Ruth felt panicked at how easily she'd let Aggie take such an important part of the day from her. Or maybe it was the other way around, maybe it was how easily Ruth had surrendered it.

Hal's room was dark from his blackout blind and he was sitting up in his cot, his hair sticking up from his head, shouting some indiscernible word. Ruth went and sat next to him, drawing in his fug of sleep. She put her hand on his cheek.

'Hello, love, did you sleep well?'

Hal looked at her, stunned. He shouted again, but she couldn't make it out. Ruth tried to pull him onto her lap but he pushed her away. 'Gie,' it sounded like, but then she was sure he said, 'Mummy.'

'I'm here, darling,' she said, feeling her heart beating faster. She'd always worried that one day Hal would wake up and his weirdness would have to be acknowledged.

He was still pushing her away. 'Mummy.'

'Hal,' she said, holding him by the shoulders. 'It's me, I'm here. Mummy's here.'

Christian put his head round the door. 'What's going on?'

'I don't know, I think he's having some sort of fit. He's calling for me, but it's like he can't see me.'

Christian came over and felt Hal's head. 'He's not hot.' He knelt down. 'What's up, mate? Mummy's here.'

Hal kicked his foot into Christian's face. 'Go way. Mummy.'

'Let's get him downstairs,' said Christian. 'It might wake him up a bit.' He picked him up, kicking and screaming and they made their way into the kitchen. Aggie was buttering toast, her face as tight as a stretched canvas. As soon as Hal saw her he lunged at her, pushing Christian away with all his strength.

'Mummy,' he shouted, over and over, the sound bouncing off the walls, cracking into all their heads.

Aggie went to him, like they were in slow motion, and he leapt into her arms, collapsing on her shoulder, weeping into her neck. 'Shh,' she was saying, 'what's all this about, silly?'

Ruth was shaking. She didn't know what she'd seen or how to react to it. 'Did he call you Mummy?' she asked as calmly as she could.

Aggie looked up. 'No, did he? I didn't hear that.' But she was pale and Ruth was sure she was lying.

'I heard,' said Betty. 'He said "Mummy".'

'Has he ever said that before, Betty?' asked Ruth.

Betty spooned some cereal onto the table and shrugged. 'I don't know. He's stupid, he gets everything wrong.' All the adults ignored this.

Ruth looked directly at Aggie and knew she had found something worse than Sarah. 'Have you heard him say that before, Aggie?'

'No, are you sure you didn't mishear? I mean, Aggie, Mummy, they sound pretty similar.'

'No, I heard it as well,' said Christian. Ruth looked at her husband, standing there still in yesterday's suit, looking like he hadn't slept and wondered what levels of shit they were in. You think it's one thing and then you realise that it's piled over your head, as high as a mountain.

'Look, it's nothing. Honestly, if I hear him do it again, I'll say something. But he is with me a lot and he'd just woken up. He was probably confused.' She shifted Hal onto her hip and Ruth flinched at the ease of the movement. 'I'll get them dressed. Come on, Betty, or we'll be late for school.'

Ruth let them leave the room because she wasn't sure how many options she had. 'What the fuck was that?' she asked Christian.

'Probably nothing. I'm sure Aggie's right.'

'The path of least resistance again, Christian.'

'What do you mean?'

'I mean, our son just called his nanny Mummy and freaked out when we tried to touch him and you're happy to sweep it under the carpet because it makes your life easier.'

'So what do you think it is then?'

'I don't know.' Ruth sat down, she felt spent. 'He probably wishes she was his mother or maybe she's a psycho who gets them to call her Mummy when we're not around. I don't know any more.'

Christian tried to put his hand on her shoulder but she shook him off. 'Look, we're both very tired and emotionally done in. Why don't we get through this weekend and talk to Aggie next week. Nothing's going to happen between now and then, she's not even going to be alone with them.'

Ruth was too tired to cry. 'Okay. Now please, go to work, I still can't stand the sight of you.'

Agatha had stars before her eyes and her breath would only come in short, sharp gasps. She leant over Hal's drawers and tried to pull the air into her lungs. Someone was coming up behind her and that someone was going to get her. She leapt, tasting her own heartbeat, the scream forming on her lips, but it was only the cat. She had to get a grip on herself, Ruth could come up any minute now.

She looked down at Hal, so innocently playing with his cars on the floor and wanted to shake him and gather him into her arms all at once. The love he showed her, the need he had for her, the preference over his own mother, it was all heart-breakingly wonderful, but at the same time so scary. He could give them away at any minute, maybe he already had. The look on Ruth's face had been one of knowledge, knowledge that you can't bear to admit to yourself. She'd seen that look once before.

When she was eleven Harry went away, no one ever told her where, but there had been a blissful six months where Agatha allowed herself to believe that he wasn't coming back. It had felt like the calmness after a great storm, which was a phrase she'd only heard a few years ago, but had immediately recognised as what she had experienced then. But weather patterns persist and storms always eventually return.

She'd been in her room when someone had knocked at her door and she'd breezily shouted for them to come in because she'd grown used to letting down her guard. But there he was, leering round her bedroom door, his revolting lascivious smile on his lips. He came into the room, shutting the door behind him, leaning his immense weight back onto it, preventing any means of escape. Agatha could see the sweat on his face, his belly straining at his T-shirt, the dirt on the front of his jeans. It was strange how she still remembered all these details and so many others, so clearly it was like a bright light illuminating everything too harshly. But it was also strange how her perception had changed over the years. She saw the same things but she understood them differently. She presumed this would change again, that over and over the image of Harry and what he had done to her would shift and blur, so that she would have to re-live it for the rest of her life.

Have you missed me, princess? he'd asked, and looking back she saw that he had been nervous, when on that day he'd seemed like an immense and powerful presence, something which couldn't be denied. She hadn't answered, but he'd gone on. God, I've missed you, he'd said, it's lonely over there and you kept dancing in my head. Agatha had put down her book at this information. All the time she'd thought she'd been free of him she'd been dancing in his head? Maybe Harry had been right, she did want it as much as him, she did love him.

He came closer, blotting out all the available light, menacing above her. He put his hand on her cheek and brushed away a tear she hadn't known she'd been crying. Then the door opened and her mum walked in.

'What are you doing in here?' she'd said, much too lightly. 'I thought you were going to the toilet and then I came up to get my cardi and there was no one in the bathroom.'

That was the moment. The moment when Agatha could have told the truth and her mother would have believed her and Harry would have been put in prison.

'I wanted to say hi to Agatha,' he said. 'Hasn't she grown since I've been away.'

Agatha's mother stepped closer to the bed. Her eyes darted nervously between her daughter and her husband's oldest friend. 'She has, hasn't she. She's getting to be a proper young woman.'

Harry and her mother loomed over her and Agatha looked up at the woman who was meant to protect her, forcing her to look back. Their eyes met and her mother's gaze twitched away. It's true, Agatha was saying, everything you've seen and much, much more is true. It's worse than you could imagine in your most terrible nightmares.

'Anyway, come down now, Harry,' her mother said. 'Peter'll be home in a minute and I want to see the photos before you two get going.'

They left together, but before she went she looked back into the room. Agatha often wondered what she'd seen. How she could look at that scared little girl sitting on the bed and not choose to save her. Because when her mother shut the door and left her, allowing the soft murmur of conversation to drift up from downstairs, was when Agatha knew that no one was going to save her, that from now on it was all up to her.

Agatha had always suspected that mothers have some form of inner knowledge, that after you give birth you become more powerful, more capable and that you can either use that knowledge or choose to ignore it. Most of the mothers she had encountered ignored it and it seemed to make them miserable, not to mention their children.

She picked out Hal's shorts and T-shirt and knelt down next to him, easing his fragile body out of his pyjamas. 'Only one more day, sweetheart,' she said, 'and then everything will be okay again.'

Ruth was thirteen when she asked her parents one summer night after supper, sitting in their country garden, what stars were. She didn't know what answer she'd been expecting, but certainly it had nothing to do with the tale of long-dead, burnt-out planets, their fire already extinguished. 'All we see,' she would always remember her father saying, 'is the image of their last explosion, which has travelled down millions of light years to appear in our sky. What you call a star isn't real, there's nothing there, it's like the light you see if someone takes a photo too close and the flash goes off in your face.'

'Did the planets have people on?' she'd asked.

'We don't know,' her father had replied, 'but it seems pretty unlikely that all of this is only for us, don't you think?' It was the first time Ruth could pinpoint feeling as if she was falling when she was sitting still; a whoosh through her brain as she tried to take in something bigger than her capacity to understand. Now she got the feeling constantly, in editorial meetings, choosing yoghurt in supermarket aisles, in deserted winter playgrounds.

Her mother had broken the spell that night by saying, 'Oh, George, I do think it's mean to be too honest sometimes. My father told me they were the sequins in a giant ballerina's ballgown and I believed it for years.' Ruth hadn't been sure which story was more preposterous.

The night sky had made Ruth uneasy since then. Not so as she was scared of it, and she could go for months, years even, without thinking about it. But if ever she did stare upwards on a clear night and see all those beautiful twinkling lights, she'd get a sudden stab of panic as she realised that their whole world was surrounded by death and destruction. The knowledge was like the definition of the word bittersweet, that something so truly magical could also be so abominably sad. That the vision which had inspired poets and lovers the world over didn't even exist. She'd written quite a good essay at university on how ironic this was and how you could interpret the whole metaphor into a description of love, which was in itself ironic. She could write a much better essay now.

For a short time in her late teens she'd became interested in astronomy. She'd studied the positions of the stars and the shapes they formed and could identify most of the constellations. She'd asked for a good telescope for her eighteenth birthday, which her parents had duly given her and which now sat unused on the upstairs landing. For that brief period of time she'd felt a fragile sense of peace because so many of the stars appeared so mapped out. The lines between them were so straight and definite and the mathematical calculations attached to them were so sure and true. The problem with maths however is that if you get good at it you soon realise that it's as lyrical and insubstantial as words on a page, which she turned back to for university as they seemed safer. Everyone expects words to have more than one meaning, to get lost in translation, to change with experience and perception, to float and glide together into sentences which can lose their thread or make an intriguing point. Words were by nature flighty and Ruth could deal with that. What she couldn't deal with was the idea that numbers also barely knew what they meant. It made the world seem too insubstantial.

Last night, when she been unable to sleep, she'd got out of bed and looked at the stars. Light pollution had obliterated most of them, but she'd made out a couple of familiar patterns and for a moment they'd comforted her. She'd expected to have her mind blown by them, but instead they'd reassured her with their steady positions. Nothing that happens to you or anyone down there will ever affect us for one millisecond, they seemed to be saying, it's all so unimportant. And of course, when you compared the breakdown of her marriage with soldiers blown apart on the other side of the world or children beaten to death by their parents in their own homes or half the world dying from curable diseases, then yes, it was meaningless. Except ... except, exactly what did any of that mean to her? What did it matter? Pictures on screens, words in newspapers. They went in and out of her mind, they touched nerves, but they didn't settle in her heart. Only Christian and her children had the ability to change the course of her life, to bring her happiness or sadness, to make her feel loved and worthy. It was, she felt, rather a tardy realisation.

She went back to bed and, as she fell asleep, she wondered if her father had been right and they weren't alone in the universe and whether or not this would be good or bad. It was true that if this whole creation was for man alone then the burden of responsibility would be great, but if that turned out to be the case then at least there wasn't anyone to witness what a fuck-up they were making of it all.

Christian only turned his phone back on when he got off the tube at Green Park. He had thirty-seven missed calls, all from Sarah. He listened to the first few. She alternated between wild, screaming accusations and pathetic, pleading nonsense. He deleted thirty-two without listening to them as he didn't see any good coming from hearing them. He had learnt something from yesterday, which wasn't a feeling he could remember having had for a very long time.

He turned off into the park and dialled Sarah's number. It rang a few times and then a male voice picked up.

'Is that Christian?'

Two days ago he would have hung up. 'Yes, it is.'

'This is Sarah's father and I don't know how the bloody hell you've got the nerve to call her.'

'I'm sorry, I was ringing to say sorry.'

'For what exactly? For fucking her life up again, for making promises you can't keep or for being a total and utter shit?'

'All of the above.'

'Have you apologised to your wife again, yet?'

'Mr Ellery, I don't think you understand, nothing happened between Sarah and I this time. We met by accident and then we went out for lunch and she told me about the abortion and I felt responsible and it was stupid of me, but I didn't promise her anything, we didn't even hold hands.'

'Don't give me any of your bullshit, Christian.' The anger in the man's voice was volcanic, Christian had never heard anyone so furious. He tried to imagine what he would feel like if anyone ever behaved like he had towards Betty and he understood. Telling this man his daughter was in the wrong wasn't going to help. 'I hope you realise that you are never speaking to her again.'

'Of course. I want to be with my wife. I was ringing to apologise for how I've behaved.'

'Well, that's very big of you. It's a shame you didn't have such a sense of decency when you seduced my twenty-two-year-old daughter the first time around, getting her pregnant and then abandoning her.'

'I know, I'm ...'

'Shut the fuck up and listen, for once in your pompous life. Do you know how long it took her to get over you? The low-life scum she ended up with in Australia because she thought she was worthless? And then, when you do meet again, you're not a big enough man to say, Look we've made this mistake once before, I'm not going to put you or my wife through this, let's shake hands and wish each other luck? No, you have to have one last look – out of curiosity, for Christ's sake! You're telling me that nothing happened, that you weren't interested in having another affair? Oh no, you just wanted to have your ego massaged one last time or assuage some fucked-up sense of guilt.'

He paused, so Christian decided to speak, even though his mouth felt as if it had been lined with sand. 'You're right.'

'Of course I'm bloody right. I've always had your number, Christian. I've met enough men like you and I thank God I'm not like that. You think you're special because you make people laugh and you get paid lots of money and you have a beautiful wife and two perfect kids, but it's not real. It's not what you are. Deep down you're a hard-hearted bastard who doesn't deserve what you've got. Sarah will be okay. She'll cry for a while and her mum will have to sleep in her room with her again, but she'll be fine. One day she'll meet some-one nice and she'll get married and have kids and you'll be nothing more than a bad memory. But if you ever, and I mean ever, try to get in touch with her again I will hunt you down and cut off your dick, do you understand?'

'Yes. I won't.'

'I hope your wife leaves you and you're miserable and lonely for the rest of your life.'

The phone went dead after that but Christian couldn't bring himself to finish the call from his end. His phone felt like a detonated bomb and he was surprised that there wasn't mayhem and carnage all around him. No one had ever come close to being that rude to him before and yet he didn't feel any outrage. He wished that Sarah's father had kept going, because it was nothing more than he deserved. He felt too big for his skin, as if the realisa-tion that his actions had consequences was trying to force its way out of his body like an alien. He put his phone back into his pocket and walked to his big office where he sat at his important desk and made large decisions. Except today he felt like a fraud. He could taste his own worthlessness like a raw onion in his mouth however many double espressos he drank.

By the time Agatha got back from taking Betty to school she had calmed down. She had stopped with Hal in the park on the way home and he'd been so happy it had lightened her heart. This was how it would always be, she realised. She'd feel sad, she'd look at him and everything would be okay again, which was as wonderful as you could get in her book. Agatha went through the list of things she had to do while pushing Hal on the swings or waiting for him at the bottom of the slide and the order calmed her mind.

She wanted to make the biscuits and the cake, to wrap the going-home presents and pass the parcel as well as Hal's birthday present. She was going to put away most of the toys, only leaving out the easier to assemble and non-breakable ones. The house was gleaming already, so a quick tidy would be all that was needed tomorrow and then she'd just have to ice the cake and the biscuits and make the sandwiches. She'd downloaded a few party games from the Internet as Ruth didn't seem to have given the entertainment any thought. She would have liked to re-arrange the furniture in the sitting room, but doubted Ruth or Christian would go for that.

Agatha gave Hal a bag of organic crunchies on the way home as she wasn't sure when she'd be able to sneak him his lunch. She was worried that Ruth might notice how few bottles he drank now, but if need be she'd say that he hadn't seemed to be feeling too good lately.

As they opened the front door Agatha glimpsed Ruth sitting at the kitchen table before she'd realised they were back and she'd known in that minute that Ruth had something else on her mind, something much bigger than Hal's party and that Agatha would be able to get away with most things today. She wondered briefly what the other thing might be, but found she didn't care. If she had to put money on it, Agatha would say it had something to do with Christian; she wouldn't be surprised if he was having an affair, he seemed pleased enough with himself to make this likely. Agatha wondered what sort of low self-esteem it took to end up with a man like Christian, or her own father for that matter. Men who made you feel weak, even when they weren't trying. In an ideal world Agatha would steer a clear path round the male of the species; she didn't think she was a lesbian, but she found men disgusting. She had always presumed that she'd need a man at least once in order to get the child she'd never for a second imagined her life without. Now it looked like this wouldn't be necessary. Good things come to those who wait, she said to herself, as she reached down to wipe the last remaining crumbs away from Hal's mouth and let him out of his buggy.

'Oh, hi, you two,' Ruth shouted from the kitchen. Hal walked towards his mother and Agatha followed, noticing that Ruth had re-applied her mask of happiness like stage make-up.

'We went park,' Hal was saying. 'Wheeee, slide.'

Ruth laughed and pulled him onto her lap. 'Did you, sweetheart? Lucky you.'

Agatha felt a violent stab of jealousy and had to turn away to compose herself. Hal chit-chatting so easily with his mother made a rage build in her stomach like a plummeting lift. Stop it, she wanted to shout at him, you're mine, not hers, you promised me. She could hear Hal giggling and the sound of Ruth kissing him and she knew exactly what feelings and smells Ruth would be getting. It made her sick. It made her want to stab them both. Calm down, Agatha, a voice inside her was saying, he's only little, he's just responding to his natural instincts.

The story of Hal's birth, how his father had abandoned Agatha and him when he was only weeks old, the struggles and tribulations they'd gone through; it was coming on so nicely that Agatha was starting to feel the switch turning on in her brain. The one where she forgot it was a story and made it become reality. Twenty-four more hours, she told herself as she stood with her back to Hal. Twenty-four hours and then we can become the people we were meant to be.

There were often cases in the newspapers about children being beaten and abused and even killed by people who were supposed to care for them. Sometimes they made Agatha physically sick in one of the loos she'd scrubbed clean at the Donaldsons'. Sometimes she spent whole nights unable to sleep, imagining the faces of the children as they were tortured again and again. Yet someone would always testify as to how much the child had loved his or her tormentors. How they had held out their arms to them.

Agatha never dwelt too much on the defectiveness of the carers; parents and their extensions were often simply shit and failed to live up to expectations. This was not a new lesson. What alarmed her instead was the fact that the babies still wanted to appeal to their torturers. They knew these people hurt them and yet they still desperately reached out. It proved to Agatha two important things. Firstly that children need love so badly they'll take it from anyone and secondly that you can get a child to do anything. Of course she was never going to hurt Hal or get him to do anything bad, but still, it made things clearer.

'So, what have you got planned today?' Ruth asked as Hal slipped off her lap and made his way to his plastic house.

'I wanted to get ahead with some jobs for the party, like making the biscuits and the cake and stuff and maybe sorting out the toys.'

'You don't have to make biscuits, Aggie, that's an awful lot of trouble to go to. And what's wrong with the toys?'

Ruth was a slob when all was said and done, lazy and unimaginative. If you didn't go to trouble for your child's third birthday then when would you? And of course she thought the toys were fine because she wasn't the one who'd spend the next month on her hands and knees looking for Betty's new Brat's missing boot because some three-year-old hadn't realised what it was. Come to think of it though, nor would Agatha have to do that, so long as her plan came off. But the thought of leaving everything all mixed up was too much. No, she'd make sure Betty's stuff was out of the way and then at least the girl would realise she hadn't disliked her, that wasn't the reason she hadn't been able to take her as well. 'It's no trouble,' she answered. 'I enjoy it.'

'Oh well, if you say so.' Ruth sounded frustrated. It was odd how these women all started off loving her industriousness and ended up hating her for the exact same thing. She hadn't been able to believe it when Jane Stephenson had screamed at her for disinfecting the children's bathroom after she'd been away for the weekend. A weekend she hadn't even wanted to go away for, with nowhere to stay except a grotty B&B. Don't you think I am capable of keeping my own children clean? she'd screamed, so close to Agatha's face that she'd felt spit fleck her cheeks. We don't all feel the need to live in a fucking operating theatre and, while we're at it, can you please stop bloody making my bed. I'll make my own damned bed if I want to and if I don't it'll stay unmade all day. She'd told Agatha to leave two days later, her hands shaking as she passed over an envelope stuffed with money, unable to look Agatha in the eye.

'I'll keep Hal out of your way, at least,' Ruth said, following her son into the sitting room.

Agatha listened to Ruth trying to entice Hal out of his house as she weighed out the sugar and flour and mixed it with the butter and eggs. It was comical how Ruth didn't know her son at all. Promises and threats didn't work with Hal, you had to pretend you were doing something super-interesting on the other side of the room and act like you didn't care whether or not he joined you. It got him in about five minutes. After a while Agatha heard the telly being switched on and the familiar sound of *Thomas the Tank Engine* starting. She let herself smile.

Ruth was dozing in front of the fifth *Thomas* episode when the doorbell rang. She'd said Hal could watch three and she felt pathetic. She knew Agatha would be listening and she hated her for it. Hated the fact that she couldn't control her son or interest him or even get up the energy to move from where she was sitting. Christian called her mobile twice but she didn't answer because she had no idea what to say to him. The initial raging anger she'd felt had been usurped by a desperate sadness which she knew made her vulnerable. They had made such a mess of it all and for what? She believed him that nothing had happened with Sarah in the physical sense, but she also thought he would never properly understand how much he had betrayed her simply by meeting the girl. And she was so young and damaged, nearly a different generation to them. If Christian had been five years older, people would have called him a dirty old man. And if she was married to a dirty old man, what did that make her?

'Come on, Hal,' she said now, standing up and turning off the telly. 'That's Granny and Granddad.'

Ruth could see her parents' outlines through the stained glass on the front door and for a second she couldn't bear to open it, was worried that she would break down and not give them what they needed. But there wasn't much of an option. If you didn't do things

like open the door to your own parents when they'd travelled three hours to get to you and knew you were standing just inches away, then you were probably insane,
you'd probably crossed some line. A line which Ruth
worried she might have already reached but wasn't ready
to admit to.

Her parents looked brown, which reminded Ruth that
they'd only been back from Portugal for two weeks. They
smiled at her and she smiled back because that's how life
went on. Her dad reached for Hal. 'Come here, young
man,' he said, 'look how you've grown.' Hal wriggled out
of Ruth's arms and ran off screaming. Ruth shrugged,
'Sorry, he's at that age.' She caught the look in her mother's eye and wondered if what she'd said was ever a reason
for anything.

'You look well, Mum,' Ruth said, to try something
different.

'Portugal was wonderful, so sunny. We just sat by the
pool every day.'

'That's the beauty of going back to the same place
every year,' said her father. 'You can do nothing without
feeling like you should be seeing some bloody church or
something.'

Ruth tried to imagine a time when she could lie by a
pool and do nothing, even for an hour, let alone a whole
holiday. Ruth and Christian always fought on holiday
because the kids were under their feet begging to be
allowed their thirtieth swim of the day or refusing to eat
the local food or staying up till ten every night and then
having a meltdown in a restaurant. She often came back
from holidays more tired than when she went. She was

starting to recognise this exhaustion as the story of her life. Time for a new chapter, as a *Viva* article might say.

'So, where's the birthday boy then?' her father was saying. 'We've come all this way and he's hiding in the kitchen.'

Ruth knew what they were going to see before they reached the kitchen, but still the sight of Hal wrapped around Aggie's legs made her catch her breath.

'Come on, Tiger,' said Ruth's dad. 'Come and give your old granddad a hug.'

'No,' screamed Hal. 'Aggie, want Aggie.'

Ruth watched Aggie pick him up and smooth his hair. 'Sorry, he's not so good with strangers.'

'Strangers? I'd hardly call his grandparents strangers, would you?' answered her dad.

'Mum, Dad, this is Aggie, our very own super-nanny. Aggie, this is my mum and dad, George and Eleanor.' She would have to think about all of this later.

Ruth's mother stepped forward and held out her hand. 'Agatha, I've heard so much about you.' Aggie looked embarrassed. 'Are you baking? It smells wonderful.'

'Yes, biscuits for Hal's party.'

Ruth's mother raised her eyebrow. Ruth took this to mean she should be doing the baking. 'How wonderful of you. And I believe you've given up your room for us.'

'Oh, it's nothing, it's fine.'

'Well, it's very kind of you.'

They had an uncomfortable lunch round the kitchen table with Hal refusing to sit down. In the end Aggie took his plate into the plastic house and said she'd sit with him there. When they came back the plate was clear but Aggie shook her head at Ruth, 'Sorry, no luck again. I finished it as it seemed a shame to let it go to waste.'

'Is he still not eating?' asked Ruth's mother.

Ruth didn't feel strong enough for this today. 'No, no progress. We went to see a nutritionist but it didn't work out.'

'Why, what did he say?'

'The same as the GP. To start him on anything, like chocolate biscuits, sweets, anything and then move forward.'

'Sounds damned sensible to me,' said her father, pushing away his plate.

'No, but it's not.' Ruth tried to control the whine in her voice which made her sound fourteen again. 'Everyone knows that children have very specific taste buds. If they get used to something it takes them ages to get away from it. He could become addicted to sweet things and then I'd never get him to eat anything good.'

'I don't think that's very likely,' said her mother. 'Children grow out of everything in the end. You don't see many sixteen-year-olds sucking bottles or only eating chocolate biscuits or cuddling their favourite teddy or sitting on their mummy's laps.'

Ruth's smile was tight. 'Maybe.' Or maybe her mother hadn't had to deal with a problem like this. Maybe her mother didn't know what she was talking about. She changed the subject. 'How do you two fancy taking Hal to the park? We could walk on and get Betty from school.'

'Great,' said her mother.

'What about Hal's sleep?' asked Aggie.

'I'm sure he could do without it,' answered Ruth.

'But it's his party tomorrow, we don't want him to be overtired.'

Ruth stood up. She felt that in a minute she was going to lose it, whatever it was; she supposed it must be worth hanging on to. 'Don't worry, Aggie. If he's overtired I'll deal with it.' No one answered her this time.

Christian couldn't concentrate at work. His mind kept drifting and he was unsure of everything he did. Soon his thoughts became too large and made him question every aspect of his life. He realised that Ruth had been saying all of this to him for a few years now. All those times she'd asked him if he thought they'd got it wrong and he'd been bemused by what she meant. Now he understood and saw her patience. It must have been like trying to communicate with someone from an Amazonian tribe. He couldn't believe she'd stuck around for as long as she had.

He tried calling her at ten-thirty but she didn't pick up. He tried again an hour later and when she still didn't answer he left a garbled message. 'I'm sorry, Ruth. Not for the Sarah thing, although obviously I am sorry for that as well. But for not being there all this time. For not understanding what you've been saying and what you needed. Maybe you've been right. I don't know. Maybe we have got it wrong. Please call me when you get this, I want to hear your voice, I feel strange.'

And he did feel strange. Unsure of himself and cast adrift. His head felt too big for his body and his brain seemed to have lost the power to control his actions. If he'd been sure of his welcome he'd have gone home sick. Instead he called Toby, who surprised him by answering.

'I've just got off the plane from Ibiza. I was about to give you a buzz about tomorrow. What time are we expected?'

'I don't know. I think three. Who's we?'

'Oh shit, I meant to ask. Is it okay if I bring Gabriella along? She's this girl I met in Ibiza. She's great.'

Christian envisaged the teenage model he would no doubt turn up with and for the first time in his life didn't wish himself into another being. 'Yeah, whatever. Listen, have you got a minute, I need to ask you something?'

'What?'

'I've been a dick.'

'That's not a question.'

'I've been seeing a bit of Sarah. Not like that. Nothing happened, but she got the wrong end of the stick and went to see Ruth and told her I was leaving.'

'Shit.'

'I know.'

'When did this happen?'

'Yesterday. Fuck, it feels like about a week ago.'

'How did Ruth take it?'

'As you'd expect.'

'You're an arse, man.'

'I know.'

'Do you think it's saveable?'

'I don't know. It has to be. I don't know what I'd do without her.' Christian surprised himself by hearing a catch in his voice. He hadn't cried in years. Not since last time.

'Look, I'm not going to lecture you because it sounds like you're giving yourself a hard enough time, but shit, what were you thinking?'

'I wasn't fucking thinking, was I? Toby, am I a total dick?'

'Is that what you've rung to ask?'

'Yeah. Am I a selfish bastard? I've been looking at my life and some of the things I've done have astonished me. I don't recognise myself. I've been repellent to Ruth. And I don't just mean the Sarah thing, I mean I haven't had any respect for her or listened to her or helped her. I don't know what she's doing with me.'

'She loves you and you're a fucking lucky bastard.'

'How do you know?'

'I've spent enough time with you two. You love her too.' Christian heard Toby light a cigarette down the phone. 'And you're not a selfish bastard or a total dick. But you do sometimes seem to lack, what's the word, maybe empathy. I have occasionally wondered if you're slightly autistic.'

'What?'

'Look, don't take this the wrong way. But Hal reminds me of you so much. Sometimes neither of you get the nuances of life. When we met in the pub just after Sarah had first got in contact with you again I knew you were going to end up seeing her and I also knew that you couldn't see what was wrong with it.'

'Yeah, but I do now.'

'But I bet you said that to Ruth. I bet you kept on about how nothing happened as if that made it all right.'

'Yeah, I did.'

'And she flipped, right?'

'Yeah. Look, I get it now, I really do.'

'Okay. Well, if you want my advice, you have to keep telling her that. You have to make her believe that you get it this time, you're not just saying what she wants to hear. She hasn't kicked you out, right?'

'Only because it's Hal's birthday. She wants me gone next week.'

'D'you want me to call her?'

'No, her parents are with her now anyway.'

'Okay. Maybe I'll be able to get a minute with her tomorrow. Go straight home after work and be your best self. It's all you can do.'

'Okay. Look, thanks, you've always been a really good friend, you …'

Toby laughed. 'Enough. You don't need to butter me up. It'll be okay. You and Ruth are made for each other, in some sick way.'

Agatha hadn't needed to be left alone. Didn't Ruth think that she'd have factored looking after Hal and Betty into her day's plan? And now Ruth had gone and spoilt everything. Don't expect us at any time, she'd said as they'd left, we might take the kids out for pizza or something. Why don't you go out, don't worry about us.

Don't worry about us? Was the woman mad? Agatha's whole body, every inch of her skin, crawled with imaginary insects when Hal was out with Ruth. She was so absent-minded Agatha could imagine her losing sight of him in the park or not holding his hand tightly enough when they crossed the road. It made her stomach lurch as though she was in a speeding car. Not to mention the added dangers of how Hal could give her away. Thankfully she hadn't ever tried him on pizza so she was sure he'd refuse to eat it. But he might refer to her as mummy again or cry for her or just about anything.

Probably she had been wrong to stay for the party. Agatha allowed herself to think this as she scrubbed the downstairs loo for the second time that day. She had only done it for Hal but now she was wondering if it was a mean thing to do to him, if it would be the one memory she wouldn't be able to erase, one which might guide him to the truth in years to come.

Agatha tried to test her theory by remembering her own birthdays. The problem was that she couldn't always separate things that far back. She remembered stories and memories the same way. There were chaotic childhood scenes with cakes and balloons and mess and cheering and Harry, often Harry, somewhere in the background, but she couldn't put an age on it. Nights out with friends, but where were they now? Had she really been taken to Monaco by a boyfriend as she'd told Laura that summer of the temp agency? Was the thin silver chain holding a miniature four-leafed clover hanging round her neck really a present from her dead grandmother?

Agatha felt hot. She stood up and avoided looking at herself in the mirror. She shook her head but the images wouldn't come. Her mind felt jumbled and disordered.

She needed Hal. She went to the kitchen, swallowed two Nurofen Plus and went to lie down in the little box room, putting the pillow over her head in an attempt to drown out the noise.

Sally called Ruth on the way to the park, which gave her a good excuse to hang back and not talk to her mother.

'Sorry, Ruth,' Sally said, 'I know you're not feeling good. What's the matter, by the way?'

No one wanted to hear the answer to that question, so Ruth gave Sally what she needed. 'Oh, it's nothing. Just a headache I can't shake.'

'Okay. Listen, I want to put the issue to bed tonight but I've had a ridiculous call from Margo Lansford's lawyer ...'

'Her lawyer? Are you joking?'

'I know, priceless, isn't it? Anyway, he's saying that she wants copy approval. Apparently the soap business is at a critical stage. I just wanted to check that you didn't tell her she could see what you'd written before it went to press.'

'Of course not. I can't believe she got a lawyer to call. Her husband told Christian that the business doesn't earn a penny and her dad's loaded, he basically paid for the whole thing.'

'What a surprise.'

'To be honest, Sally, she was a complete fake. She's one of those women who likes to make you feel bad by being fucking perfect. She gives the impression that she's got it all, kids, husband, job, dream.'

'What, you don't think it's true?'

'No. Christian said her husband was pretty fucked up, he didn't have many nice things to say about her.'

'That's not exactly reflected in your piece.'

Ruth was brought up short by Sally's tone. 'Well, no. I didn't think that's what you'd want. It's not very *Viva*.'

When Sally spoke again she sounded normal. 'No, of course not. You're right. It's fab, I loved it. I'll call her stupid lawyer back and tell him to piss off.'

'There's nothing in there that will annoy her anyway.' Both Ruth and Sally resisted the urge to take this thought any further forward.

'No, I know, it's a fuss over nothing.'

'Okay, well, I'll see you tomorrow I guess, for Hal's party.'

'Of course. What does he want by the way?'

'God, I don't know. He loves Thomas the Tank Engine, we've got him a Thomas train set.'

'Does he still sit in that plastic house?' Ruth was always surprised by how much other people remembered. 'I was thinking of getting him a tea set or something to go in it.'

'He'd love that. See you tomorrow.'

They had reached the park by the time Ruth hung up.

'I could do with a cup of coffee,' said Ruth's mother. 'Why don't you boys go on to the playground and Ruth and I will get some take-aways from the café.'

'Right you are,' said her dad, pushing the buggy purposefully onwards. 'Remember the sugar.'

Ruth felt she should protest, she could certainly see a set-up job when it was right in front of her nose, but something stopped her.

'Was that work?' asked her mother as they turned towards the café.

'Yes, it's a bad day to have off. It's the end of the issue.'

'You didn't say you had a headache. I thought you'd taken the day off.'

'It's nothing.'

'Is it going okay then, work?'

'I suppose.'

Her mother sighed and Ruth knew she had failed to provide her with the correct level of enthusiasm which was always required.

'If you don't enjoy it, Ruth, why do you do it?'

'I didn't say I don't enjoy it. And anyway, we have to pay the bills.'

'There are always choices, you know. I'm sure you could survive on Christian's salary.'

They had reached the café now, but they both seemed reluctant to go inside.

'You've always disapproved of my working, haven't you?' said Ruth, not knowing why she was doing this. 'You and Dad probably thought I should have given up like a good wife when I got married.'

'Don't be absurd, Ruth. I don't give a rat's arse whether or not you work. I don't think there's anything to be gained by staying at home and being miserable, I'm proud of what you've achieved. In fact, I wish I'd had a few more opportunities like that. But I want you to be happy. And you don't seem happy. You're a bag of bones, apart from anything else.'

Ruth had to make a decision in a split second. Ordinarily she would have denied this and stormed off into the café.

But today was the day after the night before and she didn't know how to lie that effectively. She sat down heavily on one of the wooden benches, allowing her mother to sit down next to her.

'I feel a bit lost actually, Mum.'

'Lost?'

'I know you won't understand. I bet you've never felt lost for one second. But some of us normal women find all of this quite hard, you know.'

Her mother paused for a moment, which in itself was unlike her. 'Of course I understand. Do you know what the first thing I said to your father was when he came to see me right after I had you?'

'No.'

'I said that I thought we'd made a terrible mistake. But Dad just laughed and said, Well, we can't put her back now, can we? It made me realise that I wasn't going to be able to talk to him about anything.'

Ruth looked at her mother. She'd never heard her talk like this. She looked much softer. 'What did you do?'

'I went home and I got on with it because there wasn't any other choice. But it didn't mean that the feelings went away. I used to take you to the park every day out of some stupid belief that babies had to have fresh air and I'd be pushing you up the hill and I'd feel like I was getting smaller and smaller so that in the end I'd fade away and there'd be no one there to push you.'

Ruth didn't know how to respond, she felt she was on unfamiliar territory with her mother and she didn't know how far she could let her in. Surely her mother hadn't felt the same way she had, surely she couldn't tell her mother that she was worried her bones were turning to jelly. 'I didn't know you ever felt like that.'

'You're not the first woman to find motherhood hard, Ruth. We all do, you know. But your generation have been fooled into thinking you can have it all, when that's bollocks. We all have to make choices, you have to make choices.'

'You mean choose between my children and my career?'

'Not that literally. But you and Christian seem to think you can fit it all in, when you can't. You could easily live on one of your salaries if you gave up certain things. My generation never went on holidays or had new cars or ate expensive food, that's how we survived.'

Ruth knew there was a logic to this argument, but she couldn't quite place it in her head. Now would probably be a good time to tell her mother her doubts about Aggie, maybe even what was going on with Christian, but she didn't want to give her too much information. Instead she said something silly. 'Some women have it all.'

'Like who?'

'I don't know. Bloody Nigella Lawson.'

Her mother laughed. 'Oh please, Ruth, are you joking? Don't tell me you think her life is like her stupid TV series? And even if it was, who do you think is looking after her kids while she's on the telly making those bloody cupcakes? It's not real, you know, none of it is.'

'I don't know what you're saying, Mum.'

'I'm saying that you expect too much. You've always been the same and the world we live in certainly doesn't help. Don't get so sucked in by it all. Let go a bit. Take a second off and look around you, you might find something that makes you happy. And before you accuse me of being sexist, I'm talking about both you and Christian.'

Ruth sat back. Her skin felt tight on her face. 'Are you worried about me, Mum?'

'Not especially. But Dad and I do think you seem very tired and it's as if you're not having any fun. Life isn't just to be got through, you know. It's not an endurance test.'

Ruth felt as though she might cry and she didn't want to. 'Isn't it?'

Her mother sounded urgent now. 'No, Ruth, it's not. Don't be frightened about giving up on something if it isn't working.'

'Even if that includes my marriage?' Ruth wished she hadn't said it as soon as the words left her mouth.

But her mother sounded surprisingly sanguine. 'Whatever it is, sweetheart. Just don't be hasty in the decision. What seems to be the problem at first might easily turn out not to be. It hasn't always been plain sailing for Dad and me, but we worked through it and I'm glad we did. I'm not saying that's right for everyone, but I do think there's a lot of giving up nowadays. Your generation replace everything, even when it's not broken. You want something and you go out and buy it. It's impossible for that not to have influenced how you see your relationships. We mended and made do and, I know it sounds silly, but there's a comfort in that. Newness can sometimes be a bit scary, it certainly doesn't feel familiar.'

'Familiar sounds like a pair of slippers.'

'I love my slippers.'

Ruth smiled at her mother. She had an answer for everything, but her mother had made her feel lighter, if that was the right word. 'Come on, Mum. Let's get that coffee before we drown in clichés.'

They didn't get back until half past six. Half past six! Agatha had looked out of the window so many times she'd stopped seeing what was in the street. Everything out there was only an image of reality and until Hal reappeared it would remain that way. She'd picked up the phone countless times to call Ruth but hadn't dared in case it made her angry. She couldn't even be sure if she'd be called if there was an accident. Obviously they'd let her know in the end, but in the rush to get to hospital, a call to Agatha would be very low down on the list. It was one of the many reasons that they had to leave in the morning. She didn't want to stay low down on the list.

Agatha had noticed that you get to a point in waiting where you stop believing that the thing you're waiting for will ever happen. A watched kettle never boils, her mother used to say, but Agatha had always thought that to be a stupid saying because a kettle boiled whether you watched it or not. People, on the other hand, came and went and behaved in entirely unpredictable fashions however closely you watched them or however hard you tried to ignore them.

She hadn't managed to sleep but the Nurofen or the pillow or maybe the lying down had worked because slowly her body had cooled down and the noise had quietened and she'd been able to get up. She'd boxed up the cooled biscuits and made the cake and sorted out and put away Betty's toys. She'd even had a chance to make a final sweep of her room and get Hal's stuff sorted and hide their bag in the airing cupboard outside the attic bedroom. Even the letter was written. It was perfectly neat. Now all it needed was Hal.

Agatha had been in the kitchen when she finally heard the key turn in the lock and Betty's over-excited chattering wonderfully pulling them all through the front door. She went into the hall, unable to contain her desire to see the little boy who held her heart. He was nearly asleep in his buggy, his face dirty.

'Guess what, Aggie, Hal ate a bit of chocolate ice cream,' said Ruth.

Agatha kept her smile neutral. 'Did he? That's wonderful.'

'He loved it,' said Betty.

Agatha tried to read Ruth's face, but she seemed caught up in the chaos of the situation. 'Today ice cream, tomorrow vegetables,' she was saying to her parents and they were laughing because they were stupid. Agatha was filled with hatred for them all.

'Shall I give them a bath? They must be exhausted.'

'Oh, would you, Aggie. It is his party tomorrow, after all,' said Ruth.

Yes, you stupid woman, thought Agatha, so why did you take him out and get him over-excited the day before? She reached down to unstrap Hal and he smiled up at her. She lifted his tired body and it flopped into her, all his smells wafting up her nose. He laid his head on her shoulder and she felt her heart loosen and her breath flow easily for the first time since he'd gone out that afternoon. It was becoming increasingly obvious that they had an understanding, her and Hal, that they had been made for each other.

Ruth felt light-headed. She should have been feeling terrible, but somehow she felt exhilarated and she couldn't work out why. Maybe it was Hal's eating the ice cream, or how happy Betty had been to see her grandparents, or the very unusual conversation she'd had with her mother in the park. Or perhaps it was the message Christian had left for her that morning. She hadn't listened to it until Betty had needed the loo in the restaurant and she'd checked her phone while she was waiting outside the cubicle and seen the message still flashing at her.

Ruth listened with a cavalier attitude, expecting some half-hearted apology along the 'but it wasn't me' line which Christian so specialised in. But what he said was reassuringly surprising. She had to listen to it twice. He was sorry that he hadn't understood what she'd been saying better, maybe they'd got it wrong? Even his voice sounded different, like he'd been muted. Was it conceivable that he'd finally got what life was about? Or at least life as she saw it. Which wasn't necessarily right, but perhaps more right than his version.

Ruth had to turn and look into the mirror as she listened to her husband for the second time. She looked grey, but she had two spots of red high up on her cheeks. She ruffled her hair and tried to feel resolute. She had made up her mind about Christian and she almost didn't want him to worm his way back in. There was, Ruth suspected, probably a strange satisfaction in doing it all yourself. In keeping everything neat and contained and having everyone look at you and wonder how you managed. In the end though Ruth supposed that you would probably have a nervous breakdown as too much self-sacrifice was never good for the soul.

Christian wasn't home yet and Ruth found herself feeling excited to see him for the first time in years. She wanted to see whether the message had been an aberration or if her husband had fundamentally changed. But even if he had, she didn't know if she could she trust it or be sure that he wouldn't revert to his same brash self a year or two down the line.

Ruth went to the kitchen to start on supper after Aggie had taken the kids up and her parents were safely dispatched to chairs in the garden with large glasses of wine. She was a good cook but she hardly ever did it properly any more. She still knocked up pasta sauces and salad dressings, but they were easy. Since Aggie had arrived she had hardly even done that and cooking was a bit like childcare, you got out of the habit so easily. Now, as she chopped herbs and rubbed them into the salmon, she realised that she'd missed it. That all of these little routines and rituals were good for you, kept you grounded and sane, gave you a place in the world. A thought butted her mind like a bird at a window: were all the things that made life easier actually making it harder?

The door slammed and she turned to see Christian. He came through into the kitchen and he looked as deflated as he'd sounded on the phone. As if he'd lost weight since she'd seen him that morning, which of course wasn't possible. He was pale and the bags under his eyes were dark and visible.

'Hello,' he said and as he spoke she knew what it was she was seeing; Christian was nervous, properly scared for maybe the first time in his life.

Ruth's initial response was to make him feel better, but she checked herself. 'Hi.' Her excitement from earlier fluttered in her chest, but something which resembled embarrassment held back her words. If they had both realised something new today then did that make them different people?

'Have you had a good day?'

Ruth tried to answer him, but her cheeks flushed and she turned away to stop him seeing.

'I'll just go up and say goodnight to the kids before I see your parents.'

Ruth let him leave the room and wondered what was going on.

Christian hadn't had any idea what to expect as he made his way home. Ruth hadn't called him back, which he guessed was nothing more than he deserved, but it still hurt. The realisation that his wife had probably stopped loving him made him feel as if he'd swallowed a rock. He had rehearsed some speeches on the way home but even as he was running through them in his head he knew he wouldn't be able to say any of them. He was dreading sitting round a table with Ruth's parents as if nothing was wrong. He supposed it would be worse if Ruth had told them, but he knew his wife well enough to know how unlikely that was.

Christian turned the door knob to his daughter's room and saw that Betty was already asleep. She looked so pretty lying with such abandon in her bed it made him smile. He wanted to give her a kiss but he was worried it would wake her, so he shut the door again and looked in on Hal, who was also asleep. He went on into his bedroom to change.

It was undeniably odd, his life. What was it all for if you didn't even get to see your children once a day? If the only complete time you ever spent with them was once a year on a fortnight's holiday in some over-priced European country when you tried to re-introduce yourself to them.

As he exchanged one set of clothes for another he looked at the tree which stood majestically outside their home, fluttering constantly in the view from their bedroom window. It was one of many, positioned like soldiers down their road, guarding time. It was huge, probably hundreds of years old. Christian sat on the bed, his socks lamely still on his feet, his stomach folding over onto itself. The tree would be there for so much longer than he would, it would outlast even his children, maybe the house itself. For the first time he was aware of the others who had lived within these walls, the ghosts of all the past lives in his home. He felt as insubstantial as an evaporating puddle on the floor of a forest. He was falling and no one was there to catch him.

Eventually Christian went downstairs to greet his in-laws. Ruth was sitting outside with them and he could smell something lovely on the warmth of the air. Their greetings were effusive, she definitely hadn't told them.

'Sit down,' said his father-in-law, 'and let me pour you a glass of this rather fine red I brought.'

'No thanks, George. I'm just going to have some juice.'

Ruth turned to look at him. 'Juice?' she repeated and he was pained by her surprise. 'Are you ill?'

'No, I don't feel like drinking.' That was another thing Christian had decided during the day, to cut down, maybe even stop drinking altogether. And to definitely stop smoking. He couldn't explain his train of thought. He was pretty sure he didn't have a problem with any substance, but he definitely used them to control himself in some way. Or maybe that was wrong, maybe he used them to allow himself to legitimately lose control, to negate responsibility. It resonated with what Ruth had said to him the previous night. It was potentially something else she was right about. He had yet to decide.

Supper would have been enjoyable if he hadn't had an executioner's noose hanging over him all night. Ruth looked incongruously relaxed and she drank more than her usual two glasses so that even her shoulders seemed to drop a bit. But she also looked undeniably tired and Christian was relieved when she announced she had to go to bed at ten, so releasing all of them. It took another twenty minutes to negotiate his life before he found himself lying next to his wife, who seemed to be already asleep. He lay on his back with his arms behind his head, desperate to say something, but not sure what that thing should be.

But Ruth spoke, with her back still turned to him. 'That was an odd message you left me.'

'I feel odd.'

'What did you mean?'

'What I said.' He stared into the bluey, shifting blackness, allowing his eyes to get used to it. 'I am sorry, Ruthie, for the things I said. I know it's bullshit to keep apologising about Sarah, even though I am sorry. And I get it, you know, about how whether or not I physically did anything with her is irrelevant. If you give me another chance I won't ever put you through anything like this again. I'm going to be a different man, better, I promise you.'

'I've heard your promises before.'

'I know you have, but now I can see that I didn't mean them. I thought I did, but I didn't, not properly.' Ruth didn't answer and he weighed up whether he should say the next thing to her. 'I called Sarah today to apologise for all the things I said to her and for letting her believe, well, anything about me. Her dad answered and he called me a pompous twat and said he hoped you'd leave me and that I'd end up lonely and miserable.'

'Do you expect me to feel sorry for you?' Christian could tell Ruth was making an effort to keep her voice neutral.

'Of course not. I mean, I don't know, I'm trying to be completely honest. To show you that I'm not going to hide anything from you again.'

Ruth sat up at this, hugging her knees to her chest, and Christian thought she looked so fragile he could probably snap her in two with one hand. 'You don't expect me to forgive you tonight, do you?'

'No. But please don't make me leave, Ruth. I can't bear to not come home to you and the kids. Let me stay and prove all of this to you.'

She turned to him now and he could see she was crying. He was desperate to hold her but he didn't dare. 'I'm so tired, Christian, I feel drained. And I know I say that a lot. You're not the only one who's been thinking.' She pulled a breath into her body. 'I'm sorry, too. I know it's not all you, but I don't know if I can forgive you a second time, I don't know how it would make me feel about myself. There's so much going on in my head at the moment, not all about you ...'

'What else?'

'My job, but Hal mainly. And Aggie. I can't put my finger on it, but I don't like her.'

'Really?'

'Yes, I think I'm going to ask her to leave. I know it sounds absurd, especially now, but I'm not comfortable with how she is with Hal or how he is with her.'

'Why haven't you spoken to me about this?'

'I've tried, but you're so dismissive. You make me feel like I'm mad.'

'I'm sorry.' Christian knew this to be a legitimate accusation, but still wondered how getting rid of a perfectly capable nanny made any sense right now.

'But of course you and Aggie can't leave at the same time, it would be too confusing for the children.'

'I think we should look at everything. I'm not sure we're living in the right way.'

'The right way?' Ruth made a hollow sound. 'You sound like a *Viva* tagline.'

'You know what I mean.'

'Not really. If you know the right way to live you'll solve all our problems.'

'Okay, but don't you feel maybe we've got it wrong?'

'You know I do. I've been saying it for years.'

'Ruth, please give me another chance. Let's try to sort this out together.'

Ruth lay back down as heavily as her slight body allowed and the atmosphere shifted, so that Christian knew he had misjudged some aspect of their exchange. 'God, you're annoying,' she said. 'We're not closing a fucking television deal here. You can't talk your way out of it.'

'I'm not trying to get out of anything, Ruth. I'm trying to make it better.'

'Don't you think it might be a bit late for that now?'

'I hope not.'

'I've been bloody swimming upstream all on my own for fucking years now. Dragging everything behind me while you prat around on the bank having fun and now you're suddenly all serious, like you've got all the answers and you expect me to go, Oh, okay, Christian, stay, help us all out of this shit hole. It's been what, a few hours, since you had your grand awakening and you expect me to believe that's it, a new you.'

'I don't expect ...'

'Actually, shut up.' Ruth sounded angry now. 'I'm tired and it's our son's birthday tomorrow. I need to sleep.'

Christian let her roll away from him. He knew better than to pursue the argument tonight. At least he'd said part of what he meant.

Agatha felt anxious when she woke at six the next morning. She had spent most of the night in the tiny box room going over and over all her preparations. Mentally repacking the knapsack that was hidden in the airing cupboard, containing all her possessions, plus most of Hal's, and both their passports. She was unsure how water-tight her plan was and worried by how long the media coverage might continue. She envisaged months of hiding themselves away. Months of not returning any looks, of crossing the street from penetrating eyes, of checking over her shoulder before letting them into their home, of flitting into the night, of jumping every time a policeman turned the corner. And all this whilst keeping Hal happy.

It had been wrong to stay for the party. Agatha hated the fact that she had misjudged this. She thought she had stopped making the wrong decisions years ago and she prided herself on her ability to suss out a situation and mould herself to it successfully. Naturally this way of life always had a limited time span, but moving on was never hard. Agatha had nothing but contempt for the Donaldsons now. She remembered with incredulity how she had felt about them when she'd first arrived; how she had allowed herself to believe they weren't as fucked up as the others, how she had even fantasised about making herself so indispensable that she would stay with them for ever, becoming some coherent part of their family that none of them could imagine doing without. But no one was indispensable, which was yet another reason why it was okay for her to take Hal with her tomorrow morning.

With her thoughts more ordered, Agatha felt the anxiety loosen its grip enough so she was able to get out of bed. It was coming up for seven when she got into the kitchen and the house was completely still and quiet. She had planned to slip out at six the next morning, telling Hal that they were going on a birthday treat adventure. The quietness gave her a surge of confidence, she could have at least an hour's start on them all, probably longer. You could easily get a train to the coast in that time. You might even make it on to a ferry before the police had been called.

Agatha sat at the kitchen table and waited for the house to wake up. It infuriated her that everyone would saunter around this morning, like nothing important was happening at three. She knew Ruth and Christian wouldn't do anything to stop the children spilling cereal and that they'd drop coffee granules on the floor and toast crumbs on the table. Agatha would have to sit there, holding in her anger, while they all casually trashed her cleanliness, without even apologising. If she had the power she would ban them all from the house until five minutes before the party was due to start.

Betty was the first person to appear. Agatha liked her best first thing in the morning, subdued and fuzzy round the edges. She got the little girl a bowl of cereal and a mug of juice and made herself a cup of tea and they sat together, not talking. Agatha realised that she would miss Betty, but not so as her heart would feel stretched like it did when she thought about her own sister, Louise. Walking away from her parents had been easy, but Louise had nearly been enough to make her stay. Not that her sister had shared the feeling. She was three years older than Agatha and spent most of the time they were together telling her how stupid she was. Harry once told Agatha that he'd chosen her over Louise because Louise was too feisty. She hadn't understood the word at the time, but she'd still known enough about life to see the irony in the fact that the first thing she'd ever beaten Louise in wasn't worth winning.

Agatha had googled Louise the previous year and had been surprised to see that her sister was on Facebook. The knowledge was like a worm burrowing into her brain because she could only see a picture of her sister and a few lines of text. Agatha could never be on Facebook, even though it was her perfect medium, the one way she would be able to connect with the outside world and be just like all the other people sitting behind their screens, editing their life and playing make-believe. In the photo Louise was standing in front of a glass door which Agatha thought looked like an important office. She was wearing a pink coat and her hair was long enough to blow across her face, making her smile out at whoever was behind the camera. Agatha had spent too many hours trying to see beyond the picture, but it was hard to see her sister so out of context, looking happy and successful.

She still looked at Louise as often as she could, but the picture now scared her as it made her realise that her family had continued on without her all these years. She hadn't expected them to exist in limbo, but still it was galling to see her sister so obviously full of life. One day, many years away, she was going to take Hal to see them and give them the shock of their lives; Agatha had done something useful for once.

When Agatha had first arrived in London seven years ago, with nothing more than the clothes she was wearing and a few hundred pounds she'd saved or stolen, she used to scan any missing poster she came across. Or watch those shows on the telly with people looking for relatives, as if everyone was trapped in a swirling vortex pulling you away from those you loved. She longed to see her own face staring out at her, hear her parents begging her to contact them, her mother too weak to talk and her father red-eyed as he made the statement for both of them. Even Louise would be there, huddled into their mother, saying that life wasn't the same without her sister and she'd do anything to get her back. Whatever you've done or whatever trouble you're in, we don't care, come home, we can sort it out. That was the sort of thing the other parents said on their appeals. It was not the sort of thing Agatha could imagine her own parents saying. And then, when she'd looked at Louise's photo on the Internet, she'd realised that all her hoping had been a waste of time because they'd probably never bothered looking for her or even wondered where she was. Why can't you be nice, Agatha, her mother used to shout at her. Nobody likes a liar, you know. If the truth be told, they'd all probably felt a surge of relief when she'd finally gone.

Ruth walked into the kitchen carrying Hal and for a second Agatha didn't know where she was. How had she not heard him? Betty immediately started jumping up and down, singing Happy Birthday, but Hal looked bemused.

'Can we open his presents now?' Betty was shouting.

'I don't see why not,' said Ruth. 'They're in the sitting room. Go and get Dad.'

Agatha was pleased with her present. She'd spent ages thinking about what to get him and when she'd come up with the idea it had seemed perfect. She'd gone to the Early Learning Centre and bought a pop-up tent. It was just right because it meant that Hal would be able to have his own space to retreat to wherever they were. It had been one of the first things Agatha had noticed about Hal and one of the first things to strike a chord with her. Often life seemed too much for Hal and that's why he spent so much time in the plastic house in the playroom. Ruth and Christian thought it was something to do with the house, but Agatha could have told them it had nothing to do with the place, it was the isolation Hal craved. Since she had let him dictate his own life a bit more and started removing him from situations which were too loud or chaotic, he'd stopped needing the house so much. Which was another reason why they shouldn't have stayed for the party.

By the time Agatha got back downstairs with her present the whole family was in the sitting room, all in their nightclothes, watching Betty open Hal's presents. He was sitting on Ruth's lap, curled into her, unable to give the right or any response to the gifts that Betty was shoving in his face. Next year was going to be very different; Agatha tried to catch Hal's eye to let him know this, but he wouldn't look up.

After he'd had all his family presents opened, Agatha stepped forward and handed over her offering.

'Oh, Aggie, that's so kind of you,' said Ruth. 'You shouldn't have.'

She hated Ruth. How could the stupid woman think she wouldn't get Hal a present? It made her want to scream right into her face: I spend more time with him than anyone else, I know him better than you do, he likes me the most.

Betty snatched the present out of Agatha's hand and ripped it open. 'Look, Hal,' she was shouting, 'it's a tent, it pops up, look.'

'It's a portable one.' Agatha felt her voice fading against the tide and momentarily had to put her hand to her head to stop the spinning. Ruth's father stood up to take a photo, blocking her view and sending out a flash of light which seemed to bounce around the room. Agatha heard a pop and lots of laughter as the tent opened. Betty was first in, shouting for Hal. Ruth's father was taking more pictures and Ruth and her mother were having a loud conversation about the new curtains Ruth had put up a few weeks ago. Then Hal started crying and no one seemed to notice. It's too much for him, Agatha wanted to say. She stepped forward, but as she did so Christian did the same. Hal looked up, he saw them both and then he put out his arms for his father who lifted him up and took him out of the room.

Agatha slipped out behind them. Christian was taking Hal upstairs and he already seemed calmer. She turned and went into the kitchen but it was too cramped and she could still hear all the noise from the other room. Agatha unlocked the back door and went into the garden. She walked barefoot across the still-damp grass and stood by the vegetable bed. Vegetables poured from this patch of ground, they ate them nearly every day and they tasted like the sun which made them grow. Agatha studied the sturdy plants bursting out of the soil and remembered the day when they had planted the seeds. The day which had properly made her fall in love with Hal so that everything about him became relevant and his whole being filled her head. She stared until her breathing returned to normal and she stopped seeing the white flashing lights at the edge of her vision. It's okay, she told herself, it's okay. One more day and then we'll be gone and we won't even have to remember any of this if we don't want to.

Christian only managed to get a few minutes alone with Ruth between being woken by Betty in a state of high excitement and the first guest ringing the doorbell at three o'clock. He went to put his work laptop in the bedroom and found her in there getting changed.

She was making him feel fifteen again. 'I love that dress,' he said.

'Nice try.'

'No, I mean it.' Ruth was looking in the mirror, smoothing her finger under her eyes. She often did that and yet Christian realised he had no idea why; he had never asked her. He was desperate to say something of meaning before she disappeared into their life again and he lost her for the next few hours. 'I've loved being here today.'

Ruth looked perplexed. 'Have you? I think parties are a bloody nightmare.'

'No, you know what I mean. Of course the party's a nightmare. But, you know, usually I'm looking for a way out. Or calculating how much I can drink without pissing you off. But today's been different. I don't know, it's great to be around you and the kids.'

She turned round and her tone was sneering. 'You sound like a self-help book.'

'Sorry. I can't seem to say what I mean.'

He saw Ruth's face soften at this and she came closer to him. 'I know. I know how that feels. And anyway, I do know what you mean.'

Christian reached forward and took his wife's hand. He wanted to pull her towards him but it was too far. 'Ruthie, I am so sorry. Please, please, don't make me go.'

Ruth looked down. 'Christian, I do love you. But I don't know if I can trust you again. I don't even know if I believe you.'

'I can see that. But can't I stay and prove it to you? Give me six months or something and if it's all bullshit then I'll leave.'

Ruth pulled her hand away. 'I don't know. I can't think straight at the moment. Let's get today out of the way before we make any big decisions.' And then she left the room.

Christian went over to stand by the window, swallowing down emotions he hadn't felt in years. Everything he was saying to Ruth was real and yet he had negated the meaning of his own words by who he was, or who he'd been. He found it shocking that he could have forgotten how much he loved his wife. How her presence could have lulled him into a false sense of security. Ruth's magazine was always going on about couple time and shared experience and how you had to develop interests and go out for dinner at least once a month to keep your relationship alive. But of course all of that, which he'd bought into, was nothing more than the consumer bullshit which ruled their lives. Love wasn't about watching a play together or liking the same music or sharing a plate of spaghetti. It was something primal you felt, which was no doubt why it was so hard to hold on to. Christian could see how, in a fully explained world, it was hard for mankind to make sense of an emotion that had no beginning or end or even any substance.

Was it possible to change overnight? He'd read about people who'd had epiphanies, but weren't they usually religious? Whatever this was didn't feel that momentous. What he was feeling was more like taking off a coat when you're too hot and the relief at losing the weight and the heat as cool air rushes round your skin. Thirty-nine was undeniably old to grow up, but that's what it felt like. He knew with an unusual conviction that he would not be chasing the next pint after work or night out with his friends or even promotions and money. He knew that he would be looking forward to reading Betty a bedtime story or brushing Hal's teeth with him or even sitting in front of some crap TV with Ruth. He realised that he was becoming more like his parents. That Betty and Hal would grow up finding him as boring and irrelevant as he had his own parents. That they would sit in their bedrooms listening to downloads wondering how their parents survived being so square. And the thought made him smile. It made sense, in some strange and unfamiliar way.

Ruth hated giving parties. They made her feel nervous and useless and bourgeois, although surely it was ridiculous to imagine that she wasn't any of those things. Today's was even worse as every time she tried to do something helpful in the kitchen she could feel Aggie prickle and the atmosphere became so strained she ended up leaving.

Finally, she sat in the sitting room with Hal and read him the books her parents had given him. His body succumbed in her lap and she took his tiny finger and traced it over the blue shoes, the red T-shirt, the yellow shorts.

'Blue,' she said to Hal. 'Can you say blue?'

But he turned his face into her arm and the force of her love snatched at her heart. She was struck with the realisation that it didn't matter if there was something wrong with him, it would only make her love him more, protect him from a world in which right and wrong were even a concept.

Betty sauntered in and sat on the arm of the chair they were in, resting her head on Ruth's shoulder.

'Hello, sweetheart,' said Ruth. 'I was trying to teach Hal colours.'

And, for once, Betty didn't point out that Hal couldn't talk because he was stupid or shout at Ruth. She took Hal's hand and told him about the colours in the world. Ruth sat back, her heart still fluttering. The best part of perfect moments was their unexpectedness.

The next time she checked on Aggie the icing had gone wrong on the biscuits and Aggie was scraping it off and going red. Ruth told her not to bother, but Aggie looked like she might cry and so she left again.

Ruth went to sit in the garden with her mother and a glass of wine. She felt rattled by everything and the alcohol went straight to her head. Christian was being very strange. She couldn't let herself believe that if she let him stay life would be different. She wasn't even sure if different would be better. She felt like her life view might easily be a con, that she was selling Christian a bogus reality. She certainly didn't feel confident in her ability to be right, she could definitely see how much she was to blame for this mess. But at the same time they both seemed to be letting go of something and it felt good.

The thought was intoxicating. The idea of keeping her husband, of gluing her family back together, of being in a sustaining relationship, of not having to shoulder the burden of everything all on her own, of having someone to talk to. Except, did people ever change? And if he was doing it only so he could stay and didn't mean it, then it wouldn't work and the third time would surely be even more painful than the second, which had been worse than the first because she'd had to factor herself in this time as well. But if he didn't mean it, then why was he bothering? She'd opened the door and he could walk out to a new life of nights out, young women and endless parties. It was what she'd always thought he wanted, so she couldn't understand why he wasn't grabbing it with both hands.

'Has Aggie got everything under control then?' asked Ruth's mother.

'What do you think of her, Mum?'

'I'm not her biggest fan.' Her mother was lying back in the deck chair, her face turned towards the sun.

'No,' said Ruth, 'I feel like that, but I can't put my finger on why.'

'Oh, she's too bloody perfect and polite. No one's really like that. You should never trust anyone who doesn't fuck up or tell you to fuck off.'

Ruth laughed. 'I should put that in *Viva*.'

'But it's true, darling. I've watched you offering to help in your own kitchen, it's ridiculous. And I saw how she looked at you when she was giving Hal her present this morning. Honestly, I think she's odd.'

'I think I'm going to have to get rid of her and then we're not going to have a nanny and I'll probably lose my job if I have to take any more time off and the next one will no doubt be just as bad.'

Ruth's mother sat up at this. 'Stop it, Ruth. You're like a bloody runaway train, one problem snowballing into the next. If I thought like you I'd never get anything done, it would all feel too overwhelming. There's probably a solution somewhere. Dad and I would be happy to come up for a couple of weeks if you really couldn't take off any more time.'

'Would you?'

But then the doorbell rang and Ruth had to go and answer it and within twenty minutes there were at least thirty people in their house.

Toby's girlfriend was as knockout gorgeous as Christian had imagined and he was as unbothered as he had known he would be.

'Just out of interest, how old is she?' asked Christian as he stood with Toby by the vegetable patch, watching Gabriella help his wife with an unruly game of musical bumps.

'Twenty-seven.'

'She doesn't look it. I thought you were going to say seventeen.'

'Don't be stupid. I'm pushing forty. That would be illegal or something.'

Christian laughed. 'Or something.'

Last year, after everyone had gone home and he'd drunk too much and Ruth had shouted at him for not helping clear up, he'd told her he hated her most at their children's parties. Why? she'd asked. Because you remind me of my mother, of your mother, of all the fucking mothers in history. And she'd answered, But I am a mother. And he'd been filled with an overwhelming sense of unfairness, as if his life had been snatched when he wasn't looking. What the fuck do you want me to be? she'd wept. I can't be everything, you know. He'd walked away, but he'd wanted to grab her and shake her and demand to be told why not. Why couldn't she be everything he wanted? Why couldn't it all just be for him, him alone?

'You not drinking?' Toby motioned with his bottle of beer at Christian's glass of water.

'No. Don't fancy it today.'

'How's it going with Ruth?'

'Okay. We haven't had much of a chance to talk yet. She's very angry and hurt.'

'Do you think she'll let you stay?'

'I don't know. It seems impossible right now. Even though I'm properly sorry, it's not only about me: she's had a part to play in all of this. I don't know, it feels like months of heart-ache, if we even get to that stage. I'm trying my best, but I don't think she believes me.'

Toby picked the leaves off their hedge, crumbling them absentmindedly as he did so. 'You're right, it's not just you. I love Ruth, but she's hard work, she expects a lot.'

'I know. I suppose we both are. I think, if we're going to stay together, maybe we need to get over all that crap and try to get on.'

'I guess it's time we both grew up,' said Toby. 'I'm thinking of asking Gabriella to move over here and live with me.'

'Seriously?'

'Yeah. She doesn't let me get away with shit. It's about time I met a woman who tells me to piss off when I'm being a wanker.'

'Do you think we're backward,' asked Christian, 'or are all men like us?'

Toby smiled. 'I'd take a punt on all men.'

'Ruth has been saying all this to me for years and it never meant anything before now.'

'Yeah, but it's like giving up smoking, isn't it? You know it's bad for you, but you have to want to give it up to do it.'

Christian opened his mouth to answer, but that was when they heard the noise. It was so loud and unlike anything he had ever heard that he dropped his glass. He looked around and everyone in the garden had had a similar reaction. Even the children were motionless, their shouting silenced for the first time that day. He checked for his own children and saw Betty standing in front of Ruth. He couldn't see Hal. He cast his eyes frantically around the garden in the way an animal might.

Children's parties pushed Ruth out of her head, to the point at which she felt she couldn't cope and it was only a matter of time before she would fall to the floor, a dribbling wreck. She had been negotiating a manic yet tedious game of musical bumps when she heard the scream. She was slightly tipsy, the only way she managed to get through her children's parties, so for a moment she

wondered if she'd imagined the noise. But then she saw
the look on Gabriella's face and realised it must have
occurred, out loud, in the real world. Her first thought
was shameful. She was annoyed that something like this
should happen just when she'd found out that Gabriella
wasn't a nightmare as her unfeasible beauty suggested.
She even felt guilty for laughing with Sally and her friend
Janie earlier about how women like Gabriella should not
be allowed to attend parties which contained women
over thirty, especially those whose bodies had been over-
stretched by childbirth. Believe me, Sally had said, my
body is pretty damned good for my age and I don't have
children and she still makes me feel like shit. That's rich,
Janie had said, considering you'd put her on the cover of
Viva tomorrow and I'm your target audience. Sally had
laughed and said, Get used to it, girls, it's the way of the
world.

Ruth's second thought had been much better. She had
reached instinctively for Betty, even though she was
standing right in front of her. She noticed most of her
friends moving towards their own children. Ruth did a
quick head count and saw that Hal was missing. She
turned in that instant; surely the sound hadn't been made
by a person, but still, where was Hal? She caught sight of
Christian scanning the garden and realised he too was
looking for Hal. Her heart contracted and a sickness
welled in her stomach as she tried to grab at an understanding which had been coming but was not yet fully
realised.

Agatha had had a terrible day. Nothing you could say could change that fact, not that anyone would have attempted to say anything to make her feel better. None of them even realised it had gone wrong. Which was the fucking story of her life, when you thought about it.

For starters Ruth and Christian had behaved exactly as she'd known they would. Messing up the bloody house and generally not acting with any sense of understanding for what she'd done. Then she'd made the sandwiches too early and spent the rest of the time worrying that they'd go soggy. And Ruth's fucking mother – the woman couldn't take a hint and was as thick-skinned as her stupid daughter. If Agatha had refused her help once she'd done it a fucking thousand times. And then finally the stupid woman had made Betty some lunch! Fucking lunch, two hours before a party! Lunch, which had to be cleaned up and washed and swept away. Which was better than Christian, who'd had the temerity to make himself a sandwich at quarter to two. These people were fucking insane.

Agatha wasn't sure how she'd managed to get the icing for the biscuits so spectacularly wrong, but it had tasted like shit and she hadn't had the nous to try it until she'd iced nearly all of them, which meant she'd had to scrape it off forty biscuits before bloody re-making it. Then Ruth had come in and told her not to bother. Not to fucking bother! The woman was totally unfit to be a mother.

When the party had started all these people flooded into the house. It was horrible. Everywhere Agatha looked people were laying claim to Hal and giving him presents and picking him up and shouting. Why did they all have to talk so fucking loudly? They drank glasses of fizzy wine and talked over their children's heads about the most banal crap. Nothing made any sense or had any cohesion to it. Agatha had a party plan, but Ruth had made no attempt to follow it. A few times she'd tried to talk to Ruth, to get some order back into the party, but Ruth had barely been able to hide her disdain and told Agatha not to worry, she'd handle the games. But then when the games had started Ruth hadn't handled them herself, she'd got that bloody bitch whatever her name was with the long flowing black hair and pouty lips and tight jeans. She was a bloody liar, Ruth, just like every bloody body bastard else.

Agatha had looked out of the window as she was taking the cling film off the sandwiches and arranging the biscuits on a plate and getting the little sausages out of the oven when she saw Hal holding hands with the long-haired bitch. He was jumping up and down and smiling. Agatha had a sudden pang of hatred shoot through her that was so violent it momentarily took in Hal as well. Fickle, that was the word. Every bloody bastard body was fickle as well as a liar. If she'd had a gun she'd have shot the lot of them.

Was it getting hot in here? Agatha desperately pushed open all the windows. She was sweating. It was rolling off her so that she could feel it running down her back and pooling at the base of her spine. Was it hot? Why was it so hot? Agatha pulled at her T-shirt, she wanted to take it off, she needed to take it off.

Someone was talking to her. She turned round and saw the stupid bitch of a grandmother standing there. Her mouth was moving but it was too hot for Agatha to hear anything. And they were all still shouting in the garden. She reached over to pick up the cake because if anyone was going to get Hal to blow out his candles then it was going to be her.

Too late she noticed Hal standing on a chair next to his grandmother. Her eyes went to him and she saw that he was chewing. His hand moved to the plate and he was taking another sandwich to add to the one he had already finished. Ruth's mother's voice exploded into her ears. 'Oh my God, he's eating! Quick, Aggie, go and get Ruth, she's got to see this.'

It was too hot. Had Agatha said that already? Was anyone listening? It. Was. Too. Hot. Hal had to stop. She fell towards him in one movement, dropping the plate with the cake, which smashed into fragments. It was in fragments at her feet. Feet. Fragments. Maybe she couldn't stop falling. Maybe that's why she was on the floor and the plate was harsh on her hands. Her blood felt warm and sticky.

Fragments. Floor. Falling.

Someone or something was screaming. It was loud and too close to her. It was so close it felt like it was in her head. It was hot in here. Too hot. Wasn't anyone going to help her? God help the child.

The plate was broken.

The cake was ruined.
The floor was fragmented.
Her hands and feet on the floor.
There were fragments of her on the floor.

Ruth and Christian reached the darkness of the house together. They didn't need to speak because the fear bristled on them. They were stepping into an unknown and they couldn't help each other. The familiarity of their surroundings melted into a grotesque parody of their life. Ruth went first, calling her son's name. She heard a small whimper, underneath or maybe over the screaming. She went into the hall and saw her mother holding Hal close to her. She was deathly white, as white as a pint of milk, except for the tiny pin-pricks of blood splattering both her and Hal.

'It's Aggie,' she said. 'I don't know what happened. I took Hal to the loo and then he said he was hungry so we went into the kitchen and he ate a sandwich.'

'A sandwich?' Ruth couldn't help herself.

'I know, I'll tell you about that later. I was trying to speak to Aggie, telling her what a great job she'd done, but she didn't seem to hear and she looked, I don't know, I suppose beside herself and very red. Then Hal took another sandwich and she lunged at him but she was holding the cake and she tripped and there's blood, I think she cut her hands on the plate. And, my God, that noise she's making, it's not normal.'

'Okay, Mum. Christian and I will deal with it.' A feeling of dread was all around them, enveloping and constraining them.

Ruth didn't want to see what was going on behind the kitchen door but Christian walked straight in. The noise was intensified and she could see the blood on the floor, along with shards of china and mashed cake. Aggie was still on the floor, looking like a wild animal. She had tears and snot all over her face which was red and swollen. Christian went straight to her and lifted her onto a chair. It seemed to calm her slightly and the noise dropped a decibel or two so that she sounded like a mooing cow. Ruth found a cloth and washed the blood off Aggie's hands and arms.

'I think it's mainly superficial,' she said to Christian.

Ruth looked at the girl she'd entrusted her children to these past eight months and wondered what she'd done. 'Aggie,' she said. 'Aggie, it's me – Ruth. Are you okay?' Aggie looked up but her eyes didn't connect with Ruth. She looked very young and Ruth felt a flicker of motherly love for her. She fetched her a glass of water and made Aggie drink it.

'Aggie,' Ruth tried again. 'Don't worry, it's going to be okay. Do you need to see a doctor? Do you know what's happening to you?'

'Shall I call an ambulance?' asked Christian.

'She seems to be calming down,' answered Ruth. 'Give her a minute.'

They watched the colour drain from Aggie's face, the blood moving like it was being pulled by a magnet. Then her teeth started chattering.

'Aggie, are you feeling any better?' Ruth tried again.

The girl looked up at her and started to cry. Ruth pulled her towards her and let Aggie's tears soak into her T-shirt. 'I'm sorry,' she said finally. 'I didn't want to tell you because I wanted the job so much. I'm epileptic.'

Ruth relaxed at this. There was still the thought of what would have happened if this scene had occurred when it was just Aggie and Hal in the house, but it seemed better than the other options. 'Oh, Aggie, you should have said. Maybe we could have got round it.'

'I suppose I should leave,' Aggie was saying now.

'Don't be ridiculous. You're in no fit state to go anywhere.' Ruth smoothed her hair. It felt good to be the superior one for once. 'You're going to go to bed and not worry about this and we'll talk in the morning.'

'But Hal's cake –'

'It doesn't matter. He won't even notice.'

Aggie was whimpering now and her hands were icy. But she stood up.

'Shall I come with you?' asked Ruth.

'No, I'm okay. You're right, I need to sleep.'

There was a lot that needed to be thought about, but Ruth couldn't let herself get into that now. This was a big fuck-up and she wasn't sure where to go from here.

'Shit,' she said to Christian when she was sure Aggie couldn't hear them.

'I know,' he said. 'She can't look after the children.'

'Of course not. But we can't just turn her onto the street.'

'I think we should get her to a doctor in the morning.'

Ruth wanted wine but there was a whole party still to be endured, all the questions their friends would ask, all the shock they had to absorb. 'Yes, but first I'd better rescue the cake.'

The stairs swam before Aggie's eyes and white lights darted around her head. That was as close to the edge as she ever wanted to get. Of course Ruth and Christian would ask her to leave in the morning; even they weren't desperate enough to leave a lunatic in charge of their children. She sat on her bed and calculated the possibility of them ringing a doctor or the police before the morning and decided it wasn't very likely. They'd have to deal with the party and then some guests would linger and then they'd have to get the kids to bed and have dinner with her parents. They'd imagine she was asleep and they'd leave it till morning.

She toyed with the idea of waiting till everyone was asleep and then lifting Hal from his bed and stealing into the night with him like a fugitive. But she thought it was probably unnecessary. Besides she didn't want to be made to feel like a criminal because of one stupid slip up. She was not the person screaming on the floor, she was the strong woman she had worked so hard to be. She was not afraid. She was not wrong. She was Hal's mother.

Agatha stayed awake all night. She heard Ruth and Christian go to bed just after eleven and she heard their voices rise and fall with the pitch of their argument, but they sounded too tired to get into it properly. At three she went to the airing cupboard and retrieved her knapsack. On the top were the bags of new clothes she had bought for her and Hal. It was all these little details which made her sure she would get away with it.

Agatha had studied the women in the park for weeks. She saw what they wore and looked at their labels when they left expensive jumpers on benches. She touched the real leather of their handbags, noticed the sun glinting off their dark glasses. She practised the way they walked across the grass of the park like they were in an exclusive restaurant with every right to be there. They didn't let their gaze waver over people like her, they barely even noticed their children trailing in their wake like baby ducks. Life flowed for these women because they expected it to and this sort of confidence was like a shield; no one questioned you when you were one of these women. Agatha had considered taking a few of the many clothes Ruth never wore, but she had resisted the temptation because that would have been wrong. Instead she had used her own money to buy clothes to which she could see no point other than that they opened a door to a new life.

At five she dressed and sat on the edge of her bed watching the sky lighten into a dull grey which would transform into blue in a few hours' time. Her stomach felt emptier than it ever had; she could feel her intestinal juices swirling the sick-inducing bile round her insides. Time crawled through a sewer but still she waited because it was vitally important that she performed each step exactly as she had seen it in her mind, at exactly the right time.

At six o'clock she took her knapsack downstairs and put it by the front door. She got Hal's buggy out of the cupboard under the stairs and opened it next to the bag. Then she trod noiselessly back upstairs. Agatha would have made a good burglar, she knew how to walk so that she carried her weight within her body, keeping her footsteps as light as if they really were feathers. Years of looking after children had made her an expert in this.

Hal's room was dark and she could hear him sucking in his sleep. She smoothed the hair off his face and he opened his eyes silently. His cheeks gave way to her touch like a pillow or a cashmere blanket.

'Morning, sweetheart,' she said. 'I've got a special treat for you, Hal. Do you want to come on an adventure with me?'

He held his arms up to her, the trust in the gesture so intense it caught at Agatha's throat. She lifted him up and his tiny body fitted into hers, making her sure she was right. They knelt on the floor together as Agatha eased his little limbs into his clothes.

'Now, we have to be really quiet, Hal, so we don't wake anyone else. Is that okay?'

He nodded and she picked him up and went downstairs. It was so close, her life was so close now and yet she had never felt more scared. Her heart resounded through her body, announcing itself in every muscle, every fibre, every vein of her being.

But now he was strapped into the buggy and the knapsack was on her back. She opened the front door and pushed him out. She turned and used her key to shut the door silently. The already warm summer air embraced them and propelled them down the street. The birds singing the dawn chorus stopped and stared and, when they saw what was happening, started again, but louder this time, more triumphantly, for Agatha and Hal were going home.

Christian woke with a start, his heart pumping so viciously he momentarily worried that he was having a heart attack. He turned his head and saw it was six thirty-three. He listened for the sound of crying, but none came. He was hot and he threw the covers off, letting the morning air dry the sweat onto his naked body. He had the impression of a bad dream in his mind, like a ghost at a window or a foul taste in his mouth. Ruth was still asleep, turned away from him and breathing so silently it was almost unreal. He had a desire to check on his children, but he resisted it, knowing that at this time they were too near to the day to allow any noise.

The air felt close and stifling, although it wasn't really that hot. It was never that hot in England. He tried to remember how he had got into an argument with Ruth the night before, but everything was jumbled. He doubted he could ever again say the right thing to her.

Christian got up and showered. It was Sunday and tomorrow Ruth wanted him to leave. The life that had seemed like a trap now opened up before him and he felt the knowledge of his need for it deep inside him. He might have to leave and live in a small room somewhere with a sofa which opened up into an uncomfortable bed and a kitchen which ran along a wall. Everything he owned would smell of the take-away curries he would eat or the stale beer he would breathe out night after night. He would wake up hating himself every morning and fall asleep each night wishing he was home.

By seven he was in the kitchen making coffee, looking out of the window at the mess in the garden which needed to be cleared up. But then Betty was at the kitchen door and her enthusiasm pulled him into the day so that he could busy himself with her breakfast and make believe that their life wasn't falling apart.

Ruth knew she had slept in as soon as she woke up. The air seemed different and a hazy indifference swirled above her head. The clock told her that it was twenty past eight and she wondered how she had slept through the children waking and Christian getting up. She could hear Betty shouting downstairs, the whirr of the television, the smell of coffee. The sleep had done nothing for her, instead seeping into her body like a drug, teasing her with its presence, showing her what was possible.

But today was a day that needed action and decisions and pain and torment. The day was not going to let her rest. Ruth already knew it was going to frazzle her until she might sit on her sofa in ten hours' time with a glass of wine and a dread of what Monday held in store. She pulled herself out of bed and her legs felt heavy, her head woozy. She stood under the shower in the hope it would wake her, but went downstairs feeling ravaged and distracted. Christian was busying himself with bin bags. He had already cleared most of the garden, she noticed.

'Morning,' he said. 'D'you want some coffee?'

'Please.' She wondered how she was going to do this alone. How she was going to be the one person responsible for it all. She couldn't decide if letting him stay would be weak, too much of an admittance of something she didn't want to know. 'Is Aggie up yet?' she asked instead.

'No.' Christian tied up one bin bag and shook out another. He irritated her with his unusual efficiency. 'What are we going to do about that?'

'I have no idea.' Usually Ruth was full of solutions, even when they were bad, but for this particular problem she couldn't think of anything. 'Mum said she could help us out if we need to get rid of her.'

'You definitely want her to leave?'

'Are you joking? What if she'd been alone with Hal and Betty when that happened?'

'I've never seen an epileptic fit like that.'

'How many have you seen?'

'Well, none. But I didn't know they were like that.'

Christian passed her the coffee and Betty came in from the sitting room, still in her pyjamas, the sound of cartoons following her like they cared.

'Can I get in Hal's tent?' she asked.

'I'm sure you can, sweetie,' said Ruth. 'Why don't you ask him if it's okay?'

'He's still asleep.'

Ruth looked at Christian. 'Hal's still asleep?'

'Yeah.'

She felt a constriction in her chest. 'But he never sleeps past seven.'

Christian was on his way back into the garden. 'He must be tired after yesterday.'

Ruth tried to draw something from his nonchalance. 'I think I'll go and check on him anyway.'

Ruth took the stairs two at a time, praying to an unknown God as she went, bargaining with everything for the life of her son. She opened the door to Hal's room and it was dark, but she could tell from the door that he wasn't there. She walked towards the cot pointlessly because it was empty. She had been worrying about illness, but she realised that she was about to deal with something much more sinister. There was still a chance that he had found his way to her parents or Aggie. She tried her parents first because somewhere she already knew what had happened.

She knocked on Aggie's attic room and her mother opened it. 'Hal's not in here, is he?' asked Ruth.

'No, darling. Is everything okay?'

But Ruth had turned away already, she couldn't answer. She didn't even knock on the door of the box room. It was as empty as a barren womb. No trace of Aggie remained. The bed didn't even look slept in.

Ruth raced down the stairs. Her mother was at her back trying to speak and Betty was still asking about the tent. Everything was in her way. The air was like soup so she couldn't breathe or walk. Christian was too far away, at the other side of the garden picking plastic cups out of the flowers. She went over to him and found she couldn't speak so she touched his arm to make him turn round.

'Shit, what's happened?' he said, retreating from her touch as if she was diseased.

'Hal's gone. So's Aggie. She's taken him.'

Christian put his hands over her arms, the way she'd watched actors do on soap operas. It was like he wanted to squeeze a false truth out of her. 'Don't be silly, Ruth,' he was saying somewhere over her head. 'Of course she hasn't taken him. Have you looked everywhere?'

Ruth was aware of her mother shouting behind them. It was going to take too much effort and time to explain to Christian what was happening. She knew with absolute certainty what had happened, she just didn't know how much of a head start the girl had got. 'Shut up, Christian,' she said now, shaking his hands off her arms. 'When did you get up?' A clarity which had eluded her for years lit up her mind.

'She might have just taken him to the park or something.'

'When did you get up?' Ruth shouted.

Her mother came back into the garden. 'They're not in the house. I've looked everywhere.'

Christian started to cry. 'Oh God, no.'

Ruth wanted to slap him. 'When did you wake up? Come on, Christian.'

'Six-thirty.' He looked at her and she flinched from the terror in his eyes. 'I woke with a start, I thought one of the kids was awake. I got up, had a shower. I must have been downstairs by seven. Then Betty got up. You were the next person down. I thought he was asleep.'

'She wouldn't have left in the night. Maybe her leaving woke you. It's quarter to nine now. That means she's had nearly three hours.'

Christian started towards the house. 'I'm calling the police.'

Ruth followed him, the ground giving way beneath her, pulling her into an earth that was hot and hostile. The things you see in films or read about in newspapers were happening to her. Helplessness clawed at her being like a zombie was crawling through the ground to tear the skin from her bones. Betty was crying but she didn't care.

'They're going to be here as soon as they can,' said Christian. Then he left the room and Ruth heard him retching.

Her mother and father were near her. Someone put their arms around her. Ruth looked at her mother and wondered if her misery was like her own or if you never stopped being a mother. If somewhere deep inside she was saying that silent prayer of thanks that it wasn't her child, that it wasn't Ruth.

'She won't hurt him, darling,' her mother said.

'She's mad, Mum. You saw her last night. She doesn't have epilepsy. God knows what she's got, but Hal is not safe with her.'

'The police will find them. She can't have got far.'

But of course she could already be on a ferry or in a plane. Ruth had no idea how organised she'd been. The thought made her go to the drawer where they kept the passports. Ruth didn't feel sick when she saw Hal's was missing, she felt like her insides had turned to slime and that they would seep out of her when they were ready.

The police arrived and Christian showed them into the sitting room. They looked so severe in their uniforms. A man and a woman.

'She's taken his passport,' Ruth said as she followed them into the room.

One of the men held out his hand. 'Mrs Donaldson, I'm DC Rogers and this is WPC Samuels.'

'Please,' said Ruth, 'you're wasting time. She's had three hours already. They could be anywhere.'

WPC Samuels walked forward. 'My name is Lisa. I know this is hard, Mrs Donaldson, but in order to find your son we need to ask you a few questions.'

That was when Ruth started to cry. They weren't going to help her and somewhere out there Aggie had Hal.

DC Rogers was talking again, addressing Christian now, without sharing his name. 'You said on the phone you think your nanny has left with your son without your permission. Are you sure she hasn't just taken him to the park or somewhere?'

'No, no,' said Christian. 'I've been awake since six-thirty. I thought they were asleep. She had some sort of breakdown last night. She said it was an epileptic fit, but we don't think it was. We were going to ask her to leave.' Ruth could hear the utter ridiculousness of his words.

But the policeman ignored his confusion. 'Did she know this?'

'Nothing was said, but she might have guessed.'

'She's odd,' said Ruth. 'I've known there's something wrong with her for a while now, but I couldn't put my finger on it.'

'Odd, how?' asked WPC Samuels. Ruth looked at Lisa and wondered if she had children and if she left them with odd people.

'I don't know. She was too perfect. Looking back, I'm wondering if anything she said was true.'

'Can I look at her room?' asked WPC Samuels.

'It's at the top of the house, the loft room, but she's taken everything,' said Christian, 'I've checked. And most of Hal's clothes have gone as well.'

'And his passport,' repeated Ruth.

As WPC Samuels left the room Ruth could hear her on her radio, her serious tones filling up the house.

'Where did you employ her from?' asked DC Rogers. 'We need her full name, age, family history.'

'We put an advert in *The Lady*,' said Ruth. 'I rang her referee and she couldn't praise her enough. Her name is Agatha Hartard. She said she was estranged from her family.'

'So you never met her parents? Did you ever see her passport? Are you sure that's her name?'

Ruth looked at Christian and everything was removed. 'Oh God,' she said, holding her hand over her mouth to stop herself from falling out. 'Oh God.'

Agatha had a plan. Of course she did. First they walked twenty minutes to Kilburn station where she had checked out the loos and worked out they could dye their hair and change in peace. Sure enough there was no one around and Hal was content to have himself changed dramatically without putting up any sort of fuss. She bagged everything in the bin bags she had taken and re-packed it in the knapsack, then she put them both into their new clothes. Looking into the misty mirror she could see the person she was becoming and she was pleased.

It was only seven thirty by the time they were standing on the platform waiting for the tube to Euston. Hal looked tired and she knew he was going to ask for a bottle soon. She would buy him a pain au chocolat at the station as a special treat for the train. She was also going to buy herself a latte, because that was the sort of woman she was.

Agatha thought they were probably still safe. Ruth had been tired and she hoped she might not have woken up yet. If she was awake she almost certainly wouldn't have checked on Hal yet as it would be too precious to her to have a few moments sitting on her own or arguing with Christian. And they wouldn't expect her to be up yet; they'd think she was still sleeping off her fit. It was odd to think she was epileptic, strange that she hadn't known that about herself before now. But it was fine. When things settled down she'd go to a doctor and get a proper diagnosis and drugs to control it and then everything would be fine again. Everything was going to be fine.

The tube took them to the station just as it promised it would. They bought the coffee and the pastry and they stood under the big boards which flashed the names of all the places they could go. Agatha had already decided they would go to the coast and get on a ferry headed somewhere in Europe, but as she stood on the grimy concourse she realised that if that had been her plan they would have taken a tube to Victoria station, not

Euston. Everyone knew that Victoria took you to the coast and Euston took you back, back to the heart of England. A spinning started in Agatha's head as she tried to re-capture the last thirty minutes of her life, to see herself choosing this as her destination when she'd stepped onto the tube, but nothing came. She scanned the orange words formed out of nothing more than tiny squares piled on top of each other like children's building blocks and knew why they were here. The next train going to Birmingham was leaving at 8.25, in ten minutes. Agatha pushed Hal's buggy to the ticket counter and bought a one-way ticket. They were coming back, but not yet. They were going at the moment, going back to where she had come from. Going back to where it had all started. An odd fizzing was building up behind Agatha's eyes, like someone had opened a can of coke in her skull. She had to get back and then it would be fine. Everything would be fine.

'It appears she did give you her correct name,' said WPC Samuels. She hadn't found anything in Agatha's room and had just got off the phone to someone who was trying to find Hal. 'That's a good thing. If she'd been organised, if she had come into your family with the intention of stealing a child, she would have concealed her identity.'

'She's been with us for eight months,' Ruth was saying somewhere outside Christian's ability to listen.

'Eight months is not long for a paedophile. They're often prepared to put months into the planning it takes to abduct a child.'

'A paedophile? You think that's why she's taken Hal?' Christian tried to stop listening.

'We have to look at every possibility, Mrs Donaldson. The fact that she gave you her correct name is very hopeful.'

Christian felt better when DC Rogers left. He imagined him screeching down alleys and knocking on doors, looking for his son. Also he felt freed of the policeman's contempt; because what sort of people were they, him and Ruth, that they discarded their children this way? Can I go with you? Christian had asked. What he had really wanted to do was drive around the streets screaming his son's name, but DC Rogers had told him it was vitally important they stayed where they were in case Aggie rang. She would be in an unstable state, he'd said, and she'd need everything to be normal. Other policemen and women came and went. Someone sat him and Ruth down and explained to them that they weren't going to release any details to the media yet. They were worried about spooking her because she was unstable. The word 'spooked' made Christian think about ghosts.

They had distributed the photograph of Aggie and Hal standing over the vegetable patch to the police nationwide. It was the only one Ruth had been able to find, although he'd wished to God she hadn't. They looked so complicit, so young, so innocent, so right with their spades and the earth and the sun and their wide smiles. Police were being dispatched to every train station, ferry port and airport, and she would be caught if she tried to leave the country. Soon her image would be on every police database, even the bobby on the beat would be scanning faces.

An earnest young woman in plain clothes explained to them what might be wrong with Aggie and the possible outcomes. WPC Samuels made tea and faded into the background as they held onto each other and wept.

Eventually, after what seemed like years of waiting, WPC Samuels said, 'We've traced her parents. They haven't seen or heard from her for seven years, but not because of an estrangement.'

'What do you mean?' asked Christian. 'Where are they?'

'A village called Tamworth, just outside Birmingham. A local sergeant is on her way there now. We'll know more in about fifteen minutes.'

Christian stood up, leaving Ruth behind on the sofa. Every movement seemed too large to contain himself and anyone else. 'Can I go? We could be there in what, three hours?'

'There's no point,' said WPC Samuels. 'If she's there, we'll have her in fifteen minutes. If they have any information, we'll be straight onto it. But, Mr Donaldson, she hasn't even spoken to them for seven years, it seems unlikely she'll be making her way there. At the moment, it's just a lead.'

'But I can't go on sitting here,' shouted Christian. He felt Ruth's hand pulling him down. He didn't want to sit, so redundant and useless.

WPC Samuels came towards him and he realised she wasn't going to let him leave. 'This is where you're needed, Mr Donaldson. Leave it to the police to get your son back.'

Ruth was crying again now, if she had ever stopped. 'Please, Christian,' she was saying, 'please, just do as they say. Don't get in their way.'

'We'll know more in a few minutes,' said the WPC again. 'They'll let me know as soon as there are any developments.'

At Birmingham station the connection to Stoke usually came every twenty or so minutes. She'd taken the route often enough, the platform was imprinted on her brain. There were definitely more police than usual but Agatha knew how to handle it. She pushed the buggy confidently forward, holding her head high and using her legs to make her glide. She scanned the board boldly, pushing her large dark glasses into her hair so everyone could see her eyes. When Hal moaned she told Rupert not to be silly, he would see his granny soon. She felt the police looking at her and their eyes bored into her but they failed to see beyond her surface. They looked but then they glanced away and had their attention taken up by someone else. Because there was always another mother and child. There would always be more of those.

They stood on the platform and waited for the train and it was only then that Agatha admitted to herself where they were going. She was not taking Hal to give him to Harry. In fact Harry was not going to touch a hair on either of their heads. But she was taking Hal to show Harry. It was odd that until now she hadn't realised they had the same name, even though Hal's real name was not Henry or Harry, it was just Hal. But still it was nearly the same. And she had had them both inside her. Harry in the wrong way and Hal in the right way. She was going to show this to Harry. She was going to show him that, even though he had tried his best, he had not destroyed her. Far from it, she had gone on to give birth to the most wonderful boy who had ever lived. She had become the one thing that would protect her from Harry for the rest of her life. She had become a mother.

Hal sat on her lap on the train. They watched the country-side whipping past like a painting where the colours have all run together. Mostly Agatha let her eyes relax and blur, but occasionally she would latch on to something that became a memory before she was sure what she was seeing. They would be close to her parents, maybe Louise still lived nearby. But she wouldn't be going to see them. At first she'd thought that she was going back to see them, but it had soon become obvious that this wasn't the reason at all. That there was nothing to say to them any more. She could do without them.

Ruth watched WPC Samuels take the call and she tried to work out from the way her face pinched itself together what she might be hearing. But it was as useless as holding a letter up to the light to see who it might be from.

She looked towards Christian but he had fallen in on himself. She thought they both might die if anything happened to Hal, but then she remembered Betty and realised they wouldn't even be allowed to do that.

The policewoman finished her call and came to sit opposite them. Christian started to cry, which unnerved Ruth.

'We haven't found them,' she began, 'but her parents have shed some light on the situation. Agatha ran away from home on her sixteenth birthday, seven years ago and they haven't heard from her since then. Apparently she stole some money and she'd been in trouble at school. The police were involved, her parents went on missing persons programmes, they even came to London and put up posters of her, but nothing. Then on her seventeenth birthday the father's best friend killed himself. He left a note saying he couldn't live without Agatha. It turned out that he'd been abusing her since she was nine. The police suspected that this Harry Collins had murdered Agatha, but they never found any evidence to support their theory. She hasn't been in touch with them today.'

'Oh my God.' Ruth was dumbfounded, she couldn't find words to describe how she felt.

'He lived very nearby. Just the next village. The police are on their way to his old house now.'

'Do you think she's gone there?'

'It's a possibility. By taking Hal she's done something with direct consequences. She's going to want some reassurance.'

'Can I speak to her mother?' asked Ruth.

'Why the hell would you want to do that?' shouted Christian.

'I don't know,' said Ruth. 'I just do.'

WPC Samuels didn't seem surprised, she'd seen it all before. Even in their most dreadful moment they failed to be unique. 'I'd have to make a call,' she said. She left the room and there was nothing to do but wait. Ruth thought she had spent her whole life waiting for the next thing, expecting things to be better in some indefinable way, but now she saw all the waiting for what it was. She was a queue dweller without vision.

'The mother has agreed to speak to you,' said WPC Samuels as she came back in. 'I can put you through if you're sure you want to speak to her.'

'Please,' said Ruth, holding out her hand. The ringing phone was given to her, all she had to do was place it to her ear. She felt the last remaining energy drain out of her body, as if she'd been shot and the blood was pooling round her feet. Christian put his arms around her and she let him hold her. He felt strong against her weakness.

'Hello,' said the woman on the other end.

'Hello,' said Ruth.

The woman started to cry. 'I'm so sorry,' she said. And Ruth realised she wasn't going to learn anything from this. She was simply talking to another mother and it made her feel as empty as an arid lake.

'It's okay.'

'We thought she was dead. I can't believe … Agatha was working as your nanny?'

'Yes.'

'How was she? I mean, before …'

Ruth wanted to be kind, but there was a madness to this which was circling Ruth, threatening to overtake her. 'She was great. The kids loved her. You haven't seen her for seven years?'

'No. She left on her sixteenth birthday. I suppose the police have filled you in.'

'Yes.'

'We knew she had problems. She was a very strange child, very introverted. She was always lying or saying terrible things. But we didn't realise why, we thought she was naughty.' The woman's voice caught and again Ruth wondered where this could lead. 'Then when Harry died. God, the letter he wrote. He said that he and Agatha had become lovers when she was nine. He used that word. Lovers. Like she'd agreed to it.'

'I'm so sorry.'

'So am I. I'm sorry I let her down and I'm sorry Harry killed himself because I wish I could have had the pleasure of killing him.'

'Do you think she might have gone there?'

'I don't know. She doesn't know he's dead. But why would she want to do that? I don't understand any of this.' There was a pause and then she said, 'I don't think she'll hurt your boy. I think she's got confused, the way she did when she was little. We saw a doctor once who said she was a fantasist. Do you know what that means?'

'No.'

'She makes up stories and then she can't remember what's real and what isn't. That's why we didn't take her seriously when she lied.' Agatha's mother started to cry.

'I'm so sorry. Do you know how sorry I am? I let her down. We let her down.'

'I hope you're right,' said Ruth, suddenly feeling calm. 'I hope she doesn't hurt my son.' She could not end up like this woman, but this was not something she could control. The future loomed over them like a monster, either to be endured or to be changed.

Agatha risked taking a taxi from the station to the village. Really though, it didn't feel like a risk. She was starting to believe that a divine power was watching over them and she was going to be allowed to do whatever she needed. The driver talked about the heat and asked how her son was coping, which Agatha took as another celestial sign that everything was going to be fine.

'How old is he?' asked the taxi driver.

'Just three,' said Agatha. 'We had his party yesterday. He loved it.'

'And is today his grandparents' turn then?'

'My uncle's, actually. I've always been very close to my uncle.'

A hole had opened in Agatha's head. It was bright and white and tasted of pine needles and sounded like a scream.

The house looked the same. As a child Agatha had found it imposing, but now she saw it was small. She couldn't help looking first upwards, at the bedroom window in which the curtains had always been drawn, remembering the blackness which lay within. Her legs felt heavy and her mind was too confused to work out the straps to Hal's buggy. She left it instead at the bottom of the path and picked him up in her arms as a barrier for when she rang the bell. Her hands were shaking but she hadn't expected anything else and her body was pulsating with heat. But she couldn't not do it now, so she pressed the utilitarian white buzzer next to the door.

A woman who looked not unlike Ruth opened the door. It seemed disingenuous that she should have found her way here. The possibility of collusion flicked into Agatha's mind. Was the whole of her life a set-up? But then a little girl who was not Betty ran between the woman's legs and it jolted Agatha into the present.

'Can I help you?' asked the woman.

'I'm sorry,' said Agatha. 'I'm looking for someone. Do you live here?'

The woman laughed. 'Yes, I do. Who are you looking for?'

'Harry. Harry Collins.'

The woman looked puzzled. 'I'm sorry, I don't recognise the name. Are you sure you're in the right place?'

It didn't seem possible that Harry could have got away from her. 'How long have you lived here?'

'Two years, just over. But we didn't buy it from a Harry Collins. I think their name was Anderson.'

Agatha stepped backwards and lost her footing. The house that lay within was white and bright, nothing like the one she'd known. Everything had changed. Even Harry hadn't waited for her. She heard a sob from somewhere. The woman stretched out her hand. 'Are you okay? Do you want to come in for a minute?'

'No, no,' said Agatha, and then realised it was she who was crying.

'But your son, he's upset.'

Agatha looked at Hal and saw his scared eyes. This had all gone too far. 'No,' she said again. 'We're fine. Everything's going to be fine.' The words tasted as bitter as if she was eating wood.

Agatha turned and saw the field opposite Harry's house. She knew that beyond the field would still be the wood and the river. They, at least, would not have moved. As she started to walk, she felt the woman watching her from the door, she might have even called out to her. It didn't matter any more. All that mattered was that Harry had got away. He would never know what she had been through to get back to him. He would always have the last word.

As she walked across the rutted ground which peaked and troughed beneath her feet like a dried-up sea, Agatha knew finally that this was why she had come. It hadn't been about Harry. It had always only been about this moment. It was in fact possible that her whole life had been about nothing more than this moment. She turned just before the darkness of the wood swallowed her up and saw the woman still standing at her door, still looking at her, but now with a phone to her ear. There wasn't much time, but she needed only a few more minutes.

The wood was as damp as it had been on her sixteenth birthday before she'd taken the train. She had stood outside Harry's house with her mother's kitchen knife, looking upwards, just like she'd done today. But that day she'd lost her nerve and had fallen into the wood, looking for the river and an easier way out. But again she had lost her nerve. Today though things had been different. She'd rung the bell and she'd been ready to hurt Harry. She had spent seven years gathering her courage and now it all came down to this.

You heard the river before you saw it. It was violent and deadly, Harry always said, which seemed fitting. If you fall in there, you're a goner, girly, he'd said. Your head would be crushed by all the rocks, your lungs would fill with water, your heart would stop with fear. None of this sounded that bad to Agatha; she already knew all those feelings.

Agatha stood by the side of the river and knew how easy the step would be. The only impediment was Hal. She had almost forgotten she was carrying him and she wished now she'd left him with the woman at the door. That would have been the right thing to do and it pained her that she should have got this wrong. But there was nothing to be done now. She held him tighter, he would be a comfort at least. The hole in her head was much larger now, it felt larger even than her head. Soon she wouldn't be able to make her body move and it all had to be done before then. Hal squirmed in her arms and she looked at him. It wasn't about him. Hal was nothing more than a red herring, which was what Harry always said her age was. Either way though, it didn't seem fair or right on the little boy. Agatha put Hal down on a rock by the edge. He was crying and she felt sorry for him but not overly so. He was not her child, he had never been, she couldn't even be sure she loved him now.

'Wait there, Hal,' she said. 'Don't move. Someone will come and get you.' He nodded and she smiled at him. 'Everything's going to be fine, I promise.'

Agatha turned towards the water. She was grateful to Hal for witnessing this and that was enough of a reason to have brought him. She remembered his little arms and legs and his need for her love, but as she remembered she saw herself, she felt her own littleness, her own need, her own vacuum.

Agatha stepped forward and off the edge. The water was as cold and hard as Harry had warned. It closed tightly over her head, blocking her senses. It felt as wonderful as a baptism, as new as a rebirth.

Have you ever been pulled from a burning plane? Have you ever outrun a man wearing a mask? Have you ever given a stranger the kiss of life on a dirty roadside? Have you ever watched your best mate blown up by a roadside bomb in Afghanistan but walked away yourself two days before your wife gives birth? Have you ever been the last person out of the Twin Towers? Have you ever stepped into the road without looking just a second after a lorry rushes past? Have you ever fallen under the water only to be pulled up again by someone stronger than yourself? Have you ever walked across a desert in search of food for your family to see an aid tent in the distance? Have you ever witnessed the sea rising up over your head and pulling a child out of your hands who you then find alive hours later? Have you ever been taken hostage and had a gun held to your head in front of news cameras with the sick knowledge that governments never give in to demands, just for them to release you on the side of a road three years later? Have you ever been told that your child has been found alive after being snatched from your home by a mad woman who left him on the side of a river while she killed herself?

Finally, finally they were alone together in their own bedroom, their children asleep in their bed because none of them had been able to bear the thought of not being in touching distance that night. Or every night for the rest of their lives. Ruth sat on one side of them, still fully clothed, so Christian copied her. Neither of them turned on the light, but the orange glow from the streetlamps lit up the room almost enough to read by, if it had been a normal night, if any night would ever be normal again. Ruth couldn't cry any more, she doubted her body would be able to produce the tears and Christian felt relieved for this much at least.

He stole furtive glances at his wife, desperate to ask her some questions. Because, try as he might, Christian couldn't make sense of what had happened today. It felt to him like trying to get your head round that age-old conundrum concerning the universe and whether or not it went on forever. Surely it must end somewhere, he'd said to his mother at some indeterminable moment of his youth. Well maybe, she'd replied, but then there'd have to be something. If you think about it, even nothing is something, isn't it?

Christian leant across the bed and was surprised that Ruth let him take her hand. 'You must try to sleep. You look exhausted. It'll all be clearer if we sleep on it.'

'I don't feel tired,' she said. 'I feel more awake than I've ever done in my life.'

They sat holding hands over their children's heads until Ruth said, 'I don't know what we're supposed to do now.'

'We'll do our best,' he answered.

'Yes, but what if our best isn't good enough?'

'It has to be good enough. I mean, what more is there?'

They lapsed into silence again, both listening to the steady breathing of their children. Ruth felt a deep pain in her heart. She didn't want to imagine what it would have been like to have been told that Hal had died with Agatha in the river, but her mind couldn't stop playing with the idea, like a cat worrying a mouse. He had needed her. Ruth had realised that when the policeman had handed him over as she had sat with her husband and daughter waiting for the other part which made them all whole. His little body shaking, his cheeks crusty with tears, his hands cold. If she had been able to put him back inside her at that moment she would have done. The preciousness, the precariousness, the delicacy of life stared at her from the bottom of a well of sadness. She wanted to hold on to the memory, but it was already slipping from her grasp. Moments of joy mixed with terror and shame could not be lived through too many times, they would kill you in the end.

'It's all going to have to change,' she said, feeling like she was stating the obvious.

'I know,' answered Christian.

'I'm going to talk to Sally about having some time off. Maybe I won't go back. I could go freelance.'

'I've been thinking the same thing.'

'Really?' Ruth looked across at her husband.

'Yes, I can't get a handle on what this is all about. There has to be something else. It can't just be this.'

Ruth and Christian sat in silence. They both knew what they were saying was a fantasy. If there was a way of living out there that allowed you to be all the things you were to yourself and those you loved, then everyone would be living it. It might change for them, but it probably wouldn't. Maybe the most you could hope for was knowledge, little particles dropping into you like gold found at the bottom of a river bed. Ruth wasn't even sure that the answer lay outside of themselves. She thought that now they were bound together and that this could be what saw them through. The idea that they were enough filled her.

Christian squeezed Ruth's hand and looked over at her. He wanted to know what she thought.

'Ruth,' he said. 'I don't understand. I can't get my head around it. None of it makes any sense to me.'

Ruth smiled and he knew he'd been right to ask her because he could see that she was about to tell him something important. Something that had a lot to do with why he loved her so much. Something that would stay with him for a long time. Something that maybe she wouldn't have been able to articulate unless they had been snared in this moment, which maybe gave it a meaning. Understanding whirled around them like smoke, they could nearly touch it.

'I've been thinking about that as well,' said Ruth. 'And, you know what, it's almost comforting. If nothing makes sense, then by default everything must. Don't you think?'

Acknowledgements

Thanks to my MA Creative Writing tutors at Sussex University for teaching me how to edit and, as importantly, to take myself seriously as a writer, especially Sue Roe and Irving Weinman. Thanks also to fellow students, Craig and Richard for their friendship, advice and help. Thanks to Mick Jackson for taking time to help a green writer and for the great advice to get more childcare and ditch the first thirty pages. And thanks to Lucy and Polly for the amazing childcare, which has given me the space to write this book (and for being absolutely nothing like Aggie).

Thank you Clare Reihill for being the first person to invite me in and for introducing me to my editor, Clare Smith, who has not only taken a chance on me, but has been patient, encouraging and insightful. Thanks also to Carol MacArthur for never seeming annoyed by my incessant questions.

Thanks to my amazing friends, not just for making life more fun, but also for reading my many attempts and speaking endless words of encouragement; most especially Polly, Emily M, Emily S, Dolly, Shami, Amy, Clare, Bryony, Sophie, Eve and Paula. And thanks to Penny for your help and enthusiasm.

Also my sisters Posy and Ernestina and my brothers Algy, Ferdy and Silas and their partners Jonny, Ben, Emily and Laura for staying interested and reading.

A multitude of thanks to my Mum and Dad for bringing me up in a house filled with love, books and conversation and for reading much more than just the numerous drafts of this book.

Finally thanks to my three amazing children Oscar, Violet and Edith who are too young to have read anything I've written, but old enough to make me realise what's important.

And thank you Jamie for so much, but especially always helping me find a room of my own.

Richard and Judy ask Araminta Hall

Richard and Judy ask Araminta Hall

You have children. Like so many mothers who work, have you experienced the anguish of worrying about childcare and about what might happen to your kids when you're not there?

When I had my son twelve years ago I wouldn't leave him with anyone. I ran myself ragged working as a freelance journalist and never letting him out of my sight. I relaxed a bit after the births of my daughters and now am in an amazing situation where I trust my child minders more than myself.

There were a few sticky moments before I found them, however. One woman seemed great when I interviewed her, but every time I dropped my daughter off, I got an inexplicably sick feeling in my stomach. After the fourth drop-off, I turned up to pick her up two hours early with an imagined excuse and never went back.

I think childcare is all about gut instinct; you know you've found the person who's right to look after your child in much the same way you know you've met someone you want to spend the rest of your life with. And it is just as important a decision. You trust someone with the most precious thing you have and it's not ever a decision to be taken lightly.

Christian and Ruth are a very typical young modern couple, both working all hours to pay their mortgage and fund their way of life. Their children suffer as a result. Who is more to blame – Ruth or Christian?

I find it impossible to assign blame to any of the characters, and I don't see it as black and white. We're all a messy amalgamation, which is why we can get caught up in situations that don't suit us, or those around us. Ruth and Christian both behave badly and well; they both ultimately have the best interests of their families at heart, and I think they both learn lessons from the situations in which they find themselves. We live in confusing times; I don't think it's very easy to find your place, whether you are male or female, and often the pressures of life drown out other needs. Probably they should have talked more as a couple, but not many people do.

I can't stand the media perception of the 'happy family'; it's as bad as the images of stick-thin models thrust into the minds of teenage girls. We're all so busy trying to be everything to everybody that most of us are falling flat on our faces.

Most of us who have had to pay for childcare have had some unpleasant experiences. Is there any way we could make our lives easier and things safer for our children? Be more careful about references? Or should mums not work at all?

Of course I don't think women should stop working and stay at home! And I didn't write this book with one hand, whilst blending some organic fruit and making all the family's clothes with the other. I got some childcare and I juggled things, like most of the women I know.

I truly believe that my children are happy because I am a happier person for doing something I enjoy. Being a mother is the hardest and most wonderful job in the world, but it is also isolating and confusing and a lot of women need to find a place for themselves outside of the home.

I feel incredibly lucky that I can drop my children off at the child minder's or school at 9 a.m. and pick them up at 3 p.m. I would find it hard not to have time with them every day, but that is only my experience and others will find different situations work for them. In my mind, feminism is about respecting all aspects of people and acknowledging that the domestic is as important as the commercial.

I wish we could adopt a more Scandinavian way of living in which it's the norm for both men and women to adapt their work around their families. The ideal situation seems to me to be both parents taking equal responsibility for home and work, which should create a balance in a family.

As for finding good childcare, I am a firm believer in personal recommendations – if another mother is happy then that goes a long way.

To find out more about
Richard and Judy's Autumn Book Club go to
whsmith.co.uk/richardandjudy

Chosen by us, just for you!

Read our full review and watch our author interviews at whsmith.co.uk/richardandjudy

You can also add your own review, vote for your favourite book and discover lots more online. We look forward to reading your reviews.

RICHARD AND JUDY
Galaxy
BOOK CLUB
2011
EXCLUSIVE TO
WHSmith

Download our free podcast!

Scan this code with your smart phone and download the podcast to discover more about 'Everything and Nothing' or visit http://lstn.at/everythingnothing

Available from 03 September 2011

Read the first chapter of your next Richard and Judy Book Club 2011 title for free*

Get the chapter sent to your mobile phone by texting the keyword to the number below the featured title.

Text ABBOTT to 60300

Text CAKE to 60300

Text MAY to 60300

Text LEFT to 60300

Text MATTER to 60300

Text CAROL to 60300

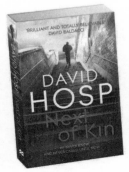

Text KIN to 60300

RICHARD AND JUDY
Galaxy
BOOK CLUB
2011
EXCLUSIVE TO
WHSmith